THE PAYOFF

I don't much like surprises. Never did. Never will. I need to know exactly what is going on at all times. Which is why I paid no attention to Johnny when he did the manly, protective bit and said, "Wait here, Brenda."

No way was I going to duck behind the Dumpster, squint my eyes closed, let Johnny expose himself to flying bullets, and hope for the best. I was right beside Johnny all the way.

We flattened our bodies against the wall and slowly crept toward the end of the street. Shards of broken glass crunched under our feet. What moments before had seemed like a stylish, edgy, slightly deliciously scary venue for my surprise birthday party, was now revealed for what it was—a dark, dank, dangerous, isolated, creepy-as-all-getout hell-hole. Where someone had only moments before popped off a few rounds at us.

Cautiously, we looked around the corner. The dark sedan had disappeared. That was very good. No more shooting. That was also very bad. No more Dweena.

BARBARA JAYE WILSON

Hatful of Homicide

A BRENDA MIDNIGHT MYSTERY

AVON BOOKS
An Imprint of HarperCollinsPublishers

This is a work of fiction. Names, characters, places, and incidents are products of the author's imagination or are used fictitiously and are not to be construed as real. Any resemblance to actual events, locales, organizations, or persons, living or dead, is entirely coincidental.

AVON BOOKS
An Imprint of HarperCollins*Publishers*
10 East 53rd Street
New York, New York 10022-5299

Copyright © 2000 by Barbara Jaye Wilson
ISBN: 0-380-80356-9
www.avonbooks.com

First Avon Books paperback printing: August 2000

Avon Trademark Reg. U.S. Pat. Off. and in Other Countries, Marca Registrada, Hecho en U.S.A.
HarperCollins® is a trademark of HarperCollins Publishers Inc.

Printed in the U.S.A.

WCD 10 9 8 7 6 5 4 3 2 1

*Dedicated to a couple of buildings
that got demolished before their time.*

ACKNOWLEDGMENTS

I would like to thank Ken Ferguson, Professor Emeritus of Ceramics, Kansas City Art Institute, who taught me a whole lot more than how to make a plate.

I had to give my friends credit. What a wonderful, fiercely creative group of individuals. This time they'd really outdone themselves. So much so, I was beginning to think they might have gone just a little bit too far.

I stood, all alone, waiting for the gang to show, on a street so dark and desolate and twisty and narrow, so devoid of traffic, that in any city other than New York it'd pass for an alley, a Greenwich Village street so remote that even long-time residents would swear it didn't exist.

At my side hung a shiny black Midnight Millinery hatbox. None of my gravity-defying hat creations nestled inside on a bed of tissue paper. This box was stuffed full of fifty thousand dollars' worth of fake fifty-dollar bills.

Impatient, I checked my watch. Where the hell was everybody?

I gazed around my dark dank surroundings, hoping to spot a telltale balloon peeking out from behind the dented Dumpster. Or, perhaps, a trail of confetti on cobblestone. I listened for hushed whispers, giggles, friendly footsteps. I sniffed the air for the scent of burning candles, cake, and ice cream.

It was my birthday.

*   *   *

I'd spent the day at Midnight Millinery, pretending to work on a new line of hats, but mostly going through the motions, mired down by a severe crisis of confidence in my design ability. Hatter's block.

My birthday is a time to reassess. I pondered life and death and millinery, put things in the proper perspective, tried to figure out where I'd been and where I might be headed. These days that pretty much boiled down to no-where fast.

One thought perked me up. My friends were giving me a surprise birthday party. I almost always throw my own party, but this year I wanted a change. For the last month I'd dropped enough big hints to choke an ele-phant.

Every so often I got up from my work table, wandered over to my antique vanity, stood in front of the beveled oval mirror, and practiced looking surprised.

All day long people called to wish me a happy birthday, although none of my closest friends. They were probably scared of giving up the surprise if they talked to me. I wondered what elaborate scheme they'd come up with to get me to the right place at the right time.

Early that evening, I got the answer. The phone rang and on the other end of the line was some guy with a very thick, very fake accent. He claimed to have kid-napped my pal Dweena.

Kidnapped. Yeah, right. Those friends of mine were too much.

I played along.

"Oh no," I said, adding a dramatic quiver to my voice to sound intimidated. If I knew my friends, one of them—probably Chuck Riley—was taping the conver-sation, so I hammed it up pretty good.

"Oh yes," sneered the fake kidnapper, "and if you want to see your friend alive again, you must cooperate fully."

In the background I could hear Dweena's hysterical laughter.

"Put Dweena on the phone," I demanded.

"No."

"How do I know she's still alive?"

"I say so."

"Not good enough."

After a long pause, he said, "All right, I'll let you talk to her, but only for a second, and don't you try any funny stuff."

Me? Funny stuff? No way.

I heard scuffling sounds, then Dweena. "Please, Brenda, you've got to help me. This maniac means business." Her voice changed pitch and cracked under the strain of suppressing giggles.

"Of course, Dweena. I'll do whatever the man says."

"Do you still have keys to my place?" she asked.

"I think they're around here somewhere." I rifled through my junk drawer, dug out her key chain. "I found them."

"Okay, here's what you do. You know that blood drain in my living room?"

I shuddered. Before she moved in and fixed the place up, Dweena's Gansevoort Street apartment had been a meat packing plant. To keep the edgy ambiance, she retained many accouterments of the former tenant. Overhead were intact racks with hooks. Nonslip ridged concrete floors sloped down to the blood drain in the dead center of her living room floor. An unsettling conversation piece.

"Pry it up," she instructed, "and reach way down inside. I've got fifty thou stashed in there."

"Gotcha," I said, like I believed Dweena kept that kind of cash in her blood drain.

More scuffling sounds. Then the fake kidnapper came back on the phone and told me when and where to bring the money. I scribbled down the instructions on a piece of pattern paper. "No cops," he warned.

"Don't worry about that."

*   *   *

Party time.

I closed up Midnight Millinery and took Jackhammer, my five-pound, redheaded Yorkshire terrier, for a quick walk around the Village. We cruised by his favorite Italian restaurant, where the owner patted him on the head, gave him a crust of garlic bread, and asked why I hadn't been in lately. When we rounded the corner to my apartment building I got a great surprise.

This surprise really was a surprise. I didn't have to fake the expression that registered on my face.

Leaning up against the redbrick wall was Johnny Verlane, dressed in all black, looking cool as ever. Thick black hair fell over his smoky gray eyes.

"Hey," he said.

Jackhammer yanked on the leash, pulling hard toward Johnny. I was more restrained, not quite sure which phase our on-again off-again relationship was in.

Johnny was supposed to be in Boston filming a cross-series special where his *Tod Trueman, Urban Detective*, character dramatically rides to the rescue when an evil New York drug kingpin moves into the territory of a Boston-based series.

"What are you doing back so soon?" I asked. "Did you finish the shoot?"

"Uh, not exactly. I . . ."

"They told you, didn't they?"

Johnny must have arranged his schedule so he could be here for my birthday. That meant we must be on-again, or at least moving in that direction.

"Who told me what?" he asked, playing the innocent. The man was a good actor.

"You know, the gang—Dweena, Chuck, Elizabeth. I know all about my surprise birthday party. Your job must be to make sure I arrive on time. Some elaborate scheme they came up with, huh?"

"I'm sorry, Brenda. I don't know what you're talking about."

"Sure you don't."

*   *   *

Johnny went with me back to the apartment. He wrestled with Jackhammer while I quickly changed into party attire.

"Nice dress," he commented on our way out, "but how come no hat?"

"Elizabeth probably picked up some of those goofy cone-shaped hats for the party. I wouldn't want to spoil the effect."

The building Dweena lived in still had a few remaining commercial tenants. The street-level door was unlocked. We went in.

"Stomp," I told Johnny.

To alert everybody that the guest of honor had arrived, I made as much racket as possible on the concrete stairs that lead up to Dweena's second-floor apartment.

I expected people to jump out from behind the furniture as soon as I unlocked the door and stepped inside. No one did, and a quick look around showed that the apartment was empty.

"Where is everybody?" asked Johnny.

I was wondering the same thing myself.

It didn't take me long to figure out what those devious friends of mine had plotted. "I know," I said. "They think I'm gonna stick my vegetarian hand down into that blood drain. Chuck has probably got it rigged up so I'll trigger something, or they're all watching us on remote video and once I stick my hand in, once I'm thoroughly humiliated and disgusted, they'll come running in with the cake."

Johnny laughed. "Very clever."

We squatted by the drain. I poked at the cover with my forefinger. It popped off easily enough. I looked down into the deep dark hole. "Yuck."

"Stand back," said Johnny. "I'll handle this."

True gallantry. I knew then, without a doubt, Johnny and I were on-again.

He rolled up his shirt sleeve and plunged his hand

into the abyss. We were both mighty surprised when he came up with a big wad of fifty-dollar bills.

I held one of the bills up to the light. "Fake."

"There's more," said Johnny. He came up with another wad. And another. When all the money was out of the drain, we had fifty thousand dollars' worth of fake fifty-dollar bills. What a coincidence, I thought, the exact amount the fake kidnapper had requested.

"You know, Brenda, these fifties look kind of real," said Johnny.

"It's amazing what you can do with a color copier these days," I said.

"So what's the deal?" asked Johnny, still pretending he didn't know what was going on.

"I guess the party's not at Dweena's after all," I said. "This diversion was to get me in the mood."

"Then where is the party?"

Fortunately, I brought the piece of pattern paper with the fake kidnapper's instructions. I handed it to Johnny.

"Way the hell over there?"

I shrugged.

Looking around for something to carry the money in, I found one of my Midnight Millinery hatboxes in Dweena's closet. Perfect.

As the sun plopped down behind New Jersey across the Hudson River, Johnny and I walked to the fringes of the West Village. I tried to be a good sport about the elusive surprise party, but if the truth be told, I wished they'd get on with it already. I mean, just bring on the cake.

Johnny seemed impatient also. "How long do you think this party is going to last?"

"A couple of hours," I said. If it ever gets started.

"Tell you what, Brenda. There's a little something I need to take care of. You go on ahead. I'll catch up with you in a few minutes."

"Yeah, sure, okay."

*   *   *

The party venue appeared deserted. Suddenly I felt very alone. I yelled out, "Come on guys, let the party begin." My words were swallowed up by the thick humid spring air.

I don't like waiting any time, anywhere, but this was especially bad. True, crime had plummeted in New York, but maybe those heartening statistics didn't apply to this particular spot at this particular time. With each passing minute I grew more ill at ease.

At last. Something was happening.

A dark shiny late-model sedan poked its chromed nose into the tiny street. Diplomat plates. Yep, that had to be Dweena.

No, my friend Dweena is not a diplomat; for that matter, she's not actually a she, at least not in the strictest sense. Formerly Edward, a stockbroker, she's now a much flashier sort, who sometimes works as a club bouncer. Her hobby is hot-wiring illegally parked diplomat cars and relocating them to out-of-the-way neighborhoods.

The sedan crunched to a stop ten feet away from me. The driver's side door opened and out stepped a small man. A long trench coat flapped around his pointy-toed shoes. His dark oily hair was slicked back into a stringy three-inch ponytail, a stick-on mustache perched atop his thin upper lip. He was the perfect villain, straight out of central casting. The Village was chock full of wannabe actors eager to do anything for a buck.

The man sauntered over to where I stood.

"You have the money?" he asked, although he pronounced it more like zsheee mooooney.

"Yeah, I got da money," I said, speaking tough-like out of the side of my mouth, once again playing out the scene for the benefit of whichever of my friends was secretly videotaping.

"Hand eet over," he snarled.

"Not until I see that my friend Dweena is alive and well," I said.

He stepped to the side and gestured toward the car. "Cheeck eet out."

I walked over to the car, cupped my hands, and peered through the heavily tinted window. Dweena lay in the backseat. She was dressed for the party in one of her finest—a tight, short neon-orange sequined dress and a platinum wig done up in a sky-high old-fashioned bee-hive hairdo. Her hands and feet were bound with duct tape. Another strip of the silvery tape was stretched over her mouth.

The backseat appeared roomy. Big enough possibly for a bunch of my friends to be hidden under the wool blanket on the floor. I figured maybe a couple more brave souls were curled up in the trunk. The other guests must be around the corner.

I tapped on the window. "Yo, Dweena, keep a stiff upper lip. Stay brave. Don't worry. I've got the situation under control."

In response, she wiggled, straining against the duct tape.

I turned away from the car and approached the fake kidnapper. "Da money," I said, holding out the hatbox.

He grabbed the hatbox away from me and threw it on the hood of the car. Then he counted, slowly and me-thodically, one fake bill at a time.

Footsteps on the cobblestones.

Johnny was walking toward me, cradling a bunch of beautiful long-stemmed red roses in his arms. So that had been the little something he had to take care of. He was truly a one-of-a-kind, great guy.

"Happy birthday, Brenda," he said.

The fake kidnapper took one look at Johnny, stopped counting money, and yelled. "I said no cops." At high volume, he lost most of his fake accent.

He reached down and pulled a fake gun out of an

ankle holster, shot off a few blanks, stuffed the money into the hatbox, jumped back in the car, gunned the motor, and took off with a duct-taped Dweena still in the backseat.

Surprise.

2

Come to think of it, I don't much like surprises. Never did. Never will.

I need to know exactly what is going on at all times. When I don't, whenever I'm forced to hand an unstable situation over to my brain, my imagination tends to run hog wild.

Which is why I paid no attention to Johnny when he did the manly protective bit, and said, "Wait here, Brenda."

No way was I going to duck behind the Dumpster, squint my eyes closed, let Johnny expose himself to flying bullets, and hope for the best. I was right beside Johnny all the way.

As he had done many times on the *Tod Trueman* set, we flattened our bodies against the wall and slowly crept toward the end of the street. Shards of broken glass crunched under our feet. Somewhere off in the distance I heard water trickling. From somewhere else, something else reeked to high heaven.

What moments before had seemed like a stylish, edgy, slightly deliciously scary venue for my surprise birthday party, was now revealed for what it was—a dark, dank, dangerous, isolated, creepy-as-all-getout hellhole. Where someone had only moments before popped off a few rounds at us.

Cautiously, we looked around the corner. The dark

sedan had disappeared. That was very good. No more shooting. That was also very bad. No more Dweena.

I gazed down at the dozen red roses scattered on the cobblestone street. When things started to go wrong, Johnny dropped them. Now, in a single suave motion he swept them up, shook off the grit, and presented them to me with a courtly flourish. "Happy birthday, Brenda."

"You shouldn't have," I said.

Then I freaked out. An observer might say I had burst into tears. I would never admit to such weakness. Besides, tears would hardly do justice to my complex emotional state. Surging around inside all at once was a dizzying mixture of fear, relief, anger, disappointment, shame, and guilt.

Worse, I also felt like a goddamned fool. After two minutes of self-indulgence I managed to get myself under control. If the situation was as bad as I thought, I needed to keep my wits about me.

It appeared my friends had not planned a surprise birthday party for me.

It was starting to look more and more like a real kidnapping.

And I had just blown the big payoff.

Not a cab in sight.

Johnny and I sped back to my building on foot. I stopped in the hallway outside my apartment and rang the doorbell of my friend and across-the-hall neighbor, Elizabeth.

I heard the scraping noise as she slid her peephole open, stepped back so she could see me, gave her a frantic little wave, and said, "Emergency meeting, my place, ASAP."

Leaving her to wonder what could possibly be so urgent, I zoomed into my apartment, speed-dialed Chuck Riley, said pretty much the same to him, and hung up before he had a chance to question me.

Then I flopped down on my banana-shaped couch. I

needed to gather my thoughts. Jackhammer scrambled up beside me, tail stub vibrating. He always senses when I am upset.

Johnny, who also always senses when I am upset, and maintains his cool no matter what, ambled into the kitchen. "Looks like we've got a long night ahead of us," he said. "I better put on a pot of coffee."

I lay back, engulfed in the aroma of brewing coffee, and tried to make sense of the evening's events.

Difficult as it was, in the face of hard evidence, I had to admit that the kidnapping and the money and the kidnapper and the gun and the bullets were all real, plug that into the equation, and reevaluate.

Except for the fact that I didn't know it was for real, the payoff had started out okay. I'd shown up at the right place at the right time with the right amount of cash and handed it over to the right bad guy. It wasn't until Johnny came on the scene, carrying those roses, that everything got screwed up.

I doubted the roses upset the kidnapper. It had to be Johnny himself.

The kidnapper, who'd warned me not to bring cops, must have seen Johnny and thought cop, as in *Tod Trueman, Urban Detective*. In a high-tension situation, in the heat of the moment, with money and lives at stake, the kidnapper did not properly analyze what was real and what was television. He didn't know my friend Johnny Verlane from a hole in the ground, but he sure as hell knew that urban detective, Tod Trueman.

Elizabeth let herself into my apartment.

Jackhammer ran into the foyer to greet her. She was his second favorite person.

To be more sociable I pushed myself into a sitting position and watched as she made her way over to the chair by the window. Her silver hair was pulled back into a single puffy braid that hung halfway down her back. She was dressed in baggy paint-splattered overalls, a sure indication she'd spent the day working at her painting studio down on Spring Street. A formerly famous abstract artist, Elizabeth had given up painting for several decades, and had only recently started again. As far as I knew, she still hadn't let anybody see her new work.

"What's the big to-do?" she asked.

"Dweena was kidnapped."

Johnny stuck his head out of the kitchen. "Hi, Elizabeth. Coffee?"

"Why yes, thank you," said Elizabeth, "don't mind if I do. And Johnny, I'd also appreciate it if you would inform Brenda that it's not nice to make up crazy stories to scare the shit out of an old lady."

Technically speaking, Elizabeth is seventy-some-odd years old. It doesn't show.

"It might be a crazy story, but I didn't make it up," I said.

"You're trying to tell me—"

The doorbell rang.

"Come on in," I said. "It's open."

Chuck Riley clomped through the foyer and into the room. Clutched in his hand was a jumbo economy-size bag of generic greasy bright orange barbecue potato chips, typical Chuck fare. "All right, Brenda, I showed up. Now tell me what the hell—" He cut himself off when he spotted Elizabeth. "Oh, Elizabeth. Hiya." He patted his giant fuzzball of carrot-red hair.

Once everybody got situated—Johnny sat on the couch, Elizabeth in the chair with Jackhammer on her lap, Chuck sprawled on the hardwood floor, and me pacing nervously back and forth—I detailed the whole sorry tale.

In retrospect it sounds incredibly stupid, but in the back of my mind I still clung desperately to the faint hope that this was all a big joke on me—kind of a mean-spirited surprise birthday party. So after I wrapped up the story, I asked, "You"—glancing from Chuck to Elizabeth—"you guys are in on this with Dweena, right?" I smiled tentatively.

"Not me," said Chuck. "I mean, it's like I didn't even know it was your birthday."

I was shocked. And terribly hurt, too. My ego took such a hard blow that for one selfish moment all I could think of was me. "How could you not know it was my birthday?" I said. "I mean, it's the very start of asparagus season. Last year you came to my birthday party and downed half a pound of fresh grilled asparagus, and the year before, and the year before that, and—"

"That's right," said Chuck, "but those birthday parties you threw for yourself, an act that relieved me, and all your other friends, from the responsibility of knowing the precise date of your birth. Asparagus, you know, gets imported all year round, so it's a lousy indicator of your birthday."

I glared at him.

Elizabeth spoke up. "Pardon me for saying so, Brenda, but a surprise party with a kidnap motif sounds more like something you'd cook up. Call me old-fashioned, but if I were to plan a surprise birthday party, it'd be more of a jump-out-from-behind-the-furniture kind of event. Festive, traditional, with a cake, candles, ice cream, and perhaps even a rousing game of spin the bottle."

Chuck stole a glance at Elizabeth and blushed.

My wounded ego would have to wait. "In that case, if you two really had nothing to do with the kidnapping," I said, "we've got big trouble."

"Poor Dweena," said Elizabeth. "She must be spitting mad and scared to death."

Chuck shook his head. "I don't get it. Why would anybody want to kidnap Dweena? She's not exactly the victim type."

"The usual motive," said Johnny. "Money, pure and simple. That fifty thousand I dug out of her blood drain must have been real honest-to-god cold hard cash."

"Where would Dweena get that kind of dough?"

"Over the years," I said, "her investments have paid off handsomely. She learned the ropes during the time she spent on Wall Street."

"Buy low," said Elizabeth.

"Sell high," said Chuck.

"There's more to it than that," I said.

"Dweena has plenty of money," said Johnny, "but she's discreet, prefers to keep her wealth on the hush-hush. How would the kidnapper know? Especially that guy. He looked like a jerk. Right, Brenda?"

"He certainly did."

"You'd be surprised what even jerks can dig up with a computer and a modem," said Chuck. "That is, if they don't mind breaking a few laws."

"Maybe," I said, "but a couple other possibilities strike me as more probable."

"Like what?" said Elizabeth.

"Well, S.O.B. for one."

"Son of a bitch?" said Chuck.

"No," I said. "Save Our Brothels, Dweena's latest cause. A couple of months ago, Dweena's landlord started eviction proceedings against her and all the other tenants living in her building. He wants everybody out so he can gut the building and turn it into expensive loftlike condos. As you can imagine, Dweena's been on the warpath."

"The landlord can't just up and throw people out of their homes," said Elizabeth. "There are laws to protect tenants."

"In this case," I said, "the law is not on Dweena's side. That building is zoned for commercial use only. She and most of the other tenants live there illegally. The landlord can do pretty much whatever he wants. She tried Landmarks, but they couldn't help. The building is just outside of the West Village historic district. So Dweena came up with S.O.B. She's trying to prove her building and some others nearby were once brothels."

"So what if they were?" said Chuck.

"Damned if I know," I said, "but she's up to some-thing and seems convinced she can save those buildings. Could be she stepped on the wrong toes. Thus the kid-napping."

"Huh?" said Chuck.

I had to admit, as the words tumbled out of my mouth, they didn't make much sense.

"I don't see the logic," said Chuck. "Most landlords would just send a bunch of junkies into the building, slip them a set of master keys, let them rob a few apart-ments. Then the tenants would leave voluntarily."

"Terrible," said Elizabeth.

"Brenda, you mentioned another possibility," said Johnny.

"Yes. You know how Dweena is. I'm thinking that in her great enthusiasm to relocate diplomat vehicles, she simply boosted the wrong car. This car came with all the options, including a kidnapper with a fake-sounding accent and a trigger-happy finger."

"You're saying the kidnapper was in the car when Dweena nabbed it?" said Chuck.

I shrugged. "Maybe. I think it's a little too coinciden-tal that Dweena, of all people, would get kidnapped by someone driving a diplomat car. And before any of you ask—no, I did not get a good look at the license number. All I remember was the *D* for diplomat."

"And I didn't even notice that," Johnny said sheep-ishly. "Some Urban Detective I turned out to be."

"Don't feel so bad," said Chuck to Johnny. "None of this is your fault."

The implication, of course, was that it was my fault, an unfair assessment, and that pissed me off, but I held in my anger. This was not a good time to fight.

"We're in over our heads," said Johnny. "I think we ought to call in the professionals."

"Meaning Turner and McKinley?"

"Sure, why not?"

I was surprised it had taken Johnny so long to bring

up the possibility of dragging in the police. He genuinely liked his pals, Detectives Turner and McKinley.

The detectives and I . . . well, we weren't always on the best of terms, however, due to the fact I'd recently saved both their butts from humiliation and probable job loss, they—Turner especially—owed me big time. I would have loved to cash in on the good will, but I was scared.

"The guy on the phone, the kidnapper, warned me, no cops. I'm pretty sure that's what started all this trouble in the first place." I explained my theory that the kidnapper had mistaken Johnny for a real cop.

Everybody agreed it was a reasonable reconstruction of events.

"Well, then," said Chuck. "If we don't bring in the fuzz, what's our next move?"

"I don't know."

Nobody else knew either.

I closed my eyes and thought back to earlier that day when the kidnapper had called.

"Do you remember hearing any noises in the background?" asked Johnny.

"No."

"Any clicks or disruptions on the telephone line?" asked Chuck.

"No."

"How about that Caller ID box I installed for you? Maybe if we found out where the guy called from, we could—"

"It's gone," I said. "One day Jackhammer was racing around the shop, and he got tangled in the phone wires, and yanked them out of the wall. When I plugged the equipment back in, my Caller ID didn't work anymore."

"You should have told me," said Chuck. "I could have fixed it for you."

"To tell you the truth, I hated the damned thing. It's not all that wonderful to know who'd called and hadn't bothered to leave a message on my answering machine."

"May I remind you all," said Elizabeth, "these days, everybody's got a callback feature, like it or not. Perhaps we can trace the bum that way."

It seemed highly unlikely that any kidnapper would be stupid enough to call from a phone that would lead back to him or any useful information. But Johnny said criminals weren't what they used to be, and nobody came up with a better idea, or for that matter any other idea whatsoever, and trooping over to Midnight Millinery gave us something to do, so we did it.

Chuck, being a reformed phone-freak and hacker, handled the callback. All he had to do, he claimed, was listen to the tones. He'd know the number, even if no one picked up.

His tone interpretation skills weren't needed. My friend Irene Finneluk answered on the third ring. Then I remembered. That evening, right after the kidnapper's call, she'd called to wish me a happy birthday.

It was a nice try, though, everyone agreed.

"Any more ideas?"

"Nope."

"Well, Johnny, what would Tod Trueman do in a similar situation?" asked Chuck.

Johnny frowned.

"For chrissakes," I said, "This is real. Dweena is in danger."

Chuck looked hurt.

"Sorry," I said. "I didn't mean to lash out at you."

By that time, we were all getting a little testy.

There was nothing we could do but wait. The kidnapper had the money. With any luck—and believe me, my fingers were crossed so hard they stuck together—he'd do what he was supposed to do and turn Dweena loose. Or, second best, maybe he'd call and make further demands.

We decided to do the waiting right where we were,

at Midnight Millinery, since that's where the kidnapper had contacted me earlier.

"I know a place that delivers pizza all night long," said Chuck.

"Hold the pepperoni," I said.

3

I caught sight of the blue-helmeted pizza delivery guy whipping around the corner at extreme speed. To head him off before he chained his stripped-down bicycle to one of the street trees, I stepped outside to pay. He pocketed the money and was gone in a flash.

As I cracked open the cardboard boxes, Chuck, Elizabeth and Johnny ran through a personalized version of "Happy Birthday." Since no one was the least bit happy, it came out sounding like a funeral dirge. It didn't much matter to me. The clock on the wall read past midnight, so technically it wasn't even my birthday anymore.

But then, when I discovered that Chuck's favorite pizza joint had neglected to leave the pepperoni off half of one of the pies, it was the last straw.

"Goddamm it anyway," I said to deflect attention away from the single tear that threatened to push out of my left eye.

"It's only pizza," said Chuck. "You don't need to get so riled up. I'll be more than happy to remove the offending pepperoni from a couple of slices."

"Don't bother," I said. "I'm not hungry anyway."

"You really ought to eat," said Elizabeth.

"Right," said Johnny. "You know how you get when you don't."

"Oh yeah? And how is that?" I snapped.

The answer was immediately apparent. An empty stomach makes me cranky. To show I was a good sport, I pulled off the pepperoni myself, tossed one greasy disk to Jackhammer, and slammed the rest onto Chuck's slice.

When we'd all finished eating, I closed up the pizza boxes, took them out to the street, and balanced them on top of the trash can. By the time I got back inside, Chuck had taken it upon himself to turn on my computer. He'd given me the machine, and perhaps saw the gift as more of a permanent loan, but I wished he'd asked first. I tried to control my expression, but a dirty look slipped out.

"I figured as long as I'm stuck here anyway," he said, "I might as well clean up your system and defragment your hard drive. Do you mind?"

"No. Go ahead. Defragment or whatever." Messing around with computers was what Chuck did; it would help pass the time.

Elizabeth wandered into the storage room and poked around until she located my roll of pattern paper. She tore off a hunk, brought it out to my blocking table, took a pencil out of her purse, and started to doodle.

Johnny sat at the vanity and made faces in the mirror.

"What in the world are you doing?" asked Elizabeth. "I'm trying to draw you."

Johnny laughed. "Face-firming exercises. It's a twice-a-day routine."

"Does it do any good?"

"Hell if I know."

I climbed into my display window to get away from everybody. Once there, I couldn't help but look around at my hats. The bad, though hardly surprising news, was that I hated all of them. Last season's styles looked mighty tired, yet I had no new hats to put up.

Thinking how awful it would be if I never got inspired to make another hat, I shifted the shopworn display hats from one hat stand to another and in the process unsettled puffs of dust. After a sneezing fit, I gave up, sat down, and stared out at the cobblestones of West Fourth Street.

By New York standards, not much was happening. A couple of dog walkers passed by, an airport limousine dropped someone off, a speeding cab overshot the stop sign at the corner.

Head resting against the window, I dozed off.

Sometime later, an hallucination.

A vision, a flash of bright sparkly orange topped with a white cloud cut through the silent murky darkness, striding straight toward Midnight Millinery. It came on high-heeled patent leather platform shoes. It looked mad as hell. It banged on the door and shouted, "Open up."

Dweena.

She needed a shave. Edward's beard stubble poked through her extra-thick layer of ultra-pale pancake makeup. Her glitter false eyelashes had come unstuck, her platinum wig was askew, and her dress no longer sported its full contingent of orange sequins.

To me, she looked fabulous.

Lots of hugs all around. Some hearty back-slapping, a few tears of relief.

Chuck got on the phone and ordered up three more pizzas. "Now we've really got something to celebrate," he said.

Once everybody settled down, Dweena asked the inevitable question. "Are you crazy, or what, Brenda? Bringing Johnny like that? For that matter, wasn't Johnny supposed to be out of town?"

"Boston," said Johnny.

"Johnny rearranged his schedule and came back to town specially to celebrate my birthday." A hell of a lot more than I could say for some of my friends. "He got me a dozen long-stemmed roses."

"Well," said Dweena, "Johnny's presence is what spooked that asshole diplomat who kidnapped me."

"That's what I figured," I said. "He thought Johnny was a real cop, right?"

"Yes. I could hardly explain that Johnny was only a cop on TV, not with duct tape plastered over my mouth."

"You poor dear," said Elizabeth.

"He could have killed me. He probably would have, too, except I got the brilliant idea to hum the *Tod True-man* theme song which, thank god, the jerk recognized."

"Great idea," said Chuck.

"Thank you. The duct tape added an interesting vibrato. The tune must have rung a bell somewhere in the kidnapper's tiny little brain and he soon realized his mistake. He actually seemed a little embarrassed at his overreaction."

"I'm glad things worked out," I said.

"You're not off the hook yet, Brenda. I'm still waiting for you to explain why you brought Johnny along to the payoff. You should have realized what would happen."

Meekly, I told her.

"You thought what?" she shrieked.

"A surprise birthday party." To avoid eye contact, I looked down at the floor. It needed a good vacuum job. When Dweena stamped her foot in anger, a dust bunny jumped up and skittered.

"That's just great," she said, stamping her other foot for emphasis. "Ever so freaking wonderful. I get kidnapped and out of all my friends and acquaintances"—she looked around at the others before turning back to me—"I determine that you, Brenda Midnight, you're the most well-grounded, the most level-headed, the most capable to deal with this particular rotten situation, so I tell the maniac kidnapper to call you, and you think it's a joke. A surprise birthday party. If that doesn't take the goddamned cake, and I'm not talking birthday cake either."

I defended myself. "It's just that it *was* my birthday, and I sort of thought you guys were gonna—"

"Oh, please, Brenda. Next time some asshole kidnaps

me, I'll be sure he times it more conveniently, so as not to conflict with any of your festivities."

She was starting to piss me off. Convenience was not the issue, nor were festivities. Thrilled as I was to have Dweena back safely, I refused to shoulder the entire blame. I'd done my part. I got the money, I made the payoff. My only mistake was to bring Johnny along.

I was not the one who started the ball rolling in the first place. I suspected Dweena herself had played a big role in that. "Dweena, what exactly were the circumstances of your kidnapping? Care to explain?"

"What do you mean?"

"Of all the people in this city to kidnap at any given moment, why did the kidnapper single you out?"

"Oh. That."

It was Dweena's turn to look down and study the dust bunnies.

"Yes, that," I said.

"Well, I guess you could say I got myself into a bad position."

"You stole that diplomat car, didn't you?"

"I most certainly did not! Dweena does not steal cars. The vehicle in question was illegally parked. It was my duty and passion to relocate it."

"I knew it," I said. "And where was the diplomat while you were performing this service to mankind? In the backseat, or what?"

Dweena threw up her hands. "Do you take me for a complete idiot?"

"No, I do not. Just curious is all." I fought to keep my sarcasm to a minimum.

With a huge sigh Dweena dramatically flung herself into a chair. "Well, you ought to, because he was. In the backseat, that is, hidden under a heavy wool blanket, which I saw the second I popped the lock. I remember thinking it was the wrong season for wool blankets and that it was the ugliest color of blue I'd ever seen. It never occurred to me the slimeball diplomat would be festering underneath. So, I go about my business, got the vehicle started, and had driven no more than thirty feet when the diplomat springs up out of the backseat, grabs me around the neck, hangs on for dear life, and screeches curse words at the top of his lungs. He's an excitable little pipsqueak. In any normal barroom brawl I'd have decked him easy, sent him sprawling. However, this was no normal brawl, this brawl was goddamned screwed up."

"Wish I'd been there," said Chuck.

Dweena gave Chuck a weird look, then continued. "So there I was barreling down Ninth Avenue, fighting off an insane angry diplomat, doing all I could to keep the vehicle on the road. You know that spot where Ninth butts into Hudson? That's where the bastard finally overpowered me." She shook her head. "Me, a victim. Can you believe it?"

"Rather odd behavior for a diplomat," commented Elizabeth. "Did you happen to catch the fellow's name? If I were you, I'd report him to his superiors. He's a bad representative, a loose cannon."

"Don't know his name, only that he's the Ambassador from Gintoflakokia. Maybe that's the way they act over there. Not everybody is as polite and restrained as we are over here in America."

"Gintoflakokia," said Johnny. "I should have known from his accent."

"I thought it was fake," I said.

"Geography is not my strong suit," said Dweena. "To tell you the truth, I'd never heard of Gintoflakokia. After the diplomat yanked off the duct tape I asked about his homeland. I thought it might calm him down. He told me Gintoflakokia was in the outer band of Dodondo, or some place like that."

I wasn't exactly great at geography either, but I didn't think a whole country could slip past me. "I haven't heard of Gintoflakokia or the outer band of Dodondo."

"It must be one of those new countries," said Johnny. "They're always popping up."

"The world is in such turmoil these days," said Elizabeth.

"Chuck," I said. "Why don't you check it out? There must be some mention on the Web."

Chuck moseyed back over to the computer and fired up the modem. A minute of hissing and fizzling and he was online.

We left him alone to search out Gintoflakokia.

The more I thought about Dweena's explanation of her kidnapping, the more it didn't totally ring true. I finally pinpointed what was bugging me. "I'm still confused about one small detail."

"What's that?" she said.

"I understand you didn't steal the car, but the diplomat thought you had. Now, why would a diplomat kidnap a car thief?"

"I dunno."

"You've gotta admit, it's weird. I mean, why didn't the diplomat just turn you over to the cops?"

"Good point," said Elizabeth.

"And that," said Dweena, "is exactly what he threatened to do. I didn't want to bore you with the complete story, but since you insist, here's how it went down. Thanks to my Wall Street experience I'm a damned good negotiator. So that's what I did. I negotiated my money for my freedom. I offered the jerk my whole stash if he'd forget he'd ever seen me. So you see, the scrawny little bastard blackmailed me."

"If you offered him the money," I said, "he's not a blackmailer."

"Right," said Johnny. "He'd be more of an opportunist."

"You had to be there," said Dweena. "Whatever, he's still an asshole."

"Back up a minute," I said. "How do we get from blackmail and/or opportunism to kidnapping?"

"Easy," said Dweena. "On the way to my place to pick up the money, I changed my mind. The money was

S.O.B.'s emergency operating fund, you know, in case I need to bribe a city official to save a building. I didn't want to waste it on some dipshit diplomat. So I made a break for it when we stopped for a light. Bastard grabbed my ankle and pulled me back into the car. After that, his mood darkened. He didn't trust me to fork over the money, not at all unreasonable given the situation, so he came up with this ransom idea. He became the kidnapper and I became the kidnapped."

"What a drag," said Chuck.

"Diplomatic vehicle relocation was never such an expensive hobby," said Dweena. "I'm gonna have to clean up my act."

The second round of pizzas arrived. I put the boxes on my hat blocking table. Everybody helped themselves. To Chuck's dismay, this time his favorite pizza joint left the pepperoni off both halves of all three pies. Disgusted, he folded over a plain cheese slice, stuffed it in his mouth, and stormed back to the computer. "Anybody know how to spell Gintoflakokia?"

"Don't ask me," said Dweena, "I can't spell for shit."

"Anybody else?"

"With a *G*?" I offered.

"Could be a *J*," said Johnny.

"Already tried both," said Chuck. "I tried various search combinations—begin strings, end strings, and in-the-middle strings."

"I wondered what was taking so long," said Elizabeth.

"I tried all the major search engines, several smaller ones, plus a couple so new nobody's heard of them yet. I've gone over lists of nations, old and new. I can only conclude that the way to spell Gintoflakokia is *B-U-L-L-S-H-I-T*. It's a make-believe country. Dweena, honey, I'm afraid you've been had. There simply ain't no Gintoflakokia on the face of the earth. No Gintoflakokia, therefore no Gintoflakokian diplomat."

Amazing. The guy really was a fake, though not an actor.

It took a nanosecond for the full impact of Chuck's statement to hit Dweena. She let loose a tirade, ending with the comparatively mild, "If there's anything worse than a goddamned son of a bitch freaking diplomat, it's a goddamned son of a bitch freaking fake diplomat con man kidnapper blackmailer. The lowest of the low. Lower than dirt. Lower than a snake belly in a wheel rut in hell. All this time I believed I was negotiating for my freedom with an honest businessman. No honor anywhere anymore. This changes everything. I want my fifty thousand dollars back. And Brenda, you and me, we're gonna get it."

4

Me? Oh no. No way.

"'Fraid not, Dweena. Much as I'd love to help you out, I'm a milliner. I create gravity-defying hats. I do not chase after kidnappers, blackmailers, opportunists, or diplomats—fake or real."

"Oh sure," said Dweena. "Brenda Midnight only does millinery. What about that time when you—"

I held up my hand. "Stop."

I knew exactly what Dweena was going to say. A few times in the past I'd managed to get myself ensnared in decidedly nonmillinery pursuits, always to right a wrong or to help a friend out of a jam. And yes, I've got to admit that once or twice, I'd contributed to that friend being in that jam in the first place. But this was different.

"It's all your fault," said Dweena.

Not this again. "How do you figure? You boosted the car and you offered the fake diplomat fifty thousand real dollars in exchange for your release."

"You screwed up the payoff."

"The payoff wouldn't have been necessary if you hadn't screwed up first."

Evidently I'd made my point. Without missing a beat, Dweena switched tactics. "Oh please, Brenda," she said all nice and sweet. "Pretty please, just one itty bitty little favor." She squeezed her thumb and forefinger together to demonstrate how small. "That's all I ask."

Later I'd hate myself for being such a soft touch, but it's damned near impossible for me to turn down a pleading friend. Much to my horror and against my better judgment, the words I didn't want to say tumbled out of my mouth, "Well, okay . . . if it's really only . . ." and I knew it was all over. Damn.

A big smile on her face, Dweena pranced over and slapped me on the back. "Thanks, Brenda. I knew you'd come through."

"She always does," said Chuck.

"You can count on our Brenda," said Elizabeth.

"Always willing to go the extra mile to help a friend," said Johnny.

It made me sick.

I noticed with disgust that nobody else volunteered to help.

Dweena's itty bitty little favor actually did seem pretty easy.

"We can trace him through the license number," she said.

"You remember it?"

"Of course. It's etched on my brain."

At least someone got the number. I glanced over at Johnny; apparently he was too embarrassed to meet my eye. I knew the feeling.

"So," said Dweena, "all you have to do is get me a name and address. I'll take care of the rest. I'll get my money back from that bastard, if I have to—"

"That's really all you want? Unless that license plate is as fake as the country of Gintoflakokia, it's easy enough to procure that information. You don't even need my help. Chuck can get it for you right here, right now, right off the Internet. Right, Chuck?"

"Wrong," said Chuck, with a shake of his head. "Time and time again I've tried to explain to you guys, the Internet is not magic. All the information in the world is not within the click of my humble mouse."

"Come on, Chuck, we're not talking NASA here. You

used to brag about how you could hack into anything."

"Yes, I did," he said. For a moment, a sparkle lit his eye and his old crooked smile showed up on his face. "But that was back when I was more into high risk. I don't do that anymore."

"I'm so glad you quit that hacking crap," said Elizabeth. "Believe me, prison is no fun."

Chuck's fairly recent respect for the law was a pain in the neck. However, I could not in good conscience encourage him to break his new moral code.

"All right then, Chuck's out. How about you, Johnny? Ask Turner and McKinley to run the license plate. They'll be more than happy to help. They like you."

"Yes, they do," said Johnny. "So why mess up a good thing by irritating the detectives with such a trivial matter? Besides, while they might *like* me, they *owe* you."

I knew when I was beat.

Later that morning, after the last pizza box was tossed away and everybody else had gone home to catch up on their sleep, Dweena went back to her place, peeled off her glitter eyelashes, traded her platinum tresses for a more conservative shoulder-length auburn pageboy, and changed into a white jumpsuit "with not too many sequins."

She picked me up and we headed down Hudson Street to the precinct.

"Promise," said Dweena, "that you won't rat on me when you talk to Turner and McKinley."

"Rat on you? What about?"

"My diplomat vehicle relocation project."

"Mum's the word."

I was positive that Turner, McKinley, and the entire precinct were already on to Dweena anyway. The only reason the cops hadn't busted her ass a long time ago was that they were on her side. Everybody from the mayor on down hates how diplomats get away with murder.

*   *   *

The uniforms who hung out on the ground floor of the precinct were accustomed to seeing me. None of them batted an eyelash when I entered. One rookie gave Dweena a quick up-and-down, then shook his head and mumbled something about Greenwich Village.

I paused before the staircase. "I think maybe it'd be a good idea for you to stay down here."

"No. I want to go with you."

"You could check out the crime map," I suggested.

"Crime map?"

"You've never seen the crime map? Well, follow me."

I led her to an alcove in back of the lobby. A gigantic map of the precinct spread over most of a wall. The map was riddled with bright colored plastic pushpins. Some of the colors were bunched together, others were scattered evenly throughout the West Village streets.

"There's a different color designated for each crime category."

Dweena brightened. "They got a special color for relocating diplomat vehicles?"

"I don't know. Ask around. I'm sure one of the nice policemen will tell you."

"That's okay. I'll figure it out myself."

Leaving Dweena to ponder pushpins, I climbed the narrow staircase to Turner and McKinley's floor, made my way over to the tiny grim cubicle the two detectives shared, and peeked in.

Turner, as usual, had his big, expensively shod feet propped up on his massive oak desk.

Detective Spencer Turner—nice-looking if you like the type, an exquisite light wool custom-made suit on his remarkably fit body—groaned at the sight of me. I could almost hear his inner self asking what he did to deserve this. Then, his inner voice must have answered and reminded him of how not so very long ago I'd saved his butt from a humiliating not-so-honorable career crash.

He swung his feet down, stuck a bogus smile on his face.

I didn't see McKinley.

"Where's Detective McKinley? Out on a doughnut run?"

My joke was a dud.

Turner frowned. "No, Ms. Midnight, Detective McKinley is not out on a doughnut run. My partner is doing his job, serving and protecting, keeping the Village safe for citizens—including milliners like yourself. Detective McKinley is out on the mean streets with a rookie apprehending a perp. A murder suspect, in fact. I'd be with them except I wracked up my knee when former Officer Gundermutter ran her Harley off the road on the way to her mother's for dinner."

"Hey, cool. Dinner at Gundermutter's mother's. Sounds like you two are serious." Though I'm not much of a cupid, I was proud of the small role I'd played in getting Turner together with Nicole Gundermutter. She'd recently quit the force to go into motorcycle repair.

"Yes, Ms. Midnight, we are. Now tell me, what can I do for you *today*?" His emphasis on the last word, reminded me that my favors were getting used up at a fast clip.

"This is a snap," I said. "All I need is for you to run a plate."

Blank stare from Turner. "Run a plate?"

"You know, like a license plate."

With a mighty sigh, Turner said, "Skip the stupid TV lingo and give me the goddamned number."

I told him the number.

He scribbled it down. "Please note that I'm not even going to ask what this is for."

I nodded.

Then he excused himself. Seconds later—way too soon for me to read the open file on his desk—he was back. "Here." He thrust a piece of paper at me.

I took a quick look before tucking the paper into my

purse: P. G. Dover. No address. Before I could ask why, Turner interrupted my thoughts.

"It's a diplomat plate."

"Really?" I said. "How interesting."

"Yes, I agree," said Turner. "Very interesting. Makes me goddamned curious. Would your inquiry by any chance happen to have anything to do with your friend Dweena?"

"Whatever would make you think that? Well, Detective, I'd stay to chat, but I've got to scoot."

"Too bad. We coulda shot the breeze about hats or crime."

Turner must be slipping, I thought, as I high-tailed it down the stairs. I got almost all the way to the ground floor before his voice boomed from above.

"Keep your nose out of police business, Ms. Midnight. Go make some hats."

I found Dweena where I'd left her, staring at the crime map, hands on hips, tapping her foot. She seemed highly agitated.

"I pay taxes for this piece of garbage?" she said. "This so-called crime map is totally messed up, not merely out of date. I can point out many instances where it's flat-out wrong. Some of my relocation endeavors aren't recorded at all, and one of the pushpins that ought to be on Bethune Street is stuck around the corner halfway down the block on Washington. I mean, did you ever? I expect much greater accuracy from highly trained professionals. I want my hard work acknowledged. If they can't even get a simple grand larceny straight—"

Suddenly, a hubbub by the front entrance of the precinct.

The ground floor came alive. Cops poured out of the woodwork. Forgetting all about the crime map, Dweena and I pushed our way through the sea of blue to get a close-up view of the action.

Turner had not been bullshitting. Together with a rookie cop, McKinley, Turner's tall, black, elegant part-

ner, actually was bringing in a perp. Very gently, Mc-
Kinley guided the handcuffed perp through the door.

The perp looked mad as hell. That was to be expected.
Unexpected, was that the perp also looked familiar. I
recognized those beady eyes, that slicked-back black
hair, the dopey little mustache. The perp was the fake
diplomat, kidnapper, blackmailer, opportunist, whatever.
His name, according to information I'd just gleaned
from Turner, was P. G. Dover.

Before I could sweep Dweena off to the side of the
room, P. G. Dover caught sight of her. He did a quick
double-take, then yelled out, "Somebody, stop that
dame." Not having use of his hands, he jerked his head
in the general direction of Dweena and me.

"Arrest that man," shouted Dweena.

"I'm pretty sure they already have," I said.

5

I didn't have the luxury of time to analyze the severity of the situation, but I knew it was bad, so I followed my gut impulse to flee from trouble. I pulled Dweena along with me.

We rushed out the side door, and ended up on the drive-through that runs along the side of the precinct building. Suspended overhead, a banner advertised the annual spring get-to-know-your-neighbors open house. On that day, the police would generously throw open the doors of the precinct to members of the community. The drive-through would be a staging area where cops would grill hot dogs and dispense sodas. Kids would climb into cop cars, set off the sirens, ride the horses, and say hello to the bomb dogs.

Today, however, was not open house. Today the drive-through was just another drive-through, notable only for a couple of oil spots on the pavement.

And, of course, Dweena and me making a quick dash-through.

Not quick enough.

We were brought up short by the long lean figure of Detective McKinley. How did he do that? Seconds before he'd been inside with P. G. Dover, now he was outside blocking our way to freedom.

I'd never before noticed how big McKinley was. Bigger than Dweena even. His face was sullen. "How nice to see you, Ms. Midnight. You and your lovely friend, Miss Dweena. Ladies, I'd think twice about bolting if I were you."

Thinking once was enough to stop me, but not Dweena. She sprinted right on by Detective McKinley and made it all the way to the other side of the street before she changed her mind, braked her platform pumps, screeched to a full stop, turned and faced McKinley. "Am I under arrest?" she yelled.

"Now what would make you think that?" asked McKinley.

McKinley herded us back into the precinct and up the stairs, all the time politely encouraging Dweena and me to stick around until this mess got sorted out. "If you know what's good for you."

"No prob," I said.

"I hope this won't take too awfully long," said Dweena. "I have a rather pressing engagement later this afternoon."

McKinley made no comment. When we reached the top of the stairs, he held the door open for us. Always the gentleman.

Dweena went first. "Oh my, I've never been all the way up here before." She did a three-sixty turn and took in the drab surroundings. "I expected it to be a tad more luxurious. I know an interior decorator who could do wonders for this shithole. If you like, I could give you his name."

McKinley grumbled some discouraging words.

I started to walk toward the detectives' cubicle.

McKinley grabbed my elbow. "Not so fast, Ms. Midnight. We have another stop to make first."

I had a bad feeling that turned out to be right. Our first stop was all-too familiar territory—the precinct's utility closet, a small multiple-use room where Jackhammer and I had once passed a tense half hour.

It was as I remembered. Metal shelving sagged under

the weight of industrial-size containers of cleaning
chemicals. Brooms and mops rested against a slop sink.
A sickening sweet odor emanated from translucent plastic tubs of liquid bathroom deodorant.

McKinley pointed a long forefinger at Dweena. "Wait
here."

She protested vigorously. When that didn't work she
tried pouting, then threats, which McKinley did not acknowledge. He turned over a bucket for her to sit on,
told her to make herself comfortable, shut the door,
locked it, and ushered me to the cubicle.

Turner glanced up, smiled at his partner, and gave me a
quizzical look. "Back so soon, Ms. Midnight?"

"Not my choice," I said.

Turner raised his eyebrows at McKinley.

McKinley did a face-twitch thing, then jerked his head
toward the door and rolled his eyes in the direction of
the corridor.

Turner pushed his chair back, got up, and limped out.
I'd forgotten all about his banged-up knee.

Now McKinley pointed his forefinger at me. "Stay."

I sat down in a folding chair and shifted around trying
to find a comfortable position. Whenever I moved, the
chair squeaked and pinched me in a new spot.

The air was lousy with burned coffee and the stench
of fear, most likely my own.

From out in the corridor I heard the low murmur of
Turner and McKinley talking. I strained to hear, but
failed.

My imagination galloped over some mighty hilly territory. I finally reined it in enough to focus on the facts.
Fact one: Turner and McKinley were homicide detectives. Fact two: Earlier, when I'd inquired about Mc-
Kinley's whereabouts, Turner told me McKinley was out
picking up a murder suspect. Fact three: Soon thereafter
McKinley escorted a handcuffed P. G. Dover into the
precinct.

Given those facts, it wasn't too much of a stretch to figure out there might be a dead body in the mix and that Dweena's kidnapper–blackmailer–opportunist–fake diplomat P. G. Dover, was involved in how that body got dead.

Turner and McKinley returned to their cubicle. Turner eased himself down in his chair and smiled at me. The smile was not genuine. McKinley perched atop his desk, casually swung his leg back and forth. He, too, wore an artificial smile.

I met their false smiles with a dazzling one of my own.

Then I closed my eyes. Maybe, just maybe, this was all a bad dream. I opened them again. No such luck. I was awake. This was real.

Turner rhythmically pounded his desk with his fist. At the rate of one pound per syllable, he pronounced, "I shoulda known the second you turned up."

I kept my mouth shut.

"Trouble," Turner said with a final pound.

McKinley stopped swinging his leg. "How come, whenever we've got trouble in the precinct, specifically homicidal kind of trouble, you turn up right smack in the middle of it?"

He exaggerated. I had never actually been in the middle. "Me?" I squeaked.

"Yes, Ms. Midnight. You," said Turner. "Cut the innocent act. As you may have deduced, this is a serious matter."

"Murder," said McKinley.

Turner continued. "Perhaps you'd care to explain how mere moments before McKinley here brings Mr. P. G. Dover in for questioning, you ask me to, in your words 'run a plate,' and the plate turns out to belong to none other than Mr. P. G. Dover?"

"I don't know," I said. "Coincidence? The random nature of the universe?"

"Don't be a smart ass."

"I'm sorry. I really don't know. Who got killed, any-way?"

Both detectives frowned.

Dead silence.

It looked like I'd used up all the favors and goodwill.

A short time later, Turner limped out of the cubicle, leaving me alone with McKinley. Except for our breath and the too-frequent squeak of my chair, we kept the uncomfortable silence going until Turner came back muttering curse words to himself.

Turner whispered something to McKinley, who then left. When McKinley returned, he had Dweena in tow. Considering that she'd been locked in the utility room, she looked complacent.

"Miss Dweena here refuses to talk without her lawyer present," he said.

Good, I thought. Dweena is using her brain.

McKinley went on. "And she maintains her lawyer is you."

Besides Turner, I was the only one in the cubicle. McKinley was looking straight at me.

I blinked. "Me?" I said for the second time that day.

"That's what the lady said."

"Oh sure," said Turner. "Brenda Midnight, Esquire and milliner. When pigs fly."

"However," continued McKinley, "it's not my god-damned job to check up on anybody's lawyer creden-tials." He glanced over at Turner. "Is it yours, pard?"

Turner cocked his head. "Uh, no. I don't remember seeing that kinda crap in my job description."

Perhaps the goodwill and favors weren't totally de-pleted, after all.

I jumped on the opportunity. "I'd like to speak with my client in private," I said.

Unfortunately, private meant a trip back to the utility room.

McKinley turned over another bucket. "For you," he said.

"Thanks so much, Detective."

"Give a holler when you're done."

The door slammed shut.

Forefinger over my lips, I signaled to Dweena to keep quiet. I put my ear up against the door, and listened for the sound of McKinley's receding footsteps. When it seemed he was far down the hall, I turned to Dweena. "Are you out of your mind? You need a real lawyer."

"You know how I hate lawyers."

"So who doesn't? Dweena, you must rise above your hatred. The time has come to transcend. The subject is murder. Turner and McKinley are involved. Dover's involved. Because he's involved, like it or not, you're involved."

"So what?" said Dweena. "I didn't kill anybody. That'll be easy enough to prove. I saw this special on TV. You would not believe all the stuff those forensics people can do these days. I don't see how anybody gets away with anything."

"You need a lawyer."

"It's bad strategy to get a lawyer right away. It'll make it look like I really do have something to hide."

"You do. Speaking of forensics, don't forget, Dweena, your fingerprints and sequins and DNA must be all over Dover's car. Who knows what he used it for or who else was in it."

"Not a problem. While I suffered alone in this awful room, I came up with a perfectly plausible explanation as to why my stuff might possibly show up in Dover's vehicle."

"Great, Dweena. I'd prefer truthful to perfectly plausible. Lying will only get you in deeper."

"You should know by now that Dweena never lies. I'm going to tell the truth, in my own way. If you just give me a chance to explain to those two fuzzbos out there what really happened, we'll be back out on the street in no time."

"I don't know, Dweena."

"Don't take this lawyer bit so seriously. All you have

to do is listen. You know Turner and McKinley. You've heard their good cop, bad cop routine dozens of times. With that experience you'll easily recognize if they try any funny business to trip me up. That happens, or if I start to lose my cool, you, as my attorney, can stop the proceedings. Then I'll get a real lawyer. I promise."

"What if I refuse to go along with this really stupid idea?"

"You won't leave me in the lurch."

I really hated that my friends knew me so well.

"So," said Dweena, "we're all set?"

I didn't answer. Why bother?

She banged on the utility room door with a broom handle. "Yo, Fuzzeroos. Turner, McKinley. Let me and my attorney out of this squalid dump. Dweena is ready to talk."

We filed back to Turner and McKinley's cubicle. Turner led the way, limping. Dweena and I came next, and McKinley brought up the rear. I didn't like the fact they were keeping such close watch on us.

They sat Dweena in the squeaky folding chair, and brought out a matching one for me.

"No thanks. I prefer to stand."

"Have it your way," said McKinley. He leaned against the wall, crossed his arms over his chest, and scowled.

Turner sat down behind his desk, made a big show of shuffling through some papers. Then he cleared his throat, and started in on Dweena. As expected, the questions all had to do with the time Dweena had spent in the company of P. G. Dover in his car.

Turner admitted that they doubted Dover's diplomatic status. He said diplomat plates were fairly easy to procure. "Everything's for sale in this city."

Throughout the grilling, Dweena maintained her composure. Sitting straight and tall and steady in the chair so that it didn't squeak at all, she spoke freely and with complete confidence.

To my horror, she was lying through her teeth. I

wanted to stop her, but feared such action would call more attention to her blatant lies.

She claimed to have stumbled onto the unlocked diplomat car. "It's like this," she said, grinning. "I merely slipped inside that vehicle for a moment."

"You 'slipped inside' a vehicle you did not own," said Turner. "Pray tell, what for?"

Dweena spread her fingers over the bottom half of her face. With a flirtatious flutter of her eyelashes, she looked from Turner to McKinley then back again, avoiding me. "It's a bit embarrassing," she said, demurely. "I was on my way to a gala occasion when a heavy breeze came up off the Hudson, and one of my artificial glitter eyelashes loosened. I don't know what the world is coming to. Subversives are messing with the weather, it's windier than ever, and glue's not what it used to be."

I closed my eyes and concentrated hard. Stop it, stop it now, stop it right now.

"Anyway," said Dweena, not picking up on my urgent nonverbal message, "I noticed Mr. Dover's vehicle parked—illegally I might add—and saw my salvation in the form of the rearview mirror. So upset was I about my appearance, and driven by the need to repair my eyelash, I didn't even think. It was, after all, a crisis situation. I discovered one of the back doors had been left unlocked. I didn't think anyone would mind if I went inside to fix my eyelash. The repair would be done in the blink of an eye."

Inwardly I rolled my eyes.

"You didn't think to use the considerably more convenient side mirror mounted on the outside of the car?" challenged Turner.

"Good heavens no. Too low. Too small. Too public. And far too unladylike. So I entered the vehicle via the back door, and had just started to climb into the front seat, when that man—the one you call P. G. Dover—pops off the backseat floor where he'd been hiding under a blanket. He had the audacity to accuse me of trying to steal the car. I mean really. At first I thought he must be joking, but then I quickly assessed the situation, and realized that I was dealing with a deranged maniac. Now you tell me he's a crazed killer—"

"Nobody said that," said McKinley.

"Sorry, I meant to say *alleged* crazed killer. I attempted to reason with the man. Finally in frustration I offered him a bit of cash, you know, to demonstrate my good intentions."

Dweena refrained from mentioning exactly how much cash equaled a bit.

"That's not quite the way Mr. Dover tells it," said Turner. "He contends he spent the entire evening motoring around the city with you, checking out the scenery."

"The little jerk is lying. You yourself said you doubt his diplomat bullshit, so he's a known liar. I'm telling you, the whole encounter was over in a couple of minutes."

"Exactly what we wanted to hear," said Turner. He smiled, and this time it looked genuine.

"Huh?" said Dweena. Finally the chair squeaked.

I too was stunned that the detectives had apparently fallen for Dweena's whopper.

Turner said, "Now that that's out of the way, we can easily place Mr. Dover at the scene of the crime, at the time of crime. I thank you, ladies. You may go now."

6

Dweena clattered down the staircase, ran through the lobby, dashed straight out the front door of the precinct, hit the street and kept going. She didn't look back.

I stuck close behind her. She couldn't run away from reality.

I knew she knew I was pissed. I also knew she'd pretend not to know, which was why a couple of blocks away when she finally slowed down to a trot, to be sure there'd be no question in her mind, I came right out and said it.

"I'm really pissed."

She stopped in her tracks, whirled around to face me. "*You're* pissed? How the hell do you think *I* feel? P. G. Dover scammed me out of fifty thousand dollars of S.O.B.'s money. I can't believe I fell for that Gintofla-kokia bit. If I ever get my hands on that little jerk... well, you don't want to know. Dig it, Brenda, the situation pisses me off much more than it pisses you off."

Hard to imagine, but it seemed she really didn't get it, didn't realize the tight hole she'd spun herself into. "I'm not talking about the situation," I said, "It's *you* I'm pissed at."

Dweena's fingertips fluttered to her chest. "Moi?"

"Yes, Dweena. You. You, in whom I placed my trust. You, who promised to tell the truth. You, who then

45

turned around and fed the cops the biggest, the stupidest, the boldest bald-face lie I've ever heard."

"You're overly dramatic, Brenda. I reinterpreted the truth. That's all. No big deal. Everybody does it. Everybody, that is, except you apparently."

"Your 'reinterpretation' could send an innocent man to prison."

"Oh yeah? Which innocent man?"

"Don't play dumb, Dweena. You know damned well I mean P. G. Dover."

"P. G. Dover is far from innocent. He's scum. He cheated me out of my money."

Talk about reinterpretation. Dweena had a warped view of the circumstances under which she gave up that money. Neither she nor Dover came up smelling like roses on that enterprise. "Forget the fifty thousand," I said.

"Easy for you to say."

"Dover didn't kill anybody, not while you were with him, which must be when the murder happened. And that's the point. Don't you understand? You're Dover's alibi."

"Well, nobody bothered to ask me if I wanted to be an alibi. Who got killed, anyway?"

"Turner and McKinley skirted that issue. They have to wait until they notify the family, I guess. That's not our concern. We have a big problem. You misled the police in a murder investigation."

"My problem, not yours."

"I was with you as your attorney. Remember? Look Dweena, it's not like you have a choice. This is murder, not an overnighter in the drunk tank. Dover could be in prison for the rest of his life. Executed even."

"Oooh, the hot chair. Cool."

"Since when do you believe in capital punishment?"

"I don't, but I could make an exception."

In our single brief encounter on that desolate street P. G. Dover hadn't created a favorable impression on me either. That didn't mean I could throw him to the wolves, unjustly accused of murder.

I tried to knock some sense into Dweena's hard head. I felt responsible for Dover's plight. Turner and McKinley would never have believed Dweena's outlandish eyelash story if she weren't my friend. The detectives might razz me, to my face they might call me a pain in the neck, but behind all the posturing, deep down they trust me.

I had to live up to that trust. I had to fix this mess—before it got a whole lot messier.

First things first. I needed to think. To that end, I shifted into automatic small-talk mode. That left me free to ponder more crucial matters, and at the same time babble on about the excessive humidity, spring rains, potholes on Hudson Street, and alternate side of the street parking—subjects Dweena could relate to, even in her present state of rage, subjects I hoped would soothe her into rational, logical thought.

As we walked along and chatted, the part of my brain doing the serious thinking came up with a solution. I had to make Dweena understand that as long as P. G. Dover remained in jail, she wouldn't get her money back. The only way she'd have a shot at it was if Dover got out. Furthermore, if he got sprung because she finally broke down and told the cops the truth thereby providing him with an alibi, Dover might return her money out of sheer gratitude.

Not so easy was figuring out the mechanism by which she would do the truth-telling. She could hardly march back into the precinct and tell Turner and McKinley she'd changed her mind, so sorry. She needed a mouthpiece to do it for her.

I had my work cut out for me.

"Come on, let's get some lunch." I whisked Dweena into a twenty-four-hour coffee shop and sat her down in a pink booth before she had a chance to refuse.

A thin, sharp-featured waiter dressed in all black swooped over, slapped gigantic plastic laminated menus down on the table. "Coffee?"

"Please," I said, suddenly aware I'd been up all night.

The waiter fluttered back with a pot of hot coffee almost before I realized he'd gone.

We got the food ordering out of the way quickly— spinach salad (hold the bacon) for me, chocolate layer cake and a large chocolate milk for Dweena.

"I see somebody is a chocoholic," trilled the waiter.

Dweena glowered at him.

She was usually very friendly. Perhaps she was beginning to understand the seriousness of her deeds. I certainly hoped so.

The waiter spun on his heel and left in a huff.

I felt bad for him. It was a tough job dealing with customers in foul moods.

While we waited for the food, I explained the facts of lying to the police to Dweena; mostly I spelled out all the reasons why she shouldn't have. I could tell, from the look on her face, that my sermon was sinking in. For my grand finale I told her that so long as P. G. Dover was incarcerated, she didn't have an ice cube's chance in hell of getting her fifty thousand dollars back.

"Oh," she said. "Now that you put it that way, I see what you mean. After we stuff our faces, I'll toddle over to the precinct and have a little chit-chat with the fuzz."

"It won't be that easy."

The waiter appeared and slammed down our plates without comment.

I nibbled at my salad, and waited for Dweena's opiate receptors to get endorphined-out by the ingestion of chocolate before explaining what she had to do.

She packed in two-thirds of the cake, rested her fork, took a long pull on the chocolate milk, scrunched back against the booth, and cracked a smile.

The time was as right as it would ever be. Very, very

gently, I suggested we go visit a mutual acquaintance on lower Broadway, Brewster Winfield.

"No. Not in this lifetime."

"Brewster Winfield can help you," I said.

"Brewster Winfield's a lawyer. I hate lawyers. We've already been through that."

"You need a lawyer."

"Maybe so, but not Brewster Winfield. He's a class-A weirdo, a freak. Anyway, I thought he gave up law-yering—too busy handling Myrtle's acting career is what I heard. You know what? I hate that stupid snake Myrtle even more than I hate lawyers, maybe more than I hate P. G. Dover."

"Myrtle's not so bad once you get used to her. Face facts, Dweena. You need a lawyer, and you'd hate a lawyer who's a stranger even more than you hate Win-field. Without him you can't tell the truth and without the truth you won't get your money back."

She picked up the fork, and slowly polished off the remaining cake. When the last bite was thoroughly chewed, she used the fork to jab at the air directly in front of me. "Okay, Brenda, if you insist, I'll go see Winfield. Just to talk."

The pay phone in the back of the coffee shop was mounted on a tiny patch of plaster wall between the kitchen and the bathroom. I dialed Winfield's home of-fice, got a recording, hung up, and tried his cellular num-ber.

He picked up immediately. "Brew Winfield here." His rich, deep voice resonated.

"Hi, Brew. It's Brenda Midnight. How about I buy you a drink?"

A sigh and then, "What kind of predicament are you in now?"

"I just thought it would be nice to get together. Haven't seen you for several months."

"A social call? Somehow, I don't believe you. I sus-pect there's more to it."

"I don't want to say on the phone."

"Sorry, Brenda. I'm otherwise occupied."

"It's really important, Brew. Life or death."

"Life or death, huh? I'm not impressed. Pretty much everything eventually boils down to one or the other, life or death."

I played my ace. "There's a large sum of money involved. Cash."

"You don't say. All right, Brenda, I'll meet you, but it'll have to be later. Right now, Myrtle and I are at an audition."

"How about I meet you there?" I had to act quickly, before Dweena changed her mind.

"I guess that'd be okay." He gave me an address in the West Forties. "Sixth floor, audition room number two."

As Dweena had mentioned, lately Brewster Winfield had been neglecting his law practice. Ever since Myrtle started to make it, he spent a considerable amount of time taking her to auditions. Legal-wise, he only took on special cases. He wouldn't be disappointed. Dweena definitely fit the bill.

"I've got to make two quick stops before we see Winfield."

"While you're running your little milliner-type errands, I'll procure us an appropriately spiffy vehicle for our journey. I think a convertible would be nice for a change. Sun and wind on my face, long auburn tresses trailing behind."

"What would be nice," I said, "is if we make it there without breaking any laws. Which is why we will take a cab."

Dweena frowned. "Sometimes you are no damned fun, Brenda Midnight."

"Do what I say today; tomorrow I'll be fun."

*   *   *

First stop, Midnight Millinery.

Dweena amused herself by trying on my display hats, but soon lost her enthusiasm. "I've seen all this stuff before. Don't you have any new hats?"

"I'm working on an idea," I said.

"Can I see?"

"It's bad luck to show works in progress."

"Really? I never knew that."

I checked my answering machine for messages. Blank. I'd hoped to hear from Johnny. So much had happened last night I never got a chance to ask when he had to be back in Boston. Maybe he was already gone. Damn. Just when we seemed to be getting along so well.

I consulted my calendar to see if any clients had scheduled a private consultation or a fitting. Not that I could remember the last time anyone had made such an appointment, but I wanted to be sure. I was tired and stressed out and could easily forget. My calendar was also blank. The entire afternoon was mine.

I took down the vaguely worded sign in the shop window, "Noonish to late or by appointment" and replaced it with the sign that read, "By appointment only."

Next Dweena and I went to my apartment. I fed Jackhammer, splashed fresh water into his bowl, and told him he had to stay home.

He looked up at me, then at the closet where his leash hung, then back at me. He vibrated his tail stub. The message was clear.

"Sorry, Little Guy. Not this time."

If he had a clue as to where Dweena and I were headed he'd have been even more heartbroken.

If Dweena had a clue where we were headed, she'd be as pissed at me as I was at her. It was my task to see that she didn't catch on until the last possible minute.

I climbed in the cab first. While Dweena maneuvered her large body into the small backseat, I leaned forward, opened the little pay slot in the bullet-proof plastic divider that separated the front seat from the back, and whispered our destination to the driver. Another time, another place I might have complimented him on his big, intricately wound turban.

"Ugh," said Dweena, wedging in beside me. "Where the hell are my legs supposed to go? This sucks. You know how I hate cabs."

"Grow up. Stop acting like a big baby."

Dweena slumped against the window and pouted, but not for long. Right away she noticed that we were headed uptown.

"What's the deal? I thought we were going down to Winfield's place on lower Broadway."

"Brew's not at home at the moment. We're meeting him in midtown."

"Midtown? What's Brewster Winfield doing in midtown?"

"Uh . . ." I stalled.

"You know how I hate midtown." She went on to tell me exactly how much. More than lawyers and cabs and Myrtle.

I got lucky. Before I was forced to give Dweena the answer that would make her so mad she might change her mind about going, the cab sailed through the intersection at Fourteenth Street, and she forgot all about the question.

She banged on the plastic divider and screamed at the cab driver. "You're staying on Eighth? Instead of taking Tenth? You nuts, or what?"

The driver, blissfully free of the nuances of the English language, ignored her, stayed on course, and slowly plowed up Eighth Avenue through impossibly dense traffic in the heart of the garment center. In the mid-Forties he missed our turn, so we got out on Eighth and hoofed it west.

7

I stood before an eight-story building, the single commercial structure on a street of indistinctive residential tenements. "This is it."

"Doesn't look like much," said Dweena. "You know, Brenda, you never finished telling me why Winfield wants us to meet him all the way up here in Hell's Kitchen."

Wrong. I'd never started to tell her, and for good reason.

"So," I said, turning my head and checking out the rest of the block, "this is the infamous Hell's Kitchen, is it? Interesting. I've heard the neighborhood has several excellent pre-theater restaurants. I don't see any on this block, do you?"

Dweena wasn't interested in pre-theater restaurants. "Does Winfield have an additional office here?" she asked. "You'd think one would be enough."

"Oh, a prestigious lawyer like Brew Winfield, I imagine he might have satellite offices all over town." Or at least did, back when he was actively practicing law.

Dweena frowned. "I detect a reticence on your part to answer a simple question. I've had enough of this crap. If you don't level with me right this instant, I'm outta here."

I had no more delaying tactics.

Dweena stepped to the curb and stuck out her arm for a cab. None were in the immediate vicinity, a situation that would not last long.

Push had come to shove.

"All right," I said. "Here's the setup: Brew is at an audition."

"I presume that 'audition' means the esteemed attorney has got that idiotic undulating Myrtle in tow."

I nodded.

"I hate Myrtle. She makes my skin crawl. Aren't I traumatized enough already? How dare you subject me, your good buddy, to Myrtle?"

"Because you, my good buddy, need a lawyer. Now, are you ready? We might as well get this over with."

I pushed open the graffiti-covered gray metal door and held it for Dweena. Muttering under her breath, she reluctantly entered the building.

The lobby was somewhat clean, and totally unadorned. A woman in a flower-print dress hummed a show tune while studying a flyer on the bulletin board that promised one hundred headshots for one hundred dollars. A guy with dark wavy hair sat on the floor with his back against the wall. An open script rested on his knees.

While we waited for the elevator I thought of Johnny and all the auditions he'd gone out on early in his career and how good he was at hiding how nervous he'd been and how disappointed he was when he didn't get a callback and how he didn't let that show either.

Of course, that was all before *Tod Trueman, Urban Detective*. I think, in a way, Johnny missed those days of exhilarating potential, when absolutely anything could happen.

I felt like that now about our relationship. I hoped he was still in town.

The elevator took forever to get down to the lobby, then forever and a day to grind up to the sixth floor. The

ascent seemed even longer because Dweena gave me the
cold shoulder. She literally turned her back to me and
stared at the fake wood patterned wall. Apparently we
were no longer on speaking terms.

The small waiting room was jam-packed with tense
hopefuls sitting on orange molded plastic chairs. Most
of the people balanced spiffy carrying cases on their
laps. Other carrying cases crowded the floor. A sign-in
sheet was taped to an interior door, behind which I presumed the actual auditions took place.

Heads turned when Dweena and I came in. Everybody
gave us a quick once-over before going back to doing
whatever they'd been doing to pass the time. Some
tapped toes, some drummed fingers, some read, and
some just stared into space.

Winfield strode over to greet us. A large black man
with a round face, wide open smile, and shoulder-length
dreadlocks, he was, as always, turned out in plush designer duds. Today's ensemble was a casually
understated melange of neutral colors, heavy on the silk
and cashmere content.

"Long time, no see," he said, giving first me, then
Dweena a showbiz-style double cheek buzz.

"Where's Myrtle?" asked Dweena. Her eyes swept
over the floor in trepidation.

With a flourish, Winfield gestured at a custom-made
leather carrying case. Myrtle's name was hand-tooled
onto both sides in fancy swash lettering and surrounded
by an elaborate circle of flowers. "Myrtle craves her privacy when she needs to get into character. She's been
isolated long enough, though. If either of you would like
to cuddle with her, I could let her out."

"Nope, not me," said Dweena. She took a step back.

"Me neither," I said, "but thanks anyway. I'm a little
stressed out today. It might rub off on Myrtle. I know
from Johnny how important it is to stay calm."

While not nearly as repulsed as Dweena, I'd never
warmed to the idea of Myrtle. I did, however, respect

her hard work and rise to success in a tough business.

She'd started out doing silly counting tricks with Winfield, little more than head-bobbing on command. It was enough to convince Johnny's agent, the inimitable Lemon (Lemmy) B. Crenshaw, to take her on as a client. Like Johnny, Myrtle's first professional gig was an appearance in an after shave commercial—she slithered on and off-screen in under two seconds. Lemmy said she had charisma. An important decision-maker saw that commercial, one thing had led to another, and from those humble beginnings Myrtle had gone on to fame and fortune as the orange and black spokes-snake for a major perfumery.

A rustling sound came from the carrying case.

Winfield said, "Oh, poor Myrtle-poo, she must think nobody loves her." He unlatched the case, tilted the top back, and gently lifted Myrtle out. She slid up his arm and buried her head under his turtleneck collar.

"What's the gig, another perfume commercial?" I asked.

"Oh no. This is Broadway, Babycakes. The Big B. A multimillion-dollar historical costume musical. Stakes are high. Backers are tense. But enough about Myrtle and our troubles. Tell me Brenda, Dweena, what kind of trouble did you two get into that requires my services to get you out of?"

"No trouble," said Dweena. "Consulting you was Brenda's idea and now that I think of it, not such a good one. Totally unnecessary. I'll mosey along now. So sorry to have taken up your valuable time."

She edged toward the exit. I grabbed her forearm. "You promised."

"I did not."

"You agreed."

"I changed my mind."

"I must admit," said Winfield, "this behavior intrigues me. What's up between you two?"

"We shouldn't go into it in here," I said. "Too many ears. Of all species. Let's step out to the hallway."

"I have to stay put," said Winfield. "I don't want to miss when they call our name. This director does not tolerate tardiness. Myrtle won't get a second chance."

"Won't somebody here tell you when it's your turn?"

"Are you kidding? These people are not a random collection of animal lovers. They're the"—he covered the sides of Myrtle's head with his hands and lowered his voice to a whisper—"Competition. With a capital *C*."

"Does money talk?"

"Hmmm," said Winfield. "Excellent idea, Brenda. I should have thought of that myself. Some truths are universal, and apply even to auditioners. Give me a twenty. Think of it as my retainer."

I thought of it as bribery, but reasonably cheap and definitely necessary. Dweena claimed not to have a cent on her, most likely a lie. I could hardly blame her. I'd probably say the same if I'd just given up fifty thousand dollars.

Since it was Dweena who needed a lawyer, I gave her the twenty, so she could personally hand it to Winfield, which she did. He palmed it and approached a woman bouncing a hamster on her lap. He bent down and said a few words. The woman smiled, nodded, grabbed the money, and tucked it down her blouse.

Myrtle slithered back down Winfield's arm and into her case. Winfield closed the lid and fastened the latch. Then we all filed out into the hall.

Dweena mistold the story. It was as if she could do no wrong. She was the perfect angel, loose in an unjust universe, and set upon by the forces of evil.

"Bullshit," I said. Then I took over and told the story the way it really happened. Every so often Winfield got fidgety, and I paused to let him peek into the waiting room. By the end of the story, specifically around the part where Dweena lied to Turner and McKinley about her false eyelash repair, I commanded his full attention.

When I finished, Dweena piped up. "However you tell

it, the situation sucks. So, Brew, what kind of contingency fee are you gonna demand to help me get my fifty thousand dollars back? Before you answer, remember, it's S.O.B. money, potentially a tax-deductible charity."

"I'm afraid that fifty thousand dollars is the least of your worries." Winfield's solemn expression confirmed my worst fears.

"What the hell's that supposed to mean?" said Dweena.

"Okay. I'll give it to you straight. No legalese, no small print, no bull. You are in deep doo-doo. You have interfered with a murder investigation. You have sent the cops down a blind alley, so to speak. Aside from the legal ramifications, you need to consider the moral and ethical—"

"Get this," said Dweena. Her eyes rolled dramatically skyward. "A lawyer lecturing *me* about morality. And ethics. The irony makes me shudder."

I jabbed her in the ribs with my elbow, a reminder that Brewster Winfield was friend, not foe, and that he was doing her a favor for a yet undetermined fee.

"So sorry," said Dweena. "I didn't intend to offend."

"No offense taken," said Winfield. "I'll grant you, in the course of my legal career I've sprung some crooks out of prison who should have been in. But I've never put someone in who should have been out. If we're really talking murder here, and it appears we are based on the involvement of homicide detectives, it could mean the death penalty."

"Dweena doesn't believe in the death penalty," I said.

"I already told you I could make an exception for P. G. Dover."

"Yeah, but you didn't mean it."

"Okay, you got me. I don't believe in the death penalty. Not for anybody, ever."

"So," I said, "you have to tell the truth. Right, Brew?"

"Don't be so hasty, Brenda," said Winfield. "We mustn't jump to conclusions. At this time, it is preferable that Dweena not admit to any wrongdoing on her part."

"What?" I wasn't prepared for this development.

"I know a better way to handle the situation."

"That's more like it," said Dweena. She offered her hand to Winfield. He shook it.

I didn't like the direction the conversation had taken. "The truth is always best," I said. "Always, always, always."

"Too simplistic, Brenda," said Winfield. "The world is not black or white. It's shades of gray."

I didn't have a come-back.

Winfield turned to Dweena. "Here's what I can do for you. Under the pretense of being Mr. Dover's attorney, I shall gain access to the man in the lock-up and discuss the matter to the degree that he is willing. After that, we'll be better able to assess our situation, and thereby effectively direct our strategy. What do you say?"

"I say, go for it," said Dweena.

"By pretending to be someone you're not, you hope to get information to help cover up a lie," I said.

"That's the spirit," said Winfield, apparently not picking up on my sarcasm.

"The beauty of it," said Dweena, "is that all the trouble started when Dover pretended to be someone he was not. Gintoflakokian ambassador. What a crock. Now, he'll get a dose of his own medicine."

Dweena was still glossing over the true facts of how the trouble began. It began when she stole P. G. Dover's car with him in it.

Before I had a chance to comment, the woman Winfield had bribed beckoned from the doorway.

Winfield picked up Myrtle's case. "That's it, gals. Gotta go. We'll touch base later."

"Break a leg," said Dweena. "Or whatever."

Dweena and I walked toward Ninth Avenue. More accurately, Dweena bopped blissfully along while I stomped in anger, chiding myself for coming up with the brilliant idea of talking to Brewster Winfield. I must have been out of my mind.

8

A solid line of parked cars stretched all the way to Ninth Avenue.

Dweena sang out, "The world is a wonder to behold, oooh, oooh, oooh, and I'm in the mood to celebrate, oooh shooby doo dooby doo."

Truly sickening. I trekked toward the avenue.

Dweena paused in front of a silver convertible sports car. "How about this honey to transport us back to the Village?"

To answer I stepped between two parked cars, stood in the street, and waved my arm at the passing traffic. Seconds later a cab rattled up.

I scrambled into the backseat and yanked Dweena in beside me.

"So maybe you don't like convertibles," said Dweena. "I can dig it. They're not everybody's cup of tea. It's because of your hats, I bet. You know, like in the wind? Gone? Blown away? Speaking of which, how come you don't have on one of your lovely chapeaux today? You never know who you'll run into, especially at an audition. You should take advantage of any opportunity to self-promote."

I was in no mood to discuss why I didn't want to ride home in a ripped-off convertible, or for that matter any subject, most especially why I hadn't worn a hat. I needed to work that out for myself.

"Gansevoort Street," I told the driver, then slumped against the side window and shut my eyes. I was completely exhausted and in a real bad mood.

Dweena took the hint. She turned her attention to the cab driver and engaged him in brisk banter about the codification of pedestrian barricades in midtown and their far-reaching effect on traffic flow in other neighborhoods, specifically the far West Village over by the meat market and the area in the East Forties around the United Nations.

I tuned out and spent the ride back to the Village tallying my stupid mistakes for the day. One, I'd aided and abetted Dweena in her big lie to the cops. Not technically my fault, but I doubted Turner and McKinley would make the distinction, especially with murder involved. Two, I'd dragged Winfield into the situation, opening up the possibility that his lawyerly lies would compound Dweena's.

What had I been thinking? I should have known better. A lawyer is a lawyer is a liar. Instead of scaring Dweena into telling the truth, Winfield had hired himself to do . . . what? Lie and make sure part of the fifty thousand ended up in his own bank account?

Not bad, I thought. Only two stupid mistakes. I glanced at my watch. The day was half over. With any luck, I might rack up a few more screw-ups before nightfall.

For whatever reason—barricades, lack of barricades, or the sheer recklessness of the lunatic behind the wheel— the cab flew downtown. Before I knew it we were on Gansevoort Street, in front of Dweena's place. We both got out. I got stuck with the cab fare.

"Do you want to come upstairs? I could show you the cool stationery Chuck designed for S.O.B. Very official-looking."

I shook my head.

"Well, then maybe we could just hang out."

Hang out? I already felt I'd been hung out to dry. "No

thanks. I need to open Midnight Millinery, at least for a couple of hours."

"In that case," said Dweena, "I guess I better say it now. Thank you, Brenda, for making me talk to Brew. You were right. I needed a lawyer. And Brewster Winfield's the best in the business."

I walked the couple of blocks back to my apartment building and stopped upstairs briefly to check for phone messages. Not a one. Weird that Johnny hadn't called. Even if he had gone back to Boston, I would have thought he'd call to find out how it had gone at the precinct for Dweena and me.

I left another message on his machine.

I took Jackhammer for a quick spin around the block, then opened up Midnight Millinery. I had every intention of working on a new hat collection. I needed fresh hats in the window.

Inspiration didn't exactly overwhelm me, a more and more common occurrence lately. Nobody who waits to get inspired stays in business very long. So I forced myself to sit down at the blocking table and spent what was left of the day tossing around an idea for a bulletproof hat, an indication of my dark mood.

Aside from my own personal distress about hats, and friends who forgot my birthday, and friends who lied to police detectives, I had to come to grips with a murder in the West Village. Violent crime is rare around here. Even putting aside my peripheral involvement, I still felt uneasy. Jackhammer and I wander throughout the neighborhood at all hours. I like feeling safe.

I turned on an all-news radio station hoping to catch details on the murder. I wanted assurance that I didn't know the victim and that it had happened on a block I never walked.

The lead story at the top of the hour round-up was the suspicious disappearance of a Greenwich Village woman, Gloria something or other. Foul play was feared. That had to be it.

Foul play feared. Not good, but a whole hell of a lot better than murder. All hope was not lost.

Not only was it not definitely murder, I didn't know anybody named Gloria. Before I had a chance to feel good about that, I felt guilty and selfish. I mean, this Gloria person was somebody.

Police had a witness in custody whom they were questioning. Listeners would be kept abreast of any late-breaking developments.

The police had to be Turner and McKinley, and the witness, P. G. Dover.

I hoped it would turn out all right for everybody.

Meanwhile, a jackknifed truck was causing traffic tie-ups and chances were good for overnight rain. I turned off the radio.

I fooled around with the scraps of fabric draped over my design head block until they took the form of a basic cloche. An appropriate shape, I thought, for protective gear—low on the forehead, close fitting, helmetlike, good for protection. I was considering whether a bow was too frivolous for bulletproof attire when the bells on the door jangled.

Elizabeth bounced through the door. "Want to grab a bite at Angie's?"

That sounded swell to me.

"Sure. Come on in. I just have to pin down a few of these loose ends first."

"Take your time. What are you working on? Summer, fall, winter, spring, cruise, holiday, or what? I don't know how you keep the seasons straight."

"None of the above." I gently lifted the rudimentary cloche off the block and placed it on my head. "A design for all seasons. Bulletproof headwear. What do you think?"

"How morbid. How not like the Brenda Midnight I know. What the hell's wrong with you?"

I told her about Dweena's lies and Winfield's dishonesty.

"Well, no wonder you feel like a pile of garbage," she said.

I stopped in front of Angie's, scooped Jackhammer off the sidewalk, and tucked him into his canvas bag. He squirmed into a comfortable position, then lay still. He knew the drill.

The deal I had with Tommy, Angie's owner and bartender, was that Jackhammer was allowed, as long as I pretended to sneak him in. He had to stay hidden in the bag until Tommy gave me the thumbs-up that no health inspectors were snooping around. Angie's had a long history. It was rumored to have started life as a speakeasy. To my knowledge, there had never, in all those years, been a health inspector anywhere near the premises, and if one ventured in today he'd have a hell of a lot more to worry about than a five-pound Yorkshire terrier with a taste for special little burger balls, but Jackhammer didn't seem to mind the bag, so I kept up the sham.

Angie's does up a pretty good grilled cheese sandwich and pours a decent house red wine, but it's the atmosphere that makes the joint—the perpetual darkness even at high noon, the soggy beer-swollen floorboards, the camaraderie of the pack of neighborhood regulars who perch on bar stools in front, the ancient wood booths in the back room where I like to sit, and beneath it all the jukebox throbbing with Tommy's hand-picked mix of jazz and blues and big band and a smattering of recent releases that make the cut.

You can tell time at Angie's by Sinatra's "New York, New York." It chimes in every hour on the hour.

But not tonight. That was the first thing I noticed when Elizabeth and I pushed through the double doors. It was nine o'clock straight up, on the dot, yet no Sinatra. No music at all and the big TV suspended in the corner at the end of the bar was turned off. The silence was crushing.

The regulars sat at their usual spots, hunched over their drinks, but they weren't engaged in their usual revelry. Smoke from their cigarettes rose, disrupted near the tin ceiling by a slowly rotating fan.

Tommy barely acknowledged us. I know he saw the canvas bag wiggle, but he didn't wink and flash a conspiratorial smile. Tommy's droopy mustache and sagging eyes gave him a dour appearance all the time, but even more so tonight. He wiped a white towel over a glass—over and over—as if the action didn't connect with his brain.

It was too strange. I didn't know how to react. I looked at Elizabeth and saw that she, too, looked ill-at-ease. What could we do? We'd been seen, so we couldn't leave without insulting Tommy, but what was the point of staying? I was wishing I could make myself invisible when Raphael ambled out of the kitchen.

Raphael, a genial guy who had a phenomenal memory for customers' usual orders, had been waiting tables at Angie's for as long as anybody could remember. He was more than a waiter. He managed all aspects of the food. During the slow part of the day he cooked. At one time a rumor circulated that he—not Tommy—owned Angie's, probably because he lived in a couple of rooms on the third floor.

"Brenda, Elizabeth, hello." He nodded his head toward the back room. "Lots of booths available this evening."

Normally, that would have been remarkable. Ever since an article in *New York Magazine* proclaimed Angie's the best neighborhood bar in all of New York, it had become next to impossible to get in around dinner time. Tonight's gloomy front room scene must have discouraged the tourist and outer-borough patrons.

It kind of discouraged me too.

I looked at Elizabeth for guidance. Stay or go? She

shrugged. I shrugged back. There was no graceful way to leave.

Following Raphael to the back, we settled into my favorite booth. When the light was just right I could still make out a spot on the tabletop where Johnny had carved our names inside of a heart. Tonight the light was not right.

Tonight, it didn't seem anything was right.

Jackhammer climbed out of the bag and rested his chin on the table.

"The usual?" asked Raphael.

"Apparently not," I said. "What's wrong with the crew out front? You'd think somebody—"

"Didn't you hear about Ria?" he asked.

"Ria?"

"About your size, brownish hair, big grin, usually sits on the stool by the front window."

"I know who you mean."

"It's all over the news. Ria Kleep."

Ria. Gloria. Gloria Kleep. Oh no. "She's the one—"

"Yeah," said Raphael. "Missing. Cops think she got killed. What happened is, this afternoon, a couple of cops came around here asking a lot of questions about Ria. Hell, I didn't even know her last name or that her full first name was Gloria, and now . . . she's probably dead."

"But they haven't found her body," I said.

"Not yet," said Raphael. "Cops got a report of loud noises in Ria's apartment, banging, screaming, gunshots maybe. When they got to the scene, the kitchen was a bloody mess, no one was around. Guess they figure she couldn't survive after losing that much blood."

"How awful," said Elizabeth.

"Makes you wonder, doesn't it?" said Raphael. "So, you two want your usuals?"

Loudmouth Ria Kleep was a regular at Angie's, one of the few women. Others had tried and failed, done in by either too much macho posturing or too much smoke.

Ria was like one of the guys. She told slightly risqué jokes, chain smoked, and drank the men under the table. For a while, I admired her.

Then she put the moves on Johnny.

"Feeling guilty?" asked Elizabeth.

"What do you mean?"

"You can't stand Ria Kleep because she went out with Johnny that time."

"Once. I never held it against her. Anyway, she made such a fool out of herself. She invited Johnny to a dinner party at her apartment. He didn't know until too late that he was the only guest."

"It's human nature to be jealous."

"Okay, so I was jealous. A little. Johnny told me she answered her door stark naked. Later Johnny admitted she looked pretty good."

"And you wished bad stuff would happen to her."

"No. Never."

"Yeah, right. Personally, I can't stand the woman either, and she never stood naked and offered herself to any boyfriend of mine."

"What did she do to you?"

"Rude bitch sneezed in my face. I politely suggested that she please in the future cover her mouth and nose before spewing spit every which way. I even offered my hankie. She had the gall to tell me that blockage was not necessary. 'It's an allergic reaction,' she said, 'not a cold.' Because she's not contagious, she thinks I want to breathe in her spit?"

"A fond memory," I said.

"Still, I'm damned sorry she's dead," said Elizabeth.

"Not dead, missing and presumed. Maybe it'll turn out okay."

"How does Dweena's fake diplomat fit in?"

"Sure wish I knew."

Later that night the phone rang. I picked up, hoping it was Johnny.

"Good evening, Brenda. Hope I'm not disturbing you."

Brewster Winfield, liar for hire, was the absolute last person I wanted to shoot the breeze with. I should have let the machine pick up.

He had a lot of nerve to call after the stunt he'd pulled. "What do you want?"

"Since you were at our little audition this afternoon I wanted you to be first to know that my sweet Myrtle beat out a hamster and a cat. She got the gig. Lemmy called a few minutes ago."

"Sure makes my day. Congratulations." A snake on Broadway. That's what the world needed.

Winfield cleared his throat. "Now, about that other matter . . ."

"You mean the matter of Dweena lying to the cops and your part in encouraging her to keep her lips zipped and then your own plan to lie to gain access to P. G. Dover? That matter? I hope not, because I'm pretty damned pissed off about that matter."

"No, not that. It's legal mumbo-jumbo, anyway. My concern. Please Brenda, don't you sweat the details. I was so quickly called away from our consultation, we didn't discuss my fees."

"Dweena's your client," I said. "Ask her."

"I plan to do that, but first, I have a question for you. I'm at a loss as to how to phrase this. I've always known, that is, I thought I knew, like, uh, you know, about Dweena. What I'm trying to say . . . is she, uh, I mean, you know . . ."

Winfield was rarely so ineloquent. It was a treat to hear him stumble for words. I had a good idea what he wanted to know. "Look," I said. "Dweena is just Dweena. Don't *you* sweat the details."

9

I needed to sleep even more than I
needed to worry.

So I did, long and hard with Jackhammer
curled up next to my belly. I awakened refreshed, although with a lot on my mind, none of which made me
greet the new day with enthusiasm.

I was tempted to visit Turner and McKinley and rat
on Dweena. I'd tell them she'd lied, that she'd been with
P. G. Dover for several hours on the night in question,
and therefore Dover couldn't be the doer of whatever
had been done, which I truly hoped wasn't murder, even
though I didn't think much of Ria Kleep.

The all-news station had no update on the story, which
was both good and bad news. They hadn't found Ria's
body, but neither had she turned up alive.

I didn't much care if Dweena's lie cost P. G. Dover
a couple of days of detainment. Dweena was right, even
if Dover hadn't committed murder, he was hardly innocent. An innocent man does not hide under a blanket
in the backseat of a car. An innocent man does not
falsely claim to be the ambassador from Gintoflakokia.
What kind of scam did Dover have going? No, he was
far from innocent. A turn in the cooler might do him
some good.

Far more serious was that Dweena's lie had the police
believing they had their man. Which meant they weren't

looking for the real killer. Which meant there might be a crazed killer on the loose who might strike again.

Then again, probably not. Even Turner and McKinley would say chances of that were next to nothing. They're always telling me that ninety-nine times out of a hundred the killer is somebody the victim knew. But what if this time were the one time in a hundred?

I had to take action. I didn't want a murder on my conscience.

"Turner here."

"Good morning, Detective."

"No, Ms. Midnight, it isn't. It's a lousy morning, shaping up to be a humdinger of a lousy day."

So much for the small talk. I plunged right ahead. "You know what we were talking about yesterday? P. G. Dover? And Dweena? And Dweena's loose eyelash? And how long Dweena spent in Dover's company?"

"What kind of question is that? Of course I remember. What are you driving at?"

"I was wondering. Is that the same case as the one on the news about the missing Greenwich Village woman? You think Dover had something to do with that?"

No answer, but his breathing was not happy.

"I'm concerned. You see, last night I went to Angie's. People there were saying that the missing woman is Ria Kleep." I paused and waited for him to speak.

Again, no response. More angry breathing.

"Because if it is Ria Kleep, I'd like to know. Ria and I are not really friends, but I do know her, and so I couldn't help but wonder. How can you and Detective Turner be so sure of the time of death, if you don't have a body and aren't even sure there was a death?"

At last Turner spoke. "Did I say we were sure? Did I give you one iota of information about our investigation?"

"No. Not in so many words. I deduced it because you and Detective McKinley seemed so concerned about whether P. G. Dover had an alibi for a particular time, and when Dweena—"

"You *deduced* it?"

"Well, yes."

"How many times have do I have to tell you to leave the police work—deduction—to the police? Whatsa matter, you got some hatter's felt stuffed in your ears so you don't hear so good?"

"So, you're not positive Dover did it? And you're pursuing other avenues in your investigation?"

"I assure you, Ms. Midnight, we're turning over every rock. That's what detectives do. Your tax dollars hard at work."

"That's a relief. Like I said, I know Ria Kleep. I sure hope she's okay."

"So do I, Ms. Midnight, so do I."

I felt better knowing their investigation didn't stop with Dover.

I opened Midnight Millinery and started to work immediately, intent on making up for the nonproductive day before. Too bad I couldn't do much about all the nonproductive days and weeks before that.

Jackhammer rearranged his bed of fabric scraps, then sniffed around for more to add to the ever-growing pile. I admired his good attitude. A crescent of bright red felt dug out from under the counter made his day.

I wished I were so lucky.

I sat down at my work table and studied the cloche under construction. My sad conclusion: derivative and uninspired. To be blunt, the design sucked. It was a stupid concept anyway—bulletproof headwear.

I didn't even know how to bulletproof a hat. I'd used a pair of Chuck's old jeans for the prototype. Denim was tough but not tough enough to stop bullets. I didn't know if civilians could legally purchase bulletproof material. Turner and McKinley might be able help me out, but now was not the time to ask a favor.

And so I scrapped the bulletproof idea. No great loss.

I'd only come up with the project as a diversion to keep from facing the fact that I wasn't much into *any* project.

That's right. I, Brenda Midnight, proprietor of Midnight Millinery, designer of gravity-defying couture hats, didn't like hats anymore. I didn't want to design them, make them, sell them, wear them, or even think about them.

I pinpointed the source of my malaise.

Several months ago I was intrigued by a hat in the window of a new boutique. I went inside to see if anyone I knew had made it, but there was no label sewn inside, no hang tags, no identifying marks whatsoever.

I tried it on. When I caught my reflection in the mirror I was shocked. I had never looked better.

The boutique specialized in sleazy prom dresses, not fine millinery. I asked the saleswoman the name of the milliner. She gave me a blank look.

I rephrased. "Do you know who designed this hat?"

"No kidding, you mean this stuff really gets designed?"

"Sometimes."

I examined the hat. The design was not as simple as it seemed at first glance. There was something tricky about the drape of the fabric. I couldn't put my finger on it.

"You want the hat or not?" asked the saleswoman.

"How much?"

The low price surprised me. Obviously, the hat was not custom made. At that price it couldn't even be hand made. There had to be thousands in existence in malls and discount stores across the nation.

I paid cash, so as not to leave a record of the purchase.

The saleswoman jammed the hat in a plastic bag and told me to have a nice day.

To avoid bumping into anyone who might ask what was in the bag, I took a circuitous route home. Once safely back in my apartment, I stored the hat high in the closet behind a box of old clothes.

That was that. An impulse purchase, best forgotten.

Except I couldn't. I thought about the hat a lot. Why did it look so good on me? Maybe I'd been in a strange mood. Maybe the boutique's lighting was exceptionally flattering. Maybe, maybe, maybe. Each day I came up with a different maybe, but when I finally screwed up my courage and put the hat on my head again—in my bathroom behind locked doors—the result was the same. I looked real good.

I wore the hat to a party. My friends are far too jaded ever to compliment me on my hats, but when I showed up in that hat, it was a different story.

"Great hat."

"You look wonderful."

"Beautiful."

"Fabulous."

It broke my spirit. I haven't designed or worn a hat since. If I kept it up, I would have no hats to sell for next season. No hats would very soon translate into no money.

Midnight Millinery meant a lot to me. Glancing around, it seemed even it had lost its sparkle. The shop looked every bit as bad as I felt. Floors erode, plaster cracks, and paint peels. Entropy, plain and simple.

A coat of paint would spiff up the place. I dreaded the job. But given my rotten mood, spending a couple of days wielding a paint roller couldn't possibly make me feel any worse. And assuming someday I'd get out of my rotten mood, it'd be nice to look up and see fresh paint on the walls. On the other hand, in the event I never got out of my rotten mood, never made another hat, and was forced to close Midnight Millinery, I'd have to paint anyway or the landlord would keep my deposit.

The paint fumes might perk me up.

As a first step, I needed paint chips.

One-Coat Joe's was a fixture in the Village. About the only change since the mom-and-pop paint store opened up decades ago were the proprietors. The original Mom and Pop were long gone. As were the second-generation Mom and Pop. The store was now in the hands of the original Mom and Pop's grandson, Joe, known around the Village as One-Coat Joe, because he boasted that his superior paint would cover any surface with only one coat.

There was no current Mom, but not because One-Coat didn't try. He never failed to ask me out. I never failed to turn him down. I didn't take it personally; at one time or another he'd tried to date every available female in the Village foolish enough to wander into his store.

That's why I waited until noon to pick up paint chips. One-Coat was a man of habit. I coordinated my visit with his invariable lunch break, which he took at a coffee shop over on Seventh Avenue, a good three blocks away.

I meandered by the paint store with Jackhammer and glanced, real casual-like, inside. One-Coat's assistant, a surly high school dropout, sat behind the counter, his nose buried in a wrestling magazine—a good sign that One-Coat was at lunch. I hurried in, helped myself to a dozen paint chips, and left. The kid didn't glance up once.

I taped the paint chips to the wall and stood back to study them. I had just eliminated a sickening yellowish white, when Dweena stormed into Midnight Millinery.

Her waist-length strawberry blond wig swirled. "You're not gonna believe the shit Brewster Winfield is trying to pull."

"Sure I will. After yesterday's stunt, Brewster Winfield is not my favorite lawyer. It's a lot more complicated than before. Turns out I know the missing woman."

"Really? Who?"

"Ria Kleep. She's one of the regulars at Angie's. You'd probably know her if you saw her."

"Drab brown hair, pointy chin, obnoxious, loud-mouth?"

"That's her."

"Didn't she go out with Johnny?"

"Once. No big deal. What *is* a big deal is the fact that between your lies and Winfield's deceptions, every time I turn around the situation gets more screwed up. I don't supposed Winfield changed his mind and advised you to tell the truth."

"He has not advised me to do so, nor will he. Winfield is no longer my lawyer."

"What do you mean? Yesterday—"

"Yesterday was yesterday. Today is today. Winfield finagled his way into the pokey to see P. G. Dover—just like he said he would, by claiming to be Dover's attorney—then the two-timing son of a bitch actually became Dover's attorney."

"Huh? Dover hired Winfield?"

"He certainly did. And I bet anything he did it with the lure of my fifty thousand dollars."

"He can't do that. Winfield works for you. It's a conflict of interest. That twenty-dollar bill you gave him yesterday was supposed to be a retainer."

Dweena laughed. "Brenda, you are so naive. It's one of your more endearing qualities, almost cute. Your friend Brewster Winfield does not play by the rules. Get this: After all this crap, he wants us to run an errand for him."

"What kind of errand?"

"I don't know. He wouldn't tell me. He says you have a cooler head than I, so he wants you to call him."

"Oh yeah? Well, I can think of a thing or two I'd like to call him."

"You can be sure I already took care of that."

I grabbed the phone and punched in Winfield's cellular number, gloating that even if he were home, taking the call would cost him.

When he picked up, I spat out a stream of curse words I'd probably later regret.

"And a good afternoon to you too, Brenda," he said. Then the son of a bitch put me on hold.

From the expression on my face, Dweena ascertained the limbo status of the phone call. "What's with the paint chips?" she asked in the interim.

"Midnight Millinery has lost its sheen," I answered. "I've got to paint."

Dweena turned around, taking in all four walls. "You're right. It's pretty shabby in here."

"Maybe you'd like to help me?"

"So sorry, Brenda. Dweena doesn't do physical labor. It's murder on a manicure."

"Dweena, you owe me."

She actually seemed to be weighing in her mind if that might be true when Winfield came back on the line. "Now, where were we?" he asked.

"We were at the part of the conversation where you were going to explain what the hell you're up to."

"Shame on you, Brenda. I am a member of a highly regarded profession. I shall triumph and prove the innocence of my client, Mr. P. G. Dover."

"What about Dweena? Only yesterday, *she* was your client."

"I spoke to Dweena as a friend. She wasn't home last night when I called. We never did get around to discussing my fee."

"She gave you a retainer."

"That was no retainer."

"You're really making me mad, Winfield."

"Trust me. I assure you, in the end, justice will be served."

"If you were so goddamned interested in the service of justice, you'd realize Dweena must tell the truth and you'd help her do it."

"Ah, yes, our Dweena, she's a lovely lady . . . or whatever. She will tell the truth. She is the rabbit I shall pull out of my hat, a metaphor you can surely relate to. Ultimately, Dweena will vindicate my client. That is, if the case gets to trial. I, for one, sincerely hope it doesn't.

However, shit happens, and if it does, I'll be prepared. As to who committed the crime, that's no concern of mine. No reason it should be yours either. You can't fight every battle, right every wrong."

"I knew the woman, the one who disappeared, the one they think got killed."

"So sorry."

"There could be a crazed killer on the loose."

"More likely not. Ninety-nine times out of a hundred—"

"What makes the cops think P. G. Dover was involved?"

"I'm not at liberty to discuss my client's case."

"Bullshit."

"However," he said, "a possibility might open up were you and Dweena to perform a little service for me in the interests of said client."

Here it comes, I thought, the favor Dweena had mentioned.

Winfield continued. "I need you to go to Mr. Dover's place of business, pay his rent, and retrieve a file from his office. I'd do it myself, but it would not be seemly. Besides, I have to prepare Myrtle for a grueling rehearsal schedule."

I was all set to tell him to go stuff it, but when he mentioned the bit about retrieving a file from Dover's office, I quickly reconsidered. Winfield was handing me a great opportunity. The cops must have already searched Dover's office. I wanted to know what they knew. Knowledge was power.

To be honest, there was yet another reason I agreed to help. For the first time in my life I was smack dab in the middle of a rip-roaring, raging, soul-shattering artistic crisis.

How boring.

So, to shake things up and rekindle my passion, I decided to throw caution to the wind, hang on to my hats, and go pay Dover's rent.

*   *   *

"The way I see it," said Dweena, "is that we're using my money to pay the rent of the jerkhole who conned me out of the money that he then gave to the bastard who was supposed to be my lawyer."

"Not your money," I said. "Winfield is fronting the money."

"Where the hell is my money?"

"My guess is the cops confiscated your money when they arrested Dover."

"Unless he stashed it somewhere first."

I hadn't thought of that.

"And as part of this errand we get to poke around Dover's office?"

"Uh, yes."

"What are we waiting for?"

10

A small red button was mounted on a metal assembly that was bolted to the side of a decayed wood doorjamb. From the metal assembly a thick black insulated wire stretched up the building all the way to the top floor where it disappeared into a high wide-arched window.

I pushed the button and waited.

Dweena, arms folded over her chest, took a critical look around. "I've always wondered about Winfield's choice of location. I mean, what kind of lawyer lives and works in a dump like this?"

We were on lower Broadway, a couple of blocks below Canal Street, standing on a busted-up chunk of sidewalk in front of Brewster Winfield's building. Dweena was not exaggerating. The six-story building appeared to be one official citation away from the wrecker's ball. One citation or a strong wind storm, and this stretch of Broadway was notoriously windy.

"You've never been inside, have you?" I said. "This mess out here is a front. Wait'll you get a load of Winfield's loft. Very luxurious, downtown chic."

Graffiti covered the lower part of the crumbling brick facade. I suspected some had been personally sprayed on by Winfield himself, especially the comments about the personal habits of a certain assistant district attorney.

"Front or not, in this day and age, at Winfield's obscene level of income, you'd think the esteemed attorney would at least spring for a two-way intercom system," she said. "Somebody like Chuck Riley could rig up a sophisticated electronic high-security device to scan people's eyeballs and print out a financial analysis and up-to-the-minute rap sheet so Winfield could screen potential clients before letting them in."

A grating sound came from above.

I looked up and saw Winfield struggling to open one of his front windows. He wrenched it open, then stuck his head out and waved at us. "Hello, ladies." He tossed down a pink and gray argyle sock. Cashmere, of course. It hit the sidewalk with a clink.

Inside the sock I found a set of keys to open the three locks on the outer door of the building. I'm no good at matching up keys to locks, so I gave them to Dweena.

She sure has a way with locks. Top to the left, middle to the right, then Dweena inserted the last key into the bottom lock, gave it a left twist, and pushed open the door. We stepped into the small lobby.

Dweena sniffed the air. "Bus exhaust, hot dog, and moo-shu pork, mingled, I believe, with a slight under note of dead rodent. Tres classy."

I punched the elevator call button. It was already on the ground floor. The door jerked open to reveal an ancient, tiny, dimly lit box.

Dweena balked. "A front, you say? I think Winfield has carried the slum motif too far. No freaking way am I gonna set one foot into this deathtrap."

"Don't you want to see what Winfield's decorator did with the place? It's really nice."

"Some day far in the future," said Dweena, "quite possibly I'll look back and regret not having ascended to Barrister Brewster's luxury loft. Right now, I'm just trying to assure that I truly do have a some day in the future. Which means, I'll wait for you right here, thank you very much."

"You sure you'll be all right?"

"Absolutely. I have plenty to keep me occupied. I can

file my nails or count cockroaches or hunt out the source of this curious odor."

With a shrug, I got on the elevator. It was probably for the best. It would have been a tight squeeze with both of us.

Winfield was dressed in casual baggy color-coordinated at-home silk lounging pajamas. "Dweena didn't come up with you?"

"She's elevator-shy."

"Hmpf. You wouldn't know it to look at her. But then, there's a lot we don't know about Dweena. Right, Brenda?"

"So," I said, ignoring his question, "where's that cute little Myrtle, the Broadway ingénue?" I sure as hell didn't want to trip over her.

"Myrtle is getting her beauty sleep."

Certainly no one has ever needed her beauty sleep more.

I followed Winfield through his hundred-foot-long loft, paying special attention to the extraordinary walls. The effect was of such richness and depth, it had to be one of those multicoat burnished-between-coats paint jobs. The result was a muted palette of mud and stone and sky. Each color defined a different zone of the vast space.

Winfield's office was all the way in the front of the loft. The windows faced Broadway. The one he had thrown the key out of was still open, a sheer curtain fluttered in the diesel fuel-tinged breeze.

He eased himself into a well patinaed leather chair behind his desk, a thick slab of glass supported by stacks of antique leather law books. It had been featured in the home decorating section of the *Times*.

Winfield motioned for me to take the chair opposite. "Now," he said, "what I need you to do—"

"No," I said. "First, *you* tell me what you learned about your new client, P. G. Dover. That's the deal we made."

Frowning, he plucked his prized antique silver fountain pen from a faceted crystal base and rotated it in his hand. "The deal we made was that you do for me, *then* I do for you. That was my understanding. However, I see no reason, since we're friends, to split hairs over such an insignificant matter. As you and your cronies and even the police correctly surmised, Mr. Dover is not the Gintoflakokian ambassador. In fact, there is no Gintoflakokia. The country is purely a product of Dover's vivid imagination."

"Why would anybody invent a country?"

"Cover up. Mr. Dover tells me he is an unlicensed private investigator. Claims he needed a country to get diplomat plates, which he did by greasing the right palms. As you well know, those plates allow him to park any place at any time with immunity, thus he can conduct surveillance, unfettered by city parking regulations. I've got to hand it to him, it's a brilliant idea."

"Dweena will freak when I tell her. Was Dover out on surveillance when she boosted his car?"

"Yes. And that explains the connection with the supposed victim. Dover was watching Ria Kleep's apartment through a concealed spyhole periscope contraption mounted in the floor of the automobile."

"Dweena said he was hiding under a wool blanket."

"Correct."

"Why was he watching Ria's apartment?"

"She was his client. Apparently, she believed someone was stalking her. She hired Dover to find out who and to protect her. Now, what I want you to do is go to Dover's office and see if you can find a file on Ria Kleep. It's in my best interest to determine if he's telling the truth."

What a refreshing change. "Why wouldn't you believe Dover's story? Don't clients always tell lawyers the truth? No reason not to because of the attorney-client privilege."

Winfield rolled his eyes.

"What about the police? Won't they have taken the file as evidence?"

Winfield smiled. "To date, the authorities have not been apprised as to the existence of the office. They arrested Mr. Dover in his car and believe him to be a drifter, passing himself off in the diplomatic community as one of their own, living off lies and political favors. Very difficult for the local police to check out."

"This changes everything."

"I don't see why it should. It's normal procedure."

Yeah, right, I thought.

"We both know Dover didn't murder anyone. It's really no big deal."

With a flourish, Winfield presented me with an envelope. "Mr. Dover's rent."

I peeked inside. Cash. "So I pay this, then the landlord lets me into the office?"

"First, you'll need the key."

"That's in the envelope too?" I hadn't seen a key.

Winfield cleared his throat. "Uh . . . no, not exactly."

I waited for him to produce the key. Instead, he tapped the silver pen on his desk. He tapped long enough for me to suspect something was wrong, long enough for me to figure out what.

The police would have confiscated any keys Dover had on him before they locked him up. That, of course, was the real reason that Winfield needed my help. It had nothing to do with Myrtle's brutal rehearsal schedule. I was simply the best—maybe the only—person for the job.

I hated being a pawn.

I stood up, better to shout. "You've got to be out of your mind if you think I'm going to try to convince Turner and McKinley to lay their butts and careers on the line to get that key without telling them what it unlocks."

Winfield stopped tapping. "Now, Brenda, you know I wouldn't dream of asking you to do that. The task should be much simpler."

*   *   *

"You've got to be kidding," said Dweena. "That little jerk is a PI?"

"So he told Winfield."

"If that doesn't beat all."

I hailed a cab, told the driver to take us to Bleecker Street.

"I thought you said Dover's office was on the East Side in midtown."

"It is, but I have to drop by the precinct first."

"What for?"

"It's like this. During the brief time Dover was in Turner and McKinley's office, after he was arrested but before they confiscated the stuff in his pockets, the two detectives battled over who'd get stuck with the paperwork, Dover slipped his office key under McKinley's desk calendar, figuring if they never found out he had an office, they couldn't search it. I have to retrieve the key from under the calendar so you and I can get the Ria Kleep file for Winfield."

"How do you propose to get that key?"

"I'd rather not say." I hadn't even decided if I would.

"Better watch your back," she warned.

We got out of the cab on Bleecker Street. Dweena went into a nearby coffee shop to wait for me. I continued on to the precinct. I sped confidently through the lobby, but on the way up the stairs I paused to consider what to do.

The idea that my further involvement would assure an innocent man didn't get a bum rap on account of Dweena's lie was overly dramatic and self-important hogwash. Despite what I often say, Turner and McKinley are competent crime solvers. They always get their man, or sometimes woman. Whether or not Dweena provided an alibi, they would find that Dover didn't do it, if indeed anything had been done. As far as I knew, no body had yet been found.

I could speed up the investigation if I told Turner and McKinley about Dover's office. I could show them where Dover hid the key and let them take it from there.

I wished it were so easy. To do that I'd have to come clean about everything, including the fact that Dweena had lied to them. I didn't want to betray Dweena, especially since I'd get blamed.

And, much as I hated the fact, I had an obligation—moral and legal—to Winfield. Technically, I was acting as his operative. As such, I was not at liberty to rat on his client.

A moral dilemma. With no clear answer, I decided to leave it up to fate. If the key was easy to get, I'd take it and proceed. If the key was hard to get, maybe I'd spill the beans. Then again, maybe I'd just leave.

As it turned out, it was easy to get the key.

Both Turner and McKinley were in their cubicle.

"Gentlemen."

From Turner, "What now?"

From McKinley, "Now what?"

Turner again, "Didn't I talk to you on the phone earlier today? And didn't I tell you to butt out?"

I plastered a big smile on my face. "Yes, but this is an entirely different matter. I'm planning a big party for when Johnny finishes that shoot in Boston. I happened to be passing by and thought I might as well pop in and invite you two fellows in person. Gundermutter, too, if she wants."

"When is the party?" asked McKinley.

In a grand gesture, I brushed my hair out of my face to hide the fact that my eyes were rapidly scanning the surface of McKinley's desk. Open files, piles of paperwork, an empty coffee mug, a half-eaten bagel. Located at the center back, just where I hoped it would be, was his calendar, the kind that has a page for each day all bound together in a plastic stand.

Keeping my smile firmly in place, I inched toward McKinley's desk, calculating the distance between me and the calendar as measured against the distance between McKinley and the calendar, taking into account the greater length of his arms.

When I got close enough, and when my body was situated so Turner couldn't see, I snatched up McKinley's calendar. Yes, the key was underneath. I palmed it with my free hand. Then, reaching across the desk I handed the calendar to McKinley. "The sixteenth. I sure hope you men are free that evening."

McKinley flipped though the calendar pages. Out of the corner of my eye, I saw Turner pick up his calendar and do the same.

"I'm free," said McKinley.

"Me too," said Turner. "And I'm sure former Officer Gundermutter would love to go."

"Fantastic," I said. "Hold the date. I'll let you know when my plans firm up."

I scooted out of there.

11

I should have known better.

Dweena is not the kind of gal to sit around and wait in a brand-new shiny coffee shop, calmly sipping some three-dollar-a-cup steamed latte confection. When I returned to pick her up, she was engaged in a shouting match with the manager.

He was a clean-cut sort, fastidiously outfitted in the latest khaki and pastel knit placket shirt combo. His taut face was red, and he jabbed at Dweena's chest with a forefinger. "You people think you own the Village."

Dweena grabbed his finger and twisted it down to his side. "Don't you 'you-people' me, buster. It's your kind, born and bred in some suburban wasteland with your cookie-cutter mentality, who are raping my Village. You speculating interlopers are knocking the life out of my home, trying to gloss it into some kind of a Times Square Junior tourist freaking wonderland. There oughta be a goddamned law."

I had enough worries without this. I approached the battling duo. "Got a problem?"

With the guy's finger still in her grip, Dweena spun her head around. "Oh, Brenda. There you are. Right in time to hear this asshole, this company man, explain why I can't leave my S.O.B. flyers next to the plastic coffee stirrers on his precious pseudo-marble counter."

She turned her attention back to the guy. "Okay, bozo breath, start talking."

The guy winced. "Let go of my finger."

One final squeeze, then Dweena relaxed her hold.

The guy wiggled his finger in front of his face, examining it from all angles. "If you fractured my finger, I'm suing."

"Fine," said Dweena. "I'll give you my lawyer's name to speed up the process. And while your lawyer is talking to my lawyer, perhaps they can touch base on the matter of your refusal to serve me, an out-and-out incident of blatant discrimination against a resident."

"But you didn't order anything."

Dweena smirked. "Hey, bub, your word against mine."

The guy swallowed hard.

"Now that we've got that all straightened out," said Dweena, "tell my friend here the corporate policy in regard to my S.O.B. flyer."

The guy addressed me. "Like I already told your friend, it's not her flyer specifically. Nobody's singling her out. The head office strictly prohibits all flyers, posters, postcards, newsletters, community notes, and the like regardless of subject matter. In the communities we serve all across this great nation, we strive to maintain the consistent look our customers expect. The president of our company insists that we come down hard on clutter."

"Clutter," said Dweena.

Before things escalated, I ushered Dweena out of the store and into a cab.

The cab crawled through midday midtown traffic toward Dover's office. Horns honked, exhaust spewed, pedestrians in suits darted in and out of the traffic, clasping tiny cell phones against their ears.

"Can you believe that toe-the-line company man?" asked Dweena.

"He was pretty amazing," I agreed. "At first I thought

he was afraid S.O.B. might somehow encourage present-day prostitution, and then, once you set him straight that the brothels in question were historic, he'd be more than happy to let you leave a whole stack of flyers, maybe even hang one up in the window."

"He didn't even look at the flyer."

The building that housed Dover's office was about twenty stories high, narrowing every few floors so sunshine could bathe the street, which might have happened had the sun not been in hiding on this drizzly gray day.

The wood-framed revolving door needed a lube job. Dweena and I lurched through, and ended up in a nondescript lobby. I stopped in front of a glass-covered directory that listed hundreds of names in a jumble of tiny plastic letters.

A quick scan turned up three entries for Dover—Dover, P. G., PI; Dover, P. G., Ambassador; and Gintoflakokia, Nation of—all located on the sixteenth floor. Given the large number of names on the directory and the relatively small size of the building, I assumed many tenants had multiple listings.

Toward the end of the lobby was a beat-up oak desk. On it, an open sign-in book. No guard in sight, so we didn't bother.

Directly across from the elevator on the sixteenth floor was a pebbled glass door with the name "Suite Sixteen" in large black letters.

"Adorable," said Dweena.

A laser-printed list of names hung next to the door in a plastic frame. In addition to Dover's three entries were dozens of other names, some individuals, some companies, with offices numbered 1601 to 1650.

"This must be one of those desk space enterprises," I said.

"What's that?" asked Dweena.

"It's a great idea, a boost for the self-employed. They rent space to many individuals and small businesses.

Everybody shares a receptionist, support staff, copy machines, and conference room. I've read that some of
them will even rent out space by the hour."

"In other words, brothels."

Dweena had brothels on the mind. "No, I don't think
so."

"What else can you do in an office for an hour?"

"Impress a client."

"Oh. That's interesting."

Suite Sixteen's reception area was decorated in low-level
corporate-compromise style. Beneath two color-
coordinated bland abstract prints, and atop a dark gray
sisal area rug, sat two tan leatherette couches at right
angles to each other. Between them, a glass and chrome
table. On it, a "Thank You for Not Smoking" sign and
a leafy potted plant.

In the center of the room a receptionist sat behind a
beige console. She seemed to be idle, though I caught a
whiff of wet nail polish in the air. A nameplate pegged
her as Deb, which seemed appropriate. Something about
Deb reminded me of bubble gum. Can't say exactly
what—she wasn't chewing any, and she was dressed in
black, not pink, and her freshly coated fingernails were
deep blood red.

"How may I help you?" she chirped.

I glanced down at the name Winfield had scrawled on
the envelope. "We're here to see Ms. Gates."

"Gates is office manager," said Deb with a nod, as if
to confirm that fact for herself. "Do you have, like, you
know, an appointment?"

"Tell Ms. Gates it concerns Mr. P. G. Dover."

"Oh right, our ambassador."

I detected a hint of sarcasm in Deb's voice.

Deb picked up the phone and related our message to
someone on the other end. Then, with a sweep of her
hand, she gestured for us to take a seat. "Gates'll be
with you momentarily."

Dweena and I barely had time to sink down into the

fake leather when a tall, hefty woman dressed in a no-nonsense navy-blue power suit strode in and announced in a husky two-pack-a-day voice, "I'm Gates." She adjusted her bifocals and gave Dweena a hard stern look. "Don't tell me you're from Gintoflakokia."

"Absolutely not," said Dweena, genuinely offended. "I live in Greenwich Village."

"Same difference," Gates mumbled. Then louder she asked, "What seems to be the problem?"

"No problem," I said. "We're here to settle Mr. Dover's rental account."

"Settle?"

"Pay."

"You should have said so sooner. If that's the case, come along with me."

Ms. Gates led us through a set of double doors and down a winding hallway past many doors. I didn't see anyone else, but I heard phones ringing, modems sputtering, chairs scooting, and people coughing. My hunch about the place being a desk space organization seemed correct.

Ms. Gates unlocked a door marked "Suite Sixteen Office Manager." She entered, and positioned herself behind a steel desk, but did not sit. Nor did she invite us to.

"You say you have Ambassador Dover's rent money?"

I handed her the envelope Winfield had given me.

Gates slowly counted out two thousand dollars in fifties. She made a big show of holding each bill up to the light before carefully placing it down on her desk.

Throughout the process, Dweena kept her composure, but I could feel her tension and see it in the set of her jaw. She looked at that pile of fifties as her own money, which it probably wasn't, but I understood why she felt that way.

When at last Gates finished counting, she returned the money to the envelope and slid it into her top drawer. She then bent over her desk and scribbled out a receipt.

"All right then, Ambassador Dover is paid up through the end of the month." She shoved the receipt across the desk to me.

I tucked it into my purse.

Then, with a manner all of a sudden friendly and relaxed, Gates asked, "Level with me, ladies. Where is P. G.? I've been worried sick about him. I saw his name in the paper in association with that terrible disappearance."

Her complete attitude turnaround threw me for a loop. I was still searching for an answer when Dweena jumped in. "I saw that article too," she said. "And, I must admit, it caused me a moment's consternation, until I realized it's a different person. Dover is a common name around these parts. There's gotta be a hundred in Manhattan alone."

"It's a different Dover?"

"Count on it."

"That's a relief."

Dweena couldn't leave well enough alone. She blathered on. "My colleague and I work through an intermediary, but we do pick up an occasional hint. We both have the distinct feeling that Ambassador Dover is on another hush-hush mission. Isn't that right, Brenda?"

"Uh, yeah," I said.

"You *know* how he is," said Dweena, with a wink at Gates. "Always up to something."

Sighing, Gates shook her head. "I certainly hope it's not another one of those insurrections. I swear, that silly country of his has a revolution every time the rent is due. It's an absolute disgrace that a man of his caliber is forced to work as a private eye. You'd think a nation would be better funded."

"You would think so," said Dweena. "Diplomats shouldn't have to chase after errant spouses and the like to make ends meet. He should be out being diplomatic. Negotiating treaties. Finding markets for Gintoflakokian folk art."

"That's right," said Gates. "Well, you be sure to tell

your intermediary to let P. G. know that this situation simply cannot go on much longer. I have to answer to the owners. I don't care how much charm P. G. oozes, this is positively the last time I'm going to cover his ass."

"I'll make sure he gets that message," I said.

"Thank you," said Gates. "Now, if you'll excuse me, I have many duties to attend to. Suite Sixteen clients are very demanding."

"One more thing," I said. "As a formality, the intermediary would like us to take a look around Mr. Dover's office, to make sure all is in order. You don't mind, do you?"

"Did the intermediary happen to furnish you with a key?"

"Yes." I held it up so Gates could see.

"Hmmm," she said. "You paid the rent. You have a key. I suppose you've got as much right to be in that office as anybody. Sure, go ahead. Remember to turn off the lights when you leave."

12

Gates called after us. "Make a right at the end of the hall. The Gintoflakokian Embassy will be the first door on your left."

"Thank you," I said.

"It was pleasure doing business with you," said Dweena.

"I assure you, the pleasure was mine." With that, Gates stepped back inside her office and pulled the door shut.

When we'd walked twenty feet or so down the hall, Dweena turned to me. "You don't think the Gates woman actually fell for Dover's Gintoflakokia bull, do you?"

"It's possible. *You* fell for it."

"That doesn't count. I fell for it under extreme circumstances. The slimy little bastard had his hands around my throat, for chrissakes. I was in no position to determine the veracity of his story."

"I don't know about Gates, but I'm pretty sure the receptionist knows he's a fake."

"Yeah, I picked up on that too."

We rounded the corner and came up on the first door on the left.

"This must be the place."

Dweena cocked her head at a round object stuck on

the door. "And this, I suppose, is the seal of the great nation of Gintoflakokia."

I squinted at the swirling psychedelic letters of super bright chartreuse, orange, and blue. "Afraid not. What we have here is a refrigerator magnet touting a new fruit-flavored high-caffeine carbonated soft drink." I pried the disk off the door, then restuck it a few inches to the left.

"Metal door," commented Dweena.

"Door frame too. Tough to crowbar."

"Why would anyone want to bother with such a crude tool? This lock is a joke. A bumbling idiot with a hairpin could pop this sucker in two seconds."

With the key, it took four seconds.

"I see that Gintoflakokia has quite a rich decorative heritage," said Dweena. "We better hurry up before *Architectural Digest* arrives on the scene."

Down and Out Digest was more like it.

The room was no more than eight-by-eight, small even for New York. I immediately noticed the walls—cracked, peeling, and stained, in much worse condition than Midnight Millinery's. An overhead flickering fluorescent tube bathed the room in a sickly glow.

Dweena slammed the door. "Get a load of this," she said, pointing to a trench coat and felt fedora hanging on the back of the door. "Private eye duds."

In the dead center of the room, a standard-issue dented gray-green metal desk hogged most of the square footage. A couple of chairs, a folded-up cot, a coat rack, and a black two-drawer file cabinet with a small refrigerator on top squeezed into the remaining space. Everywhere papers spilled out of fat reddish-brown accordion folders.

The air was stale.

I maneuvered around the desk and climbed over a chair to get to the window. I pulled the cord and the wooden blinds clattered up. Then I opened the window. The moist air that strayed in was not particularly fresh, but at least it was different.

I leaned out the window into the shaftway. After seeing the coat and fedora I halfway expected a glowing neon motel sign. But no. Not exactly a dramatic skyline view of the Big Apple either. Straight up was a dark patch of sky. The neighboring building was so close I could almost touch its yellow bricks. City sounds, mixed together into the ever-present New York background buzz, reverberated. I listened for a moment, fascinated, before directing my attention back to Dweena.

She was saying, "If you were a pathetic PI, a man with a scheme and a scam and diplomat plates, and you'd conned a lovely dame such as myself out of fifty thousand smackers, where would you stash the loot?" She yanked open the top drawer of the file cabinet and dumped the contents out on the floor.

"Not here," I said, hoping to discourage her search.

It's not that I didn't want Dweena to get her money back. I just didn't want her to find any cash hidden in Dover's office. Before, I thought it highly unlikely she'd find money, but now that I knew the cops hadn't been here, I realized it was possible. And if she did, she'd insist on taking it, and I'd tell her it wasn't as simple as finders-keepers, we'd fight, she'd never help me paint Midnight Millinery, and somehow sometime somebody— probably me—would be in big trouble.

I focused on my immediate goal, which was to find the file Winfield wanted as quickly as possible, and get out. Unlike Dweena, who was in the process of gleefully tossing the joint, I was not comfortable invading the privacy of another, even when the other was a shady character, and even when directed to do so by the shady character's lawyer.

I never should have agreed to do this, especially after Winfield admitted the cops were in the dark about the office. I could imagine Turner and McKinley's reaction if I tried to convince them that I really truly thought it was okay because Winfield had sent me. Once again, despite my good intentions, every time I turned around,

I found myself more deeply involved and more likely to get caught.

I desperately needed to get into some serious hat making. Fine millinery keeps me out of trouble.

I got to work. The sooner this was over, the better I'd feel.

I figured Dover would keep his active case files on his desktop. Wrong. Or in the large right-hand desk drawer. Wrong again, but close. I found the Ria Kleep file in the left-hand desk drawer. That probably meant Dover was left-handed. Inside were notes scrawled on a few sheets of yellow legal paper. I slipped the file into a large brown envelope.

That wasn't so bad.

"Good news, Dweena. I found the file. We're done. We can go now."

"What'd you say?" Dweena's voice was muffled.

Both file drawers were totally out of the cabinet. Dweena was down on the floor on her hands and knees with her head inside the cavity. I walked over to her, leaned down, and repeated.

"That's super you found the file so quickly," she said, backing out. "Now you can help me look for my money."

It would have been futile to argue.

My halfhearted search through the remaining desk drawers turned up foil-wrapped packets of cheese, boxes of crackers, and bags of low-sodium pretzels. The flat middle drawer was a jumble of pencils and erasers and ballpoint pens and paper clips and little reinforcement rings and rubber bands and several fresh yellow legal pads. "That's interesting," I said. "Seeing all this junk makes me realize Dover doesn't have a computer."

"He's just an old-fashioned kinda con guy gumshoe," said Dweena.

"How could he do his job without Internet access?"

"Nobody ever said Dover was a successful private investigator. Take a look around. This dump is not a high-profit center. He couldn't even pay the rent. Remember? We did that. With my money, I might add."

I was beginning to feel sorry for P. G. Dover, a man who lived by his wits, struggling to survive in a world moving too fast, left in the dust of his competition. The felt fedora hanging on the door got to me.

His communications system consisted of two old telephones placed side by side on the desk, one red, one black. Each was hooked up to its own ancient answering machine. One must be for Gintoflakokia and the other for his private eye business.

I held up the two receivers so Dweena could see. "Which phone for Gintoflakokia?"

"The red one," she said. "I hear those Gintoflakokians are a bunch of commies."

There were no incoming messages and I couldn't figure out how to play back the outgoing messages, so I wrote down the phone numbers from the keypads. Later I'd call and see if one of them really was for Gintoflakokia. I wanted to know to how far Dover had taken his diplomat ruse.

"Did you find my money?"

"Not even an old subway token. How about you?"

"The top drawer of the filing cabinet yielded boxer shorts, jeans, and tees all wadded up together. Dover's a slob. The bottom drawer's got an electric razor, toothbrush, toothpaste, spray deodorant, and a half-full bottle of Jack Daniel's. Considering this evidence and that cot leaning up against the wall, I'd say His Excellency resides on the premises."

"Makes sense," I said. "Winfield told me the police believe Dover's a freeloader with no known address."

"What about Gates?" said Dweena. "You'd think she would have caught on to Dover's living arrangements. I would imagine it's against the rules of the Suite Sixteen outfit."

"Most likely, but the tenants probably work all hours of the day and night. It'd be impossible to prove who's doing what when. Or, maybe Gates knows but lets it slide. She did seem genuinely fond of Dover."

"I noticed. 'Oozes charm,' I believe she said. Ha. She's got to be some kind of weirdo."

"No accounting for taste."

"That's for damned sure."

We got back to work. Dweena refused to leave until we'd combed every inch. She tapped the walls. I turned back the threadbare rug, reached under the desk, and even felt along the wall outside the window. Nothing.

"Check inside the refrigerator for me, okay?" said Dweena.

"Do it yourself. You're standing right by it."

"I thought maybe you'd want to do it."

"Not particularly. Though it would be the perfect place to hide cool cash."

"I know. So do me a favor and take a look inside."

"What's the matter. You scared of festering sesame noodles or pizza with green fuzz?"

"I just don't like strange refrigerators."

I couldn't believe it. Dweena, who hid her money down a vile disgusting blood drain, was terrified of a pint-size harvest-gold refrigerator. And, I am ashamed to say, armed with that information, I used it against her.

"You want a favor? Gee, Dweena, that reminds me, you never told me if you were available to help me paint."

Dweena frowned. "Really? I thought I did."

"No, you didn't."

"Oh."

"So . . . ?"

She looked at the refrigerator, then back at me. "Sure, I'll help you paint. That's what friends are for, right?"

"Tomorrow," I said.

"So soon?"

"Yes. Tonight I'll decide on the color. Tomorrow I'll

pick up the paint as soon as One-Coat opens up. Then I'll have to do a little prep work. I'll need you to come by, say, around eleven."

"Okay dokey. You can count on me."

I stepped up to the refrigerator. Dweena stood back as far away as possible. She pinched her nose between her thumb and forefinger.

With a dramatic flourish I fearlessly yanked open the door.

"How bad is it?" she honked.

"Not at all," I said. "Two six-packs of Bud. Beer does not go rotten."

At the top was a tiny freezer section. About enough room for a single ice cube tray, empty, and behind that—nothing.

"Sorry, Dweena. The cops must have your money."

Neither of us said much on the way back to the Village. Dweena was disappointed she didn't find money. I was upset for a million other reasons, none of which I cared to discuss, most especially not with her.

Dweena got out of the cab in front of her building.

"See you tomorrow," I said.

She gave me quizzical look, it lasted a beat, then she said, "Oh yeah, right. Painting. Elevenish. I'll be there."

I called Brewster Winfield from Midnight Millinery. He put me on hold.

While I waited, I studied the paint chips on the wall. The color I'd liked earlier didn't fare so well in the late afternoon light.

Winfield came back on the line. "Did you get the file?"

"Yeah." I'd considered telling him I couldn't find it and turning it over to the police.

"Any trouble along the way?"

"No. One thing bugs me though. It looks like Dover lives in his office. Don't you think somebody ought to tell the police?"

"Get serious, Brenda. That would only create unnecessary complications for my client. You don't want that on your conscience, do you?"

"I suppose not. It's just that—"

"We've already established that Dover is not a murderer. Who cares if he lives in his office? I remember a time when a certain young milliner lived illegally under her blocking table in a commercial space, not to mention Dweena's current domicile."

"That's different."

"Not so very, not when you think about it."

I had to admit Winfield had a point.

"Now tell me," he said, "how large is the Ria Kleep file?"

"Five or six handwritten pages. If you don't need the originals, I'll fax them over."

"Fine. Good work, Brenda."

"I still have Dover's key."

"That's all right. He has no immediate need for it. Just don't lose it."

My fax machine, a relic from the time Chuck and Elizabeth ran a resume typing and desktop publishing business out of Midnight Millinery, was exceedingly slow. I read the pages while feeding them through.

No surprises. The chronological list of terse summations confirmed what Winfield said Dover had told him.

Ria Kleep had first contacted Dover several weeks ago. She told him someone was stalking her. Dover's job was to find out who. His time-honored method was surveillance. Very straightforward.

And then Dweena stole his car, and disrupted the surveillance.

I shuddered. Could that disruption have provided the stalker with the opportunity to harm Ria? Or kill her?

If so, that had to weigh heavy on Dweena's conscience. Despite outward appearances, I knew Dweena had a seriously sensitive side. She just didn't like to flaunt it.

13

"If Ria Kleep did get killed that night, on my birthday, Dweena's responsible."

I hadn't meant to dump on Elizabeth. I'd gone over to her apartment with a batch of paint chips to get her artistic opinion.

Always gracious, Elizabeth did the hostess bit. She uncorked a bottle of California red, then bustled off to the kitchen to get Jackhammer one of her homemade dog biscuits. He trotted along behind her.

Left alone, I went over the day's events. By the time she returned, settled down on the couch, and asked how things were going, my mind overflowed with terrible thoughts, the kind of stuff that would give me nightmares.

And so, I couldn't stop myself. It gushed out, all the sordid details, including how Dweena and I had searched Dover's office.

"That was stupid," she said.

"Yeah, I know."

"If the cops ever do find out about the office, they'll search it, right?"

"I suppose. Unless Dover's completely in the clear by then."

"Dover doesn't sound like the kind of guy who'll ever be completely in the clear. So, they'll search. And when they do, what do you think they're gonna find?"

"Not much. Dweena and I—"

Elizabeth stopped me. "Think," she said.

It took a moment to get what Elizabeth was driving at. When I did, I could literally feel the color drain out of my face. "Fingerprints," I said. "Mine and Dweena's. All over."

"Right."

Not enough that I'd kept the fact of the office a secret, I had to go search the place, no doubt destroying evidence in the process, and then I left my calling card behind.

"You better hope Ria Kleep turns up alive," said Elizabeth.

"I doubt she's alive."

"You say she was being stalked?"

"That's why she hired Dover."

"Maybe the stalker took her away somewhere to talk to her."

"And left a bloody mess in her kitchen."

"I forgot about that."

"It doesn't look too good for Ria. I shouldn't say this, it sounds totally selfish, but even if Ria is okay, and the cops never find out about Dover's office, I could still be in hot water for the whopper Dweena told Turner and McKinley. She was in top form."

"I can imagine."

"As Dweena's so-called attorney, I'm responsible. I should have forced her to tell the truth, or at the very least, shut her up before she lied."

"Since when did anybody force Dweena to do anything? Besides, lies are a dime a dozen. The cops are used to it. Every single second of every single day millions of liars are out there in the world, doing what they do best, telling millions of lies to anybody who'll listen, which is just about everybody who isn't in the process of lying. It's not your business to determine who did or did not lie to whom and about what. Nor is any of it your fault. If you think otherwise, you'll go nuts, and if I were you, I'd go with the ultra pale pink."

"Huh?"

"Paint. For your shop. Isn't that the purpose of your visit?"

"Oh yeah, right. Paint. You like the pink?"

It would be nice to think about paint for a while.

Elizabeth pointed at one of the paint chips. "This pink in particular, an almost pure white with a mere blush of warm color. As you know, pink flatters most skin tones. Even Chuck Riley might look almost healthy with a little pink light dancing off his green freckles."

I picked up the chip and flipped it over to read the information on the back. I recognized the name. "Midnight Millinery is already painted this color. Or was. Over time, it's darkened up."

"Then you made a good decision way back whenever when you chose the color. When exactly *was* the last time you painted?"

"When I first opened the shop. I'm sick of pink. I want a change, something like this blue." I held the chip up so she could see. "It too is almost white. An unschooled eye would never know, yet will respond subconsciously to the depth and sophistication and complexity of color, and transfer that association to my hats."

Elizabeth chuckled. "Surely you don't believe that load of crap?"

I thought a moment. "Uh . . . no. I know I could never get that kind of complexity with a pastel. For true color sophistication, I'd go for a deep tone made up of several coats of slightly different colors. You should see Brewster Winfield's loft. His walls are stunning."

"Simplify your life, Brenda. Go for the pink. Speaking of pink, I'll loan you my cart to transport your supplies."

Before I could say no thanks, Elizabeth darted into the foyer. Soon she was back with her souped-up hot pink collapsible shopping cart. "Wheel this baby over to One-Coat's tomorrow. You can get all the paint—whatever color—in one trip."

      *   *   *

I still wasn't sold on the pink. Later that night, back in the apartment, I put the pink chip and the blue chip into a velvet pillbox hat, closed my eyes, spun the hat, reached in, and picked a chip. Pink. Okay, I thought, best two out of three would be more scientific. I put the pink back in, spun the hat, and picked again. Blue. I put that chip back in, and held the hat out to Jackhammer. "Here, you pick the tie breaker."

He stuck his nose into the hat. The first chip his nose poked was pink. Who was I to argue?

I dragged my TV out of the closet, set it up, and tuned in the local station, hoping for good news, expecting no news.

Two seconds into the news the phone rang.

Figuring it was Dweena punking out on helping me paint, I let the machine pick up. It was Johnny. Finally. "Sorry I didn't get back to you sooner. I need to talk to you about—"

I grabbed the phone.

"Back from Boston?"

"Well . . . yeah, I am, that's what I wanted—"

An image on the TV caught my eye. "Hold on. Did you see that?"

"See what?"

"On the news."

"I'm not watching."

"Angie's is on the news. It must be about Ria Kleep."

"Ria?"

That's right. Johnny didn't know. "Wait a minute. Let me listen. Oh shit. Some kids found Ria's body in an abandoned building on Little West Twelfth. Shot. Tommy IDed it. There's Angie's again. That's it. Story's done. Poor Tommy. He must be shook up."

"Tommy? Ria? You mean Ria Kleep? Shot? Brenda, what the hell's going on?"

I gave him a quick rundown, edited so as not to upset him so soon after he got back.

"I can't believe Ria Kleep is dead," he said. "She was so vivacious."

Vivacious? I didn't want to get into that. "Do you think we ought to go over to Angie's?"

I hoped Johnny would come up with the right words to rationalize why we need not go, but he didn't. "Yeah, I guess—for Tommy. I'll be by for you in a while."

I threw on a sweatshirt and jeans and went down to the lobby to wait for Johnny. Too rattled to sit, I stood by the door and stared out into the misty night.

The doorman was in a talkative mood. "Didya hear, they found the body of that woman, the one who disappeared?"

"Yes, I heard. It's very sad. I knew her, although not very well."

"Man, that's tough. No place is safe anymore."

I didn't consider anyplace safe ever, even in this time of low crime, but I knew what he meant, so I nodded.

"If you ask me," he said, "it's a love triangle. That's what the cops should look into."

Of course he would think that. He didn't know about Ria's stalker, so he blamed her murder on the motive everybody in the entire world could relate to. "It's possible," I said, to make conversation. But then, I realized he might not be too far off base.

I hadn't given much thought as to why anybody would stalk Ria Kleep.

Even Johnny, as famous as he was, had never been stalked. The closest was when some fan sent him a fuzzy pink bunny suit. I thought that was perverse, but nothing bad ever came of it, except that the zipper got stuck when he tried it on.

Ria was not a celebrity. Anyone stalking her probably would be an ex-husband or a jilted lover. Of course, I didn't know if Ria had either in her past. I didn't know much about her at all.

When Johnny showed up, I asked him. After all, he'd dated her, sort of.

"I dunno," he said.

* * *

Even from across the street, we could tell something was wrong. Angie's was subdued. No one hung out in the doorway. Dark green velvet curtains were drawn over the front window. I remembered how awful it had been when Elizabeth and I were there. Now, with Ria's death confirmed, it had to be even more depressing. "Do we really want to go through with this?"

"We don't have to stay long," said Johnny.

"Right," I said. "We'll just make an appearance and say a few words to Tommy."

"God, I hate this kind of stuff."

"Me too."

Reluctantly, we crossed the street. Soon we were close enough to make out a handwritten sign thumbtacked to the door: "Closed Due to Death."

I let out a sigh of relief.

"So much for our good intentions," said Johnny.

"Can't say we didn't try."

"It's the thought that counts."

"We could go to the White Horse instead."

"Great idea."

We turned to leave, but got only a few steps away before the door opened and Raphael called out. "Brenda. Johnny. Don't go. Please, come in. The sign was not meant for you. You two are always welcome."

The bar was empty. Raphael ushered us into the back room where Tommy was sitting at the big round table, along with half a dozen or so of the regulars.

Tommy acknowledged our arrival with a solemn nod. "Please, sit."

Raphael, though distraught, was a considerate host. He had one of the regulars switch chairs so Johnny and I could sit next to each other.

Drinks were on the house. I didn't feel like drinking, but to be polite I let Raphael pour me a red wine. Grief didn't seem to be slowing down any of the regulars. The tabletop was littered with empty glasses and bottles, and the ashtrays overflowed with cigarette butts.

When I looked around at the sad faces, I realized and immediately felt guilty about the fact that I'd never before considered the regulars as individuals. They'd always seemed more a dark and brooding drunken collective presence. Except for Ria, I didn't know any of their names. And the only reason I knew her name, aside from recent events, was because of that time she'd invited Johnny to dinner.

Naturally, the conversation revolved around Ria. The time she did this . . . and then there was the time . . .

I didn't know Ria well enough to contribute to the eulogies, but I listened carefully, and made sympathetic sounds at the appropriate times. I learned that Ria loved the Yankees, played the lottery every Saturday, and was one goddamned good arm wrestler.

"What'd she smell like?" asked one of the regulars, a red-faced, bearded guy.

That was a real conversation stopper.

After several seconds of dead silence, the guy went on to explain. "A few days old, that body must have been mighty ripe. They say that's the absolute worst. How about it, Tommy?"

"I wouldn't know," said Tommy. "They showed me a photograph."

I've been to the morgue. I had an idea what Tommy had been through. He seemed to be holding up well.

After that gruesome moment, the talk turned back to more pleasant remembrances of Ria Kleep. At one point, I managed to slip in a question about boyfriends and ex-husbands.

Tommy quickly put that idea to rest. "No one," he said, then qualified, "at least not around here."

"And Ria was always here," said a regular.

"Too bad," commented another regular. "That'd make it easier for the cops to find out who did it. They say ninety-nine times outta a hundred it's the spouse, or the boyfriend, or the ex, or whatever."

Around one o'clock, Johnny and I excused ourselves.

We both gave Tommy a hug. "Thanks for coming," he said.

Then Raphael spoke. "We all appreciate it."

Johnny and I stood outside my apartment building and talked.

"Boy, did I ever feel out of place," I said.

"I know what you mean," said Johnny. "I thought there'd be lots more people, but even most of the regulars stayed away. That was the real hardcore bunch, the inner circle."

"It's too bad Raphael spotted us lurking around outside. We could have stolen away into the night. I don't think anybody would have missed us."

"Maybe Raphael thought we'd already seen him and didn't want to hurt our feelings."

"Could be," I said. Then to change the subject I asked Johnny how the Boston shoot had gone.

"Okay."

"I was concerned. It lasted a long time."

"I guess."

"Well, I'm glad you're back. I missed you."

"Missed you too."

"Are you back for good?"

"Hard to say. You know how these things go. What have you been up to?"

"Not much." I would eventually level with Johnny about recent events, but now was not the time. "Oh yeah, I decided to paint Midnight Millinery. I'd ask you to help, but Dweena already volunteered."

Jackhammer raced into the foyer to greet me. He sniffed at my ankles.

I picked him up and scratched the top of his head. "You didn't miss out," I said. "Raphael wasn't making special little burger balls tonight."

14

I had a dream about Ria Kleep. She was sitting on her regular stool at Angie's, blowing smoke rings at the TV, watching the story of her own murder.

I woke up with a sense of dread. The world was a different place and the change was not good. The worst had happened. Ria Kleep was dead. Very soon, I feared, the repercussions would come.

I still had to paint. Taking Elizabeth's advice, I bounced her shopping cart over to One-Coat Joe's to pick up the paint. Yesterday I had wanted to avoid One-Coat. Today I hoped he'd be minding the store. It was worth fielding a fresh remark or two and turning down a date. One-Coat had a magic touch. He was the best paint mixer in the entire city. I sure didn't trust that kid he'd hired to get it right.

I could see One-Coat through the window, hard at work wiping down his counter. I had to give the guy credit. Except for his problem with women, he was a capable, intelligent, dedicated man. Not bad-looking. Tallish, reasonably fit, fluffy sandy-brown hair, and a pleasant face. Only when he leered was it revealed that he was a throwback to another age. Perhaps someday a woman would come along with the patience to educate him as to which century we were in.

An electronic bell gonged when I entered. One-Coat glanced up. A network of crinkles formed around his soft hazel eyes.

I steeled myself.

"Brenda Midnight," he said. "How nice to see you, *and* I see you're looking nice too, though I do wonder why you're not wearing a chapeau atop your lovely head."

His eyes flickered away from my hatless head. He squinted and I got the predictable all-over scrutiny.

Which I ignored.

"Good morning, Joe."

"It is now," he said. "How may I be of service? Dinner at eight? La Reverie? Or shall we dispense with the preliminary crap, go straight for the nightcap at my place, and see what develops?"

I placed the pink paint chip on his counter. "I need three gallons of paint for Midnight Millinery."

"Mmmm, fleshy pink. Nice choice." He flicked his tongue over his lips. "Very yummy."

That did it. Screw the pink. I made a split-second decision. I fished around in my purse and located the other paint chip. "I changed my mind. Give me this blue instead."

"Just like a woman, always changing her mind. In your case, at the drop of a hat." He yuk-yukked at his own joke, then came up with proposition number two. "What say I come by tonight and give you my official paint estimate? After that who knows what we'll find to occupy ourselves."

"No."

"You don't know what you're missing."

"I can deal with the loss."

"You should see what my new computer can do. I finally broke down and got one. The goddamned competition was killing me what with the big discount chains springing up all over. Now I have the digital edge. The computer's a humdinger. It came with a state-of-the-art program that does my job better than I ever did. All I do is punch in the measurements and enter a code for wall age and composition. In two seconds it calculates hours of labor and gallons of paint. No more guesstimating."

It sounded like a big waste of money. "Thanks, Joe, but I don't need a computer estimate for my little job. I'm doing the work myself with the help of a friend. It'll take as long as it takes. All I need is the paint. I already know the square footage, and I remember that last time three gallons was more than enough."

"That was a while back, wasn't it?"

"Yes. When I opened."

"Your walls have aged since. These dry old buildings absorb an incredible amount of product. I should come by to check your porosity. If you don't let me do a proper estimate, I can't guarantee one-coat coverage. You'll end up watering down the paint, and then blame me when it doesn't cover in one coat."

"My walls are fine, Joe."

"Don't be so sure. I recently did an estimate for Angie's, the entire building, upstairs and down, inside and out. The building your shop's in is about the same age. Angie's has the worst walls I've ever seen. Like sponges."

Oh . . . Angie's.

"I went to Angie's last night," I said. "It was so sad. Ria Kleep, that woman who was killed, she hung out there, one of the regulars."

"Ria was a customer."

"Did you know her well?"

"Not really. She painted her apartment about a year ago. Ivory bedroom, light green living room, and sunny yellow kitchen. I remember teasing about her suburban tastes. This morning's paper said she was shot in that kitchen, then dragged into an abandoned building in the meat market. Kind of gives me the creeps."

Me too.

*   *   *

Once One-Coat accepted the fact I didn't want a dinner date, or a nightcap, or a computer estimate, he turned into the consummate professional.

It was a pleasure to watch him work. He squeezed the tiniest amount of blue into a cool white base, gave it a thorough stir, and fastened the can to the mixing machine. While it jiggled, he squeezed pigment into two other cans of base.

We chatted entrepreneur-to-entrepreneur. He told me he'd installed a new security system the same time he got the computer.

Jackhammer was my only security system. Lately, I'd been thinking of upgrading. Even before Ria's murder, there'd been two high-profile robberies in the Village. Perhaps the time had come to take precautions.

"I'm totally wired," said One-Coat.

He had me lean over the counter. For once, he was not conducting a cleavage inspection. He showed me strategically placed alarm buttons. "These alert the company and the precinct." He gave me a brochure from the security company. "Be sure to mention my name. They'll give you a special rate and knock twenty dollars off my next monthly bill."

The paint mixer stopped jiggling. All three gallons were lined up on the counter. One-Coat helped me load them into Elizabeth's cart.

"Anything else?"

"A few supplies."

We took a tour through the aisles. I selected the cheapest possible brushes, rollers, drop cloths, and paint pans.

"Why do you want my bottom-of-the-line junk?"

"Budget dictates."

"You'll be sorry."

"It'll be okay. A true artist learns to make do."

He rang up my purchases.

What a shock. The price of paint had gone way up

since I'd last painted. Even the cheap supplies were more than I expected. I guess One-Coat had to pay for his new security system and computer somehow.

I paid and started to roll out of the store, when I thought to ask him about the Angie's job. It hadn't been painted yet. I imagined they'd probably have to close for a couple of days. I hadn't heard anything about it.

"When are you going to paint Angie's?"

One-Coat shook his head and sighed. "I'm not."

I shouldn't have asked. "Gee, Joe, I'm sorry you didn't get the job. Did one of the chains beat you out?"

"Hell no, not with my trusty computer. I got my sub-contractors lined up, we were all set to start the job, when Tommy got in trouble."

"What do you mean, trouble?"

"Haven't you heard?"

"I guess not."

"I thought everybody knew. Tommy can't afford to stay in the building. Angie's has to close."

I was shocked. It took a moment to recover. "Wait a minute, doesn't Tommy own that building? The place is always jam-packed. He must make a pile of money."

"Tommy owns the business, but his ex-wife owns the building. What he told me was that all of a sudden she gets a bee up her behind, wants to move to the West Coast, sell the building, and buy some hunk of junk out there that'll probably slide down a hill or fall into a crack in the earth when the big one hits. Tommy makes enough to stay in business, but not enough to buy the building, especially on such short notice. It's a damned shame."

And I thought I felt lousy before.

I couldn't imagine the West Village without Angie's. That would be a terrible loss, not only for me personally, but for the entire neighborhood, and even beyond. Bars throughout the country modeled themselves after Angie's. I doubted any of them got the ambiance right, but at least they had a good place to start.

*   *   *

I made a quick pass by Midnight Millinery, unloaded the cart, then returned it to Elizabeth.

"I heard you come in late last night," she said. "Hot date?"

"Hardly. My worst fears came true. They found Ria Kleep's body. Johnny and I thought we should go to Angie's for a little while."

"Oh, I'm very sorry to hear about Ria. How were the Angie's regulars coping?"

"With lots of booze. The story gets much worse, though. It's not just Ria they were so broken up about. No one let on last night, but One-Coat just told me Angie's is closing."

"No. That can't be. Angie's has been in that spot forever."

I told her what One-Coat had said.

"Maybe One-Coat got it wrong. Maybe he misunderstood. Or maybe Tommy found someone to paint cheaper and made up the story as an excuse to cancel the job with One-Coat."

Like me, Elizabeth was pretty good at denial.

"I don't think so," I said. "It's not like One-Coat wouldn't eventually find out if Tommy lied."

I wanted to get all the preparation out of the way before Dweena arrived. I snatched my hats off the displays, moved them into the storage room, unbolted the hooks from the walls, shoved my blocking table and vanity to the middle of the room, and unfurled the thin plastic drop cloths over everything. Jackhammer took care of his own bedding, tossing up fabric scraps and moving them into the closet one by one.

We finished right on time, by eleven.

Dweena, as usual, was late.

I, as usual, got mad that Dweena was late. Actually, I got madder than usual. I was not only mad that she was late, I was mad about all the other stuff she'd done recently. And now, with the discovery of Ria's body,

Dover could definitely be charged with murder. Some-
how I had to get Dweena to level with Turner and Mc-
Kinley. That wouldn't alleviate the problem about
Dover's office, but it was a step in the right direction.
I'd try to talk some sense into her while we painted. If
she ever got here.

I waited a half hour. Damn her anyway.

I yanked the drop cloth off my desk, picked up the
phone, and dialed Dweena's number. I got the S.O.B.
message on her machine. I had no way of knowing if
she was still asleep, on her way over, or had decided to
give me the slip.

I tried very hard to think positive and give her the
benefit of the doubt. I closed my eyes and concentrated
on an image of Dweena barging through the door with
one of her imaginative excuses. I further envisioned her
carrying two cups of fresh-brewed coffee and a bag
blueberry muffins as a peace offering.

The image faded.

I gritted my teeth and started to paint without her. I
began close to the floor. I wanted to have someone
around before getting up on a ladder. I have a tendency
to step back to look at my work—from four rungs up.

Another half hour went by. Still no Dweena.

By then I was fuming. After finishing up the lower
section of the back wall, I took a break. I tried Dweena
again. Got her machine with the S.O.B. message again.
I threw the receiver down on the desk. It dislodged a
scrap of paper under the phone. I'd forgotten all about
it—the paper with P. G. Dover's two telephone numbers. That made me even angrier by reminding me of
everything I was mad about.

Well, hell, I thought. Now was as good a time as any
to call Dover's two numbers. Perhaps the diversion
would calm me.

Like Dweena, I figured the red phone was Dover's
Gintoflakokian embassy. I tried that number first.

Dweena's voice. "You've reached the offices of S.O.B."

Now that was weird. I stared at the receiver. I must have hit the redial button by accident and got Dweena's machine.

I dialed again. Got Dweena's machine yet again.

Nothing like this had ever happened before. Somehow Dweena's number must have got stuck in my telephone circuitry.

Taking extra special care, I dialed P. G. Dover's other number, the one I presumed was his private investigator line. I got Dweena's machine again.

That confirmed it. My phone was definitely screwed up. I hated that memory feature. I jerked the phone out of the wall jack and got my old black rotary dial telephone out of the closet. It's a great phone. The receiver has real heft, enough to cause major damage.

Chuck had showed me how to hook it up with alligator clips. It was, as he would say, a piece of cake. In seconds, I had a dial tone. So, once again, I dialed the number for P. G. Dover's red phone. This time I was dialing on a real dial, not punching in numbers. However, the results were the same. I got Dweena. I dialed P. G. Dover's black phone. Dweena.

I dialed Chuck. Obviously, I needed an electronics expert.

"No way," said Chuck.

"I'm telling you, it's happening. Every time I dial, I get Dweena's answering machine. Her number is stuck in my wire."

"That's not possible, and besides it not happening *every* time," said Chuck. "You dialed me and I answered."

"Maybe it got fixed."

"Whatever you say, Brenda. Why don't you take a deep breath, settle down, and try again?"

I hung up from Chuck and dialed P. G. Dover's red phone. Dweena. I went through the rest of the drill.

Dweena once. Dweena twice, Dweena three times.

I was in the middle of dialing Chuck's number, to tell him to come over and see for himself if he didn't believe what my phone was doing, when suddenly another possibility occurred to me.

I put the receiver back. Chuck was right. There was nothing whatsoever wrong with my phone.

For the first time I truly understood, felt deep down in my gut, why murder victims are usually killed by people they knew. People they'd pissed off. Lovers, spouses, exes. And friends. Dweena was damned lucky I'm scared of weapons.

15

Driven by extreme anger, I barely remembered pouring the paint out of the roller tin back into the paint can, or rinsing out the rollers and brushes, or closing Midnight Millinery and pulling down the gates, or taking Jackhammer back to the apartment, or changing out of my paint-splattered overalls, or hailing a cab.

I must have done all that, because I found myself in a cab hurtling up Sixth Avenue on the way to midtown hoping the driver would take Thirty-eighth Street east so I could see if any more millinery supply stores had been forced out of business since my last visit.

He took Thirty-fourth.

So I leaned back and closed my eyes.

Gripped tightly in my fist was P. G. Dover's office key—exactly what I needed to find out what the hell was going on. And if I was right . . .

Whoa there.

The cab jerked violently across two of lanes of traffic, pitching me to the side. I righted myself, cursed. I saw that he'd turned off Thirty-fourth. We were headed uptown again, about three blocks away from Dover's building, and closing fast. I checked the cab meter, calculated the fare plus tip, and got my money out.

Ready to pay, I settled back and looked out the window at all the buses and cabs and cars and buildings and hundreds of people surging by in a big herd.

And over there, a woman in a silly hat with a big portrait brim scurried along the sidewalk in front of a marble-facaded bank . . .

Ria Kleep?

It couldn't be her.

Ria Kleep didn't wear hats. Then there was the cold hard fact that Ria Kleep was dead. The dead don't walk Manhattan streets, at least not in broad daylight in silly hats.

No, I had not seen a ghost or a zombie. I was familiar with the phenomenon. It had happened to me before.

For many months after my friend Carla died, I saw her everywhere I went. My heart would skip a beat, and then I'd realize it was someone else, someone alive, someone who resembled Carla in some tiny detail—the arch of an eyebrow, the sweep of a hand, the way she glided along. Yet that hint was all it took to trigger my response.

Carla had been my best friend. I wouldn't have expected such a reaction with a mere acquaintance like Ria Kleep. Nonetheless it had happened. I looked again; the woman was gone.

The cab shot through an intersection, braked, and deposited me in front of Dover's building.

Technically the security guard was on duty, though in his case "on" wasn't very. The sound of his snore rattled throughout the hard-surfaced lobby.

I decided to sign in anyway, in case he happened to be more awake than he seemed. I approached on tiptoe, and silently scrawled my Jane Smith in the open book on his desk.

I watched the guard. He hadn't budged. His snoring kept a steady rhythm.

Emboldened, I flipped back a couple of pages in the book. Among the late night entries I discovered that a certain Maude Meatmarket had penned her signature at

four in the morning using bright purple ink. Maude
Meatmarket. I had to hand it to Dweena. Not a bad mon-
iker. In a year or so I might even get a chuckle out of
Maude Meatmarket.

Now, however, was another story.

"Good morning, Deb," I said to the Suite Sixteen receptionist. The air again smelled of nail polish.

Deb had the phone receiver to her ear, but she smiled
and waggled her wet fingertips at me in greeting.

Glad that she seemed to recognize me, I strode pur-
posefully up to her station. She punched the hold button
on the phone and asked how she might help me.

"Any messages come in for S.O.B.?" I asked.

"A couple," she said, "but I already gave them to that
other lady, the big, tall one who was with you yesterday.
She's got different hair today, but I remembered her. I
mean, who wouldn't? Was that okay? I wasn't sure exactly who's in charge and I didn't want to bother Gates."

"No problem," I said. "Thanks, Deb. Carry on."

I crept up to the door and slowly inserted the key into
the lock. I didn't have to jiggle it. It worked first try.
One quick quiet turn, a shove of the door, and I burst
into P. G. Dover's office.

My suspicions were confirmed.

"Goddammit, Dweena." I slammed the door behind me.

Dweena's laptop computer sat in the middle of Dover's desk, her inkjet printer balanced precariously atop
the little refrigerator, and she'd draped fake leopard skin
ultrasuede over the chairs. Maude Meatmarket had
moved in.

Dweena herself sat behind the desk. She was dressed
for success in a jet-black chin-length pageboy wig with
bangs. It went well with her purple and black polka-
dotted miniskirted suit. She was on the telephone, the
red one.

At the sight of me her eyes got big and round enough to strain the glue that bonded her false eyelashes to her real eyelids. Then her eyelids began to blink rapidly, out of control.

"I'll have to get back to you on that," she said into the phone. She cut the connection and turned her attention to me. "Uh, hi Brenda. This is a nice surprise. What brings you—oh my god—I just this second remembered. I was supposed to help you paint, wasn't I? Oh my, Dweena is *so* forgetful. I'm *so* sorry. I've been *so* overburdened, it totally slipped my mind. Will you ever forgive me?" She tried out a smile. It faded when she saw the expression on my face.

"Forget about painting," I demanded. "Explain what the hell you're doing in Dover's office."

"Well, there's not really very much to explain."

"Good, because I don't want to listen very long. And I don't want any of your bullshit either."

Dweena took several deep breaths. "All right, here's the lowdown. Remember yesterday, when we paid Dover's rent with my money?"

I nodded.

"And how that Gates woman said we had as much right to the office as anybody since we'd paid and had the key?"

Again, I nodded.

Her voice cracked and changed pitch. Like a slip peeking out from beneath a hem, a bit of Edward showed.

She cleared her throat, popped a throat lozenge in her mouth, and continued. "I took Gates's statement to heart. It's only fair. I thought it would be cool if S.O.B. had an office, where I could meet with city officials and landlords. My money paid slimeball Dover's rent. He can't use the office because he's still in the pokey. I suppose you know they found Ria Kleep's body?"

Yet another nod.

"Last night after I heard the story on the news, I called Brew Winfield. He said Dover's probably gonna stay locked up for a while because of the body and some other complications. So I thought, why not utilize the office in the interim? I hate to see good space wasted."

"Did you happen to tell Winfield of your takeover plans?"

"Oh, yes. Absolutely."

I glared at her.

"Well, sort of." She looked down and studied her false fingernails.

"Care to elaborate on that 'sort of'?"

"I mentioned that maybe somebody should keep an eye on the office in case the tense Gintoflakokian situation suddenly worsened."

"There is no Gintoflakokia, therefore, there is no situation, and Winfield knows it. And you know damned well he knows."

"Of course he knows. That's why he laughed. For a lawyer with a prima-donna pet snake, Brew can be rather jolly at times."

"And you took a lawyer's late-night chortle as greenlight go-ahead?"

"No. I simply went ahead. That's how things get done in this world—somebody forges ahead, rises above adversity to scale that mountain, to achieve their dream, to succeed where others have failed."

"Oh, please, Dweena."

"So anyway," she said, "I've been here for hours. The lobster shift receptionist, a guy, didn't give me an ounce of trouble. All it takes is the proper attitude. I sailed right by him. Then I utilized skills developed and finely honed in my diplomat vehicle relocation program to achieve access to the office."

"You broke in."

"Nothing's broken. Actually the lock works better now. You could say I fixed my way in."

"No, I couldn't say that."

"Whatever."

"You changed the messages on Dover's answering machines, didn't you?"

"That was my very first task, that is, after fixing the lock. It took awhile to determine how the machines worked. They must be over twenty years old."

"The messages were how I figured out where you were."

"I wondered how you did that."

"First I called you to see why you hadn't shown up as promised."

"I said I was sorry."

"Then, while taking a much needed break from painting all alone, I called Dover's phones to see which was for Gintoflakokia and which was the PI line. No matter which number I dialed, I got your S.O.B. message. At first I thought—well, never mind what. Bottom line is, I had a pretty good idea what you'd done."

"Clever," said Dweena.

"I see you've redecorated. What else have you been up to?"

"Lotsa stuff. Made a slew of telephone calls, set up appointments, intimidated evil landlords, and sucked up to various city officials. I love this place. I've even got the day receptionist, Deb, taking messages for me. It's part of the Suite Sixteen package."

As if on cue, a loud buzzer sounded.

"The intercom," said Dweena. "Do you think I should answer it?"

"I guess you have to. Deb knows we're both in here."

Dweena leaned into the intercom. "Yes?"

Deb's voice squawked back. ". . . a lady out here to see Mr. Dover. I sent her on back. I hope that's okay. I didn't know what else to do."

Just then, a sharp knock on the door.

Dweena gave me a what-the-hell-are-we-going-to-do-now? look.

I countered with a hell-if-I-know look.

Another knock, this time sharper and louder.

In the short time it took me to traverse the slightly more than three feet of faded ratty carpet to the door, approximately seventeen million possibilities spun through my mind, all twisting and turning and teaming up with each other and conspiring and diverting off into new directions. Not one of those seventeen million possibilities prepared me for what I was about to see. Not one of them even came close.

16

I was surprised.

Dweena, on the other hand, was horrified.

Her mouth stretched wide open and she let out one incredibly long, loud, spine-tingling screech. While that was still resounding around the room, she propelled out of Dover's chair and backed up against the window, crashing into a metal wastebasket on the way. A firm believer in the supernatural, she held her arms in front of her body and made the shape of a cross.

"Oh stop it, Dweena," I said. "You'll find that the apparition before you is quite alive."

I turned to the apparition in question. "Isn't that right, Ria?"

Ria—yes, that Ria. Ria Kleep. Not dead, but very much alive, and she was standing just inside the door to P. G. Dover's office, wearing that hat with the big portrait brim I'd spotted from the cab window. So, it really had been her after all.

I felt a surge of relief. Ria Kleep wasn't dead. Very good for Ria Kleep. Very good for me. With Ria Kleep alive, the cops would eventually let Dover go, and no one would care whether or not I knew of his office-home. Oh sure, there was still that matter of Dweena's lie, but like Elizabeth said, that wasn't my fault.

Before I could fully appreciate my initial relief, it was

replaced by serious questions. What about the dead body? If Ria Kleep wasn't dead, who was. Why had Tommy identified the dead body as Ria Kleep? I was confused.

So apparently was Ria Kleep. Her eyes darted from me to Dweena and back. "I know you from Angie's," she said to me. Then to Dweena, "And you, I've seen strutting around the Village. What are *you* two doing here? Where's Dover?"

I come from a long line of polite people. And so, my first instinct was to respond politely to Ria's questions. I caught myself in time. With great determination I broke through generations of inherited etiquette. "You," I said, pointing my finger at Ria, and sounding more like Detective Turner than me, "you're the one who's got the explaining to do. You're the one who's supposed to be dead."

Dweena had recovered sufficiently to pipe up with, "Yeah, Ria, how do you explain that?"

Ria said, "Well, obviously I'm not dead."

That was not the explanation I wanted.

Ria didn't seem all that willing to elaborate. She frowned, then with a large dramatic movement shifted her bag from one shoulder to the other. The movement wasn't large enough or dramatic enough to hide the fact that she'd also backed up a step and her right hand was groping around for the doorknob.

I had to stop her.

I am notoriously not brave. That trait is not inherited, but learned. My brain churned in an effort to determine if the stakes in this particular situation were big enough to throw caution to the wind. Then I remembered I was not alone. For whatever it was worth, Dweena was along for the ride.

Now, nobody ever called Dweena brave either. In fact, she's a much bigger chicken than me. She's also a much bigger human. Big enough to intimidate Ria, who weighed in at about my size.

I made a dive for the door and wedged my body be-

tween Ria and freedom. I nudged her hand aside and
closed mine over the doorknob. "Not so fast, Ria. I really think it would be in everybody's best interest if we
all had a little chat."

"The only thing I'm going to say to you two is good-
bye."

She grasped at the doorknob.

"Dweena," I said, "perhaps you could persuade our
friend Ria to stay." I tried to make it sound threatening.

It worked.

Ria decided to stick around. With a sigh of defeat, she
collapsed into one of the leopard skin–covered chairs,
buried her head in her hands, and began to sob——great
loud wails of extreme distress. Her entire body shook
and heaved. The hat fell off and tumbled to the ground,
revealing a matted-down mass of mousy-brown hair.

Dweena rolled her eyes, expressing my exact senti-
ments. Ria was faking it, and doing a rotten job. Unlike
Myrtle, she'd never make it to Broadway.

"Hey, Ria," I said, "Cut the melodrama already."

Her blubbering sputtered to a stop. A few seconds of
silence, then with a mighty sniffle Ria lifted her head
and glared at me.

I met her glare with an easy good-cop smile. "Want
to tell us what's going on?"

Ria wiped away a stream of fake tears with the sleeve
of her jacket, and blinked at me. "I swear," she said, "it
wasn't supposed to go down this way. My plan got all
screwed up."

"Well," said Dweena, "I *guess* it did."

I made sure Ria was watching, then gave that bad cop
Dweena a look to shush her from further mean-spirited
sarcastic comments. Then I turned to Ria and said with
kindness in my voice, "Tell us about your plan. Take
your time."

Her story unfolded at a painfully slow pace. She
hemmed and hawed, backed up and started over, and
insisted she didn't know what had gone wrong. ". . . And
so," she said winding down at long last, "I trashed my

apartment, sliced my arm, and smeared blood on the kitchen floor. Then I walked around for a while, thinking. When I was sure I wanted to go ahead, I called nine-one-one from a pay phone on the street, reported hearing sounds of a violent disturbance and possible gunshots in my apartment, and disappeared into the night. I never planned on a dead body turning up. I only wanted to be missing and *presumed* dead."

Dweena, who had been making a commendable effort to keep her lips zipped, burst out. "Give me a break. You expect us to believe that crap?"

Actually, I did believe her. I understood why Ria wanted to disappear. In her shoes, maybe I'd have done the same. "You wanted to get away from that stalker," I said with genuine sympathy.

"How'd you know about that?" asked Ria.

"Stalker?" said Dweena. "Nobody told me about any stalker."

I attempted to answer them both at once. I turned to Dweena. "Somebody had been stalking Ria. She hired Dover to find out who." Then to Ria, "I read your file." Back to Dweena, "You know, the file we got for Winfield."

"Who the hell is Winfield and why's he got my file?" asked Ria.

"Brewster Winfield," I said. "He's P. G. Dover's attorney, so your file is in good hands."

"Oh yeah, right," said Dweena. "It's in great hands."

"Where *is* Dover? Do you two work for him?" Ria looked around the office again as if she thought Dover might crawl out from under the rug. "I'd *really* like to talk to him."

"I bet he'd like to talk to you too," said Dweena. "Only he's still in the hoosegow."

Ria cocked her head and gave Dweena a questioning look.

"You know, in the pokey," said Dweena.

Still, Ria looked perplexed.

Dweena shook her head in disgust. "Jail. The jerkhole is locked up."

"I'm hip to the lingo," said Ria. "What I want to know is why. Why is Dover in jail?"

"Surely you know."

Ria shook her head.

"It's all over the goddamned news," said Dweena. "They don't come right out and say it, but it's clear the cops think Dover whacked you."

Surprise registered on Ria's face. It looked real to me. It took quite a while to sort it all out.

"Dover's a lousy private investigator," said Ria.

"You don't say," said Dweena.

"I hired him to find out who was stalking me."

"You didn't know?" I asked.

"Of course not. It's just some guy following me. I could feel him. Oh yeah, and sometimes I'd get these calls and the person would hang up. So I contacted Dover. About all he did was watch my building a couple of hours a day."

"What did you expect?" I asked.

"I don't know. Something. Anything. It was Dover's job to figure out what."

"Any possibility you were stalked by an old flame or an ex-spouse?"

"Uh, no."

"With no leads, it seems to me that watching your building wasn't such a bad idea."

"Dover didn't produce results. I was scared, so I took matters into my own hands and faked my own death."

An act of desperation. I smelled a rat. The sympathy I'd felt for Ria was rapidly dissipating, escaping through the holes in her story. I couldn't comprehend how she could just all of a sudden give up all that made her life a life. "What about your friends? Your job?"

"Friends? You know about my social life. I hang around Angie's with a bunch of losers. As far as my job goes, I hate it. I'm a secretary at a crummy import-export firm. Boss goes gallivanting all over the globe, I get stuck with the hassles. A fresh start, no stalker, a whole new me, sounded good."

"I can dig it," said Dweena, who had some experience in fresh starts.

Ria continued. "Then I heard they'd found my body."

"Back up a minute," I said. "If you knew they found your body, how come you didn't know they were holding Dover?"

"I didn't listen to the whole report. I couldn't. Until I decide where to go, I'm staying in a boardinghouse in Hoboken. It's not fancy—bathroom's at the end of the hall, TV downstairs in the living room. I was watching the news with a couple of the residents when the story came on. I was afraid any second a picture of me might flash by on the screen, and my secret would be out. Lucky for me, I had the remote control. I switched over to a game show, then cleared out fast. I called Dover to see if he knew what was going on, but the phones were screwed up. I kept getting somebody else's answering machine. It was weird."

I knew what she meant.

Ria continued. "I couldn't get through so I had to come in person. I borrowed this hat from one of the old women at the rooming house so no one would recognize me. I guess you know the rest."

Not all the rest. Probably not even a little of the rest, but I nodded agreeably. Ria had switched gears and seemed almost friendly. The nicer she got the less I trusted her. "Do you know whose body they found?"

"Of course not. How could I? Why do they think it's mine?"

"I don't know." I wasn't about let Ria know that it was Tommy who had identified the body as hers. Not until I knew what was going on. I wanted to hear what Tommy had to say.

I pulled back and let Dweena take over the conversation. She told Ria how she put the S.O.B. messages on both of Dover's answering machines.

"That's good to know. I thought I was losing my mind. What's S.O.B.?"

And Dweena was off.

When my friends lie they do it in a big way.

Dweena's lie had brought me a lot of grief. Her lie paled in comparison to Tommy's. What could possibly have motivated him? When the cops found out—and they surely would—they'd be around asking Tommy some hard questions.

Better me than them. If I could talk to him before the cops got to him, maybe together we could figure a way out.

Meanwhile, I had to deal with Ria. I didn't want her back out on the street. It was a big city, but it was also a small world. If somebody recognized Ria and blabbed to the cops, they'd be knocking on Tommy's door.

Back to the conversation.

I waited for a lull in Dweena's brothel rundown.

"Ria," I said, "were you planning to go back to Hoboken?"

She shrugged.

"Why not stay here?" I jerked my head toward P. G. Dover's fold-up cot.

Dweena shot me a dirty look.

"At least until you talk to Dover. It's safer than going back out on the street."

17

"Is Tommy around?"

It was Angie's slowest time of day, that vague period after the lunch rush and before the after-work crush.

The TV was tuned to a true-life courtroom drama. A couple of regulars sat at the bar.

One of them pointed with an elaborately carved unlit pipe. "Yeah, back there. He's in the kitchen with Raphael."

"Thanks."

When I was several steps away, the other regular called out. "Did you hear about Ria Kleep?"

Knowing all that I knew, his question rattled me. Then I realized what he must be asking, knowing only what he knew. "Yes," I said, "I was here the other night not long after—"

"Damned shame," he said. "A dirty damned shame."

"You said it," said the other regular.

Chili spices filled the air. I could almost taste the heat.

Like two witches intent on their brew, Tommy and Raphael huddled over a two-foot-tall stainless steel caldron. Tommy ladled out a sample of reddish brown chili and lifted it to his lips.

"Perfect," he announced. "Raphael, my man, you are a genius. I just wish—"

"Hey," I said.

Tommy glanced up and smiled. "Brenda. You're just in time for a bowl of Raphael's chili."

"Smells great, but I bet it's got meat in it."

"Oh yeah, sorry," said Tommy. "I forgot you're a freak for green leaves. What about Jackhammer? I know he eats meat."

"He sure does," said Raphael. "I make him my special burger balls."

"Where is the little rascal?" asked Tommy. "I don't see his bag."

"He's at home."

I'd made a conscious decision not to bring Jackhammer, thinking his absence would signal that my visit was different from usual—business, not pleasure—something I would find hard to express in words.

"He's not sick, is he?"

"No, Jackhammer's fine."

"Well," said Tommy, "you know he's always welcome at Angie's, as long as—"

Raphael ambled to other end of the kitchen, reached for bottle of spice, opened it up, and sniffed the contents.

I took the opportunity to lean close to Tommy and say, "I need to talk to you. In private."

Tommy knitted his brow. "I'm pressed for time. Can it wait?"

I shook my head, leaned even closer. "I saw Ria Kleep. Less than an hour ago. Alive."

Color drained out of Tommy's face. "Raphael, if anybody needs me, I'll be up in my office with Brenda."

Tommy led me into the back room. He unlocked the heavy wooden door to the upstairs. "Ever been up here before?"

"No."

"Watch your step. These stairs are uneven. I snagged my toe the other day and fell head over heels."

"Are you all right?"

"Bruises, cracked rib maybe. Hard to tell. Damned lucky I didn't break my neck."

On the second-floor landing, he unlocked another door and we stepped into the hallway. A bare lightbulb hanging from the ceiling cast harsh illumination on the stained and dingy walls—a sad reminder of One-Coat Joe's canceled paint job and the imminent closing of Angie's. I wanted to ask Tommy about that, but there was only so much upsetting stuff I could do in one day.

"The office," said Tommy, opening the door.

Dust particles danced in the beam of late afternoon sun that filtered in through a grimy window. I could hear the squeal of a blues guitar from the jukebox down below. I figured the office had to be directly over the bar.

"Not much to look at, I'm afraid."

"Cozy," I said, taking in the mismatched assortment of dark oak furniture.

He dragged two heavy straight-back chairs into the middle the room. We sat, knee-to-knee. Neither of us spoke.

A final spine-tingling guitar wail cut through our silence. Then the blues gave way to Frank Sinatra singing his hourly tribute to New York. I waited for the song to end, took a deep breath, and said, "I saw Ria Kleep."

Tommy nodded solemnly. "So you said."

"She's alive. Which is very, very good."

"I agree," said Tommy, "that is very, very good."

"Except for one detail."

Tommy's sad hound dog eyes got a little sadder, a little droopier. He looked years older.

"Why'd you do it? Why'd you ID the dead body as Ria Kleep?"

"How much do you know?"

"I don't know how much I know because I don't know how much there is to know. The one thing I do know for sure is that you're in a heap of trouble. You've got to make this right."

Tommy looked up at the ceiling, then the floor, then

at me. "Ria wanted to disappear. She was having, uh, some difficulty."

"The stalker."

"I thought it would help if I told the cops that body was hers. It stands to reason, if you want to disappear, being actually confirmed dead is better than being presumed dead."

"Unless you're the dead person," I said. "What about her?"

"Well, hey," said Tommy, with a shrug. "She looked a little like Ria. Size, hair, enough to meet a general description. The dead woman was already dead, and couldn't get any deader, so I figured what harm would it do?"

"Lots. You sent the cops down the wrong path, investigating the death of someone who's not dead. They won't be able to find the killer that way. Any idea whose body it was?"

"No." Tommy pushed himself out of the chair. The floorboards squeaked as he crossed the room. He went over to the window, pulled back the dark curtains, and gazed out.

"What you did is seriously illegal," I said. "You interfered with a homicide investigation. There's a killer on the loose and an innocent man about to be charged if he hasn't been already."

Tommy turned back to me. "I didn't think it through very well. There wasn't time. Put yourself in my shoes. It was just a regular day, getting on about evening. I was behind the bar, like always, taking care of business. All of a sudden the door opens and two cops come barging in. Next thing I know, wham bam, I'm at the morgue. You ever been to the morgue?"

I had, but that was not relevant. "Did you catch the names of the cops?"

"No."

"Does Turner ring a bell? Or McKinley?"

"Maybe. One black, one white, both well-dressed."

"Could be Turner and McKinley. Those are the detectives I know."

Tommy brightened. "That's good for me, right?"

"Hard to say. I might be able to smooth the way. Tommy, you have to tell them it's not Ria's body."

He shook his head.

"They'll be back, Tommy, asking tough questions, expecting good answers. Truthful answers. They won't be very nice about it. I know. I've seen them in action."

"They won't be back. I already did my civic duty."

"No. You misdid your civic duty. They'll find out you lied."

"How?"

"A thousand ways. The dead woman must have friends or family somewhere. They'll be looking for her, reporting her missing. A description might make the cops wonder. Also, Ria smeared her own blood on her kitchen floor. That blood's not going to match up with the corpse. These are just possibilities off the top of my head."

A tortured expression on his face, Tommy sat in the chair again, tilted back, and shut his eyes.

I left him alone with his thoughts, hoping he'd make the right decision.

I got up and looked out the window. Raphael was down below. I watched as he unpadlocked the metal flap doors in the sidewalk, pulled them open, and descended to the basement. A couple of minutes later, he came back up carrying a cardboard carton. The way he struggled, it must have been heavy. Bottles of booze probably.

The streets were empty. The midtown workers weren't home yet, and the people who stayed home had already done their errands.

Now that I was several blocks and an hour or so away from Ria Kleep's story, it bothered me even more than it had when she told it. For somebody supposedly so traumatized by a stalker that she'd do a disappearing act . . . I couldn't pin down why, but I didn't believe her.

It was a bizarre coincidence that the other body

showed up. Dead bodies are rare in Greenwich Village. I wondered why Ria cared that the cops thought the dead woman was her. Wasn't that exactly what she wanted? Tommy thought so. If the rest of her story was true, she should have been pleased. But she claimed to be so upset that she wanted to find out what happened, upset enough to risk her own disappearance scheme by walking around Manhattan.

I suspected she knew something about the dead woman. There had to be some connection.

"All right," said Tommy. "I've thought it through. I'll do whatever you say."

"Good," I said. "I'll call Turner and McKinley and tell them that you got in touch with me. You knew I was acquainted with a couple of detectives at the precinct. You're deeply troubled. You can't sleep. The more you think about it, the more you're not so sure the body you identified was really Ria Kleep. You think you might have made a mistake. You were tired, confused, and upset."

"Do you think they'll go for it?"

"I don't know."

"And if they don't?"

"It doesn't matter. You've got to tell the truth whatever the consequences. If I remember correctly, the other night you said you were shown a picture, not the actual dead body."

"That's right. And thank god for that."

"Good. It should be relatively easy for them to show it to you again. With any luck, they'll have a duplicate at the precinct and you won't have to go back to the morgue. This time, tell the truth. Tell them it's not Ria Kleep."

"Okay," said Tommy, without much conviction.

"It's important that we make the first move."

Tommy handed me his phone.

"All right, Brenda. Go ahead, make the call."

18

"Will you be okay up here alone?" asked Tommy. "I've got to do some prep work before the happy hour bunch streams in."

"Go ahead. I'll be fine."

"Thanks, Brenda. On your way out, pull the door all the way closed behind you."

I was grateful for the privacy. Despite my brave front, it would not be easy to get up the nerve to call Turner. No reason Tommy had to know it was a bigger deal than I'd let on.

With the freedom to procrastinate, I did, and it occurred to me that many things were much bigger deals than I ever let on to anybody. It's not healthy to keep so much bottled up.

I never even told my friends how devastated I'd been on my birthday. Bad enough they hadn't thrown me a surprise party. Except for Johnny, nobody had even remembered it was my birthday, and sometimes I wasn't so sure about him. Lately, he was acting so weird.

My bruised feelings got buried in the avalanche of activity surrounding Dweena and P. G. Dover and Ria Kleep, and now Tommy. Someday that snow would melt and expose me.

Enough moping.

It was important that I make the call to Turner. I stared at the telephone still in my hand.

A big band number on the jukebox ended. From downstairs I heard the ring of the cash register opening, Tommy murmured something to Raphael, then the jukebox started up again with a rap cover version of "Jailhouse Rock." An appropriate background for my call to Turner. I took it as a sign.

I punched in the number fast. When Turner answered I spat out the reason for my call all at once, before he had a chance to tell me how utterly swell it was to hear from me again so soon.

"Why does this not surprise me?" Turner said, sarcasm turned up full-tilt.

That wasn't a real question, and he probably didn't expect any kind of an answer, but he got one anyway. "Well," I said, trying to sound nonchalant, "I suppose because misidentification of dead bodies by civilians is a relatively common occurrence."

"Yes," agreed Turner, "your normal average civilian screwing up an ID, that kind of crap happens all the time. But that's not what I'm talking about. What I'm talking about is *you*, Ms. Midnight, and the fact that you continue, despite numerous warnings, to be involved in this case. Bug off. Butt out. Go make some goddamned hats."

"I know how it must seem, Detective, but in this particular instance I'm actually not involved. It's just that Tommy knows me, and he knows that I know you, so he came to me for advice, which I was more than happy to give him. That's all."

"I'm gonna hate myself in the morning," said Turner, "but go on, Ms. Midnight, and tell me what you've got in mind."

"Thanks, Detective. Tommy's afraid he goofed up when he saw the photograph of the dead woman. He was intimidated by the whole scene at the morgue, so he didn't study it as closely as he should have. The image didn't connect with his brain. He'd like to take another look at the photograph."

"I can arrange that."

"Is it possible for him to do it at the precinct? Tommy says the morgue creeps him out."

Turner sighed. "The morgue 'creeps out' most civilians. All right, Ms. Midnight. I've got a duplicate of the photo. Have your friend Tommy stop by."

"If it's all right with you," I said, "I'd like to come along with him. I knew Ria Kleep. Perhaps I can help."

"That's what we police need more of—helpful milliners. I don't care. Bring the whole goddamned neighborhood if you want."

An idea had started to form. I needed time. Gently, I stalled. "Is early evening okay? Tommy should probably hang around Angie's to greet the regulars who drift in after work."

"It's okay by me," said Turner. "I'm gonna be stuck here most of the night anyway. Got a shitload of paperwork to catch up on."

I cradled the phone.

That hadn't been so bad. If he didn't watch himself, Turner might turn into sort of an all right guy—for a cop, that is. I hoped so. His girlfriend, former Officer Nicole (Gung-Ho) Gundermutter, deserved the best.

I took a moment to soak up the atmosphere of Tommy's office. It felt safe and comforting, a warm coat against a sharp wind. That's what Angie's was all about. Its loss would rupture the neighborhood's soul. The wound would be a long time healing.

I pulled the door closed behind me.

The bar was moderately crowded and rapidly filling with cigarette smoke and boisterous laughter. In another half hour people would be jammed in subway-tight.

I pulled Tommy off to the side. "We're all set."

"I don't know about this, Brenda. I'm starting to get cold feet."

"Don't worry. Detective Turner said normal everyday civilians frequently screw up this kind of stuff. The good news is we can see the photo at the precinct."

"We?"

"Yeah. I thought I'd go along as moral support. Turner said it was okay. You don't mind, do you?"

"Of course not."

"Good. I'll meet you back here in a couple of hours. We can walk down to the precinct together."

"Why not stick around?" said Tommy. "Dinner and drinks are on the house. It's the least I can do."

"Thanks, but there's something I want to take care of before we go."

Like I said, in the middle of talking to Turner I got this great idea—at least I thought it was great—a possible way prove my hunch that although Ria was not the dead woman, she was somehow connected to her.

I'd need a camera to implement my plan.

I called Chuck Riley from Midnight Millinery.

"Did you ever get that problem with your phone fixed?" he asked.

"It was all a mistake," I said.

"I told you so. The effect you described could not happen without breaking a couple of real important laws of physics. A major catastrophic event might do it. I'm sure I would have heard if a meteor had smashed into the West Village this morning."

"Can I borrow your digital camera?"

"What for?"

"To take a photograph."

"That's a smart-ass answer, leading me to suspect there's more to the story. So, divulge."

"I need to photograph a picture of a dead body."

"Ah, now that sounds more like it. Who's the stiff?"

"All I know for sure is who it isn't. I'll fill you in when I see you. If I manage to get the shot can you print it out right away?"

"Piece of cake. Speaking of nutrients, I'm running low

on an essential food group. Do me a favor and stop by
the deli on your way over and pick up a jumbo bag of
chips, the saltier and greasier and brighter the better."

The cab dropped me off at the end of Chuck's street.
Since I'd last visited, a black and chrome sushi bar had
sprung up in the ruins of a burned-out liquor store. In
the middle of Chuck's block a notorious squatter's building, the scene of several violent battles between squatters
and cops, had been gutted. Renovation was well under
way. A sign affixed to the frontage advertised that fifteen
loftlike condos—"edgy East Village ambiance in a full-
service building"—would be available in the early fall,
all priced under a million and a half. The roof, where
squatters armed with bottle rockets had made their last
stand, sported a brand-new big white satellite dish.

From revolution to renovation in a geologic blink of
an eye.

"You got the chips?" asked Chuck.

I handed over the bag. "The deli counterman promised
these glow in the dark."

"Cool. I haven't eaten since my morning jelly doughnuts." He flung the bag on top of an ancient oscilloscope.
"Have a seat. I'll be with you as soon as I find the
camera. It's gotta be around here somewhere."

He disappeared behind the wall he'd built out of
stacked-up computer magazines. It was now two layers
thick and topped out at various heights right up to the
sagging ceiling.

I sank down into one of the red beanbag chairs. Chuck
had skillfully managed to keep any hint of neighborhood
renewal far away from his boarded-up storefront apartment. It was, as always, crammed with scores of computers, electronics equipment, and junk, piled up all over
the place, all running at the same time, little lights blink-
ing, doing things that Chuck found fascinating, but that
I never quite understood.

"Got it," said Chuck. He popped into the room holding a palm-size camera that he dangled enticingly in front of my face. I made a grab for it; he snatched it away.

"Not until you level with me. I'm afraid all this talk about snapping photographs of cadavers has got me nervous. I need to know what kind of trouble you're stirring up."

"You sound like Turner." This was the new reformed exceedingly paranoid Chuck. "I assure you I am not stirring up trouble. In fact, I'm doing quite the opposite. I'm fixing existing trouble, righting a terrible wrong, making the world a better place."

"Spare me the theatrics and clarify."

I updated him on Ria Kleep's disappearance, supposed death, and subsequent reappearance. "All I know for sure is that Ria Kleep is not dead. Everything else . . . I'm not so clear about, except I think Ria knows more than she's telling. I want to see how she reacts when I show her the picture."

"But first you have to take it."

"Right. And for that I need your camera. So how about it?"

"I'm still confused," said Chuck. "How come the cops thought the dead body was Ria's?"

"I told you, Tommy identified it."

"I mean, before that? Why did they go to Tommy in the first place?"

"They'd already been to Angie's asking a bunch of questions about Ria even before there was a body, when she was just missing. They must have found out from a neighbor or somebody that Ria hung out at Angie's. Since they already suspected foul play, when a dead body turned up that met Ria's general description, the pieces fit good enough to check it out. They took Tommy to the morgue, he IDed the picture, and their theory was confirmed."

"I don't get it. Why would Tommy do such an incredibly stupid thing?"

"To give Ria's disappearing act credibility."

"Do you think maybe there's some funny business between him and Ria? She is sexy, you know, in a low-rent kind of way."

"You've got to be kidding."

"Trust me, Brenda, as a male I know of what I speak."

"Well, I don't think she's sexy and I don't think she was involved with Tommy, but I do think there's more to the story."

"Like?"

"I don't know. Maybe Tommy is afraid one of the regulars is the stalker and wants to keep him out of trouble."

"Wouldn't he want to get rid of the troublemaker?"

"That does make more sense. So, it's probably nothing. Tommy admitted he didn't think it through carefully. That's why I'm trying to fix it. Now, can I have the camera?"

He handed it over. I tucked it into my purse.

"Thanks, Chuck. You're a pal."

From Chuck's I took a cab straight to Angie's. The place was really hopping now. Raphael was working the bar. I elbowed my way through the noisy crowd. "Where's Tommy?" I hoped he hadn't chickened out.

"Upstairs putting on a fresh T-shirt. He'll be down in a couple of minutes. Want a glass of wine while you wait?"

"No thanks." I almost blabbed to Raphael how I wanted to be stone-cold sober when talking to the police, then I realized he might not know where Tommy was going, so I shut up.

I wedged myself in next to one of the regulars. He gave me a friendly nod, then turned his attention back to a game show on the TV. I pretended to watch it too, but I was really staring into space, worrying a little about how Turner would react to Tommy and a lot about how I was going to manage to take a photograph of the picture of the dead body.

*   *   *

"Will you get a load of this?" said one of regulars down at the other end of the bar.

Everybody looked in the direction he pointed.

Tommy swaggered through the masses. He'd changed more than his T-shirt. He had on a jacket. And a shirt with a collar. And a tie. Blue with a touch of maroon.

"Now I've seen everything. Lay me down to die," said the guy next to me.

"Take my advice," I said to Tommy. "Lose the tie."

"What's the matter, don't you like blue?"

"It's not the color, it's the tie. Or, more precisely, it's the tie on you. It makes you not look like you. Turner will get the idea you're trying too hard to impress him that you're an upstanding citizen. It might make him think you're up to something."

"But I am an upstanding citizen."

"Trust me, as a stylist and as a friend."

Tommy took the tie off, rolled it up, and put it in the pocket of his jacket. "Better?"

"Much."

19

At one time or another, almost everyone in the West Village has wandered
into Angie's. If not to eat or drink or hang
out, then to use the phone, or make a quick bathroom
stop, or catch the game scores on the big overhead TV.
In passing, they say a couple of words to Tommy, and
he says a couple of words back.

Tommy is a fixture. Everybody knows him, but they
know him as the guy behind the bar.

Which was why it was very strange out on the street.

Dozens of people we encountered had the exact same
reaction on seeing Tommy—first a quick smile and nod,
then a puzzled double-take, like they knew him, but
couldn't quite place him. Those who finally made the
connection commented that they'd never in all these
years seen Tommy outside Angie's. "Thought you'd
grown roots behind the bar," said one.

It's an absurd perception. Tommy has a life. I often
see him in the morning when I'm out with Jackhammer.
And then late each night after Angie's closes, Tommy
walks over to Seventh Avenue and takes the subway to
his apartment somewhere deep in Queens.

Once people fit you into a convenient slot, it's hard
to change their mind-set. It's like how I'm so closely
identified with Midnight Millinery some people don't
recognize me unless I've got a hat on my head. Lately,

I've been hatless a lot and I've felt anonymous. I wondered who I'd be if I never made another hat.

Tommy forged ahead, seemingly oblivious to people's reactions to his out-of-Angie's presence. He was probably too nervous, and focused entirely on the unpleasant job ahead.

As we neared the precinct, he slowed his pace, turned to me, and said, "You must know these detectives pretty well to call them up out of the blue."

"Hardly. They owe me a few favors, that's all."

"I wouldn't want you wasting any favors on my account."

"Don't worry about it. The way I keep running into situations with the detectives, there's bound to be plenty more favors looming on the horizon."

That's what I said. I didn't want Tommy to know that I too was worried, although not so much about favors. I was wrestling with major moral issues. I had encouraged, insisted even, that Tommy go to the cops and tell the truth. Yet, at the same time, I was holding back information about Dweena, and Dover's office, and also about Ria Kleep. I had damned good reasons, but I was starting to doubt if they were equal to the risk.

Truth was truth and the whole truth up front would have been a far better route. Easier, too, than keeping who knew what sorted out.

We rounded the corner to the precinct. "You ready?" I asked.

"Yep."

I escorted Tommy through the precinct lobby, up the stairs, and over to Turner and McKinley's cubicle. I peeked in the doorway, but Turner didn't see me. He was alone, cursing a blue streak at his computer monitor, both index fingers fully extended, pounding on his keyboard. His hunt-and-peck method probably clocked in at about thirty words a minute.

I rapped on the door frame. Turner looked up and scowled his greeting.

"Good evening, Detective," I said.

"It isn't, Ms. Midnight. Not at all. In fact, after a quiet start, this is shaping up to be one humdinger of a shit-filled night. McKinley's already gone and half the late shift called in sick with food poisoning. One of the men brought in his wife's potato salad last night, only it rode around with him all day in his car before the shift. By the time he got here, the stuff turned lethal. So if you don't mind, can we speed this up?"

And he'd sounded almost in a good mood when I'd called earlier.

Tommy spoke. "I'm very sorry about this, Detective. Sir."

Turner leveled his gaze at Tommy. "Yeah? Well, don't sweat it. Sorry if I seem gruff. You're not the first and you sure as hell won't be the last to screw up. Nine outta ten civilians fall to pieces when you show them a stiff. You'd think they'd be used to it by now, with all the crap that gets on TV, even the news for godsakes." He reached for a folder, opened it, and removed a picture. "Most people do much better the second time around."

"I hope so," said Tommy. He took the picture from Turner. His brow wrinkled and his lips pressed together as he studied it.

Even from where I stood it was obvious that the woman in the picture was not Ria Kleep, though they were of the same general type.

"Well?" said Turner.

Tommy shook his head. "I made a mistake before. I've never seen this woman."

"Then it's *not* Ms. Kleep? You sure about that?"

"Positive. Her hair's the same though. That must be what fooled me. Same color, same length, same style, but the face, no, that's not Ria Kleep."

"And you've never seen this woman before?"

"No. Never."

"What about you, Ms. Midnight?" said Turner.

I was definitely one of the nine out of ten civilians Turner mentioned who fall to pieces looking at pictures of dead people. Fortunately I didn't have to look at this one too carefully. All I had to do was pretend to look and figure out a way to take a photo of the picture.

I picked it up, squinted, focused elsewhere, and tilted it this way and that.

"Hmmm." I tapped my fingernail on a spot near the center of the picture. "That mole on her cheek, you know, I think maybe it could be a tattoo. It could be significant, the mark of a cult."

"I didn't see any tattoo," said Turner. "Neither did McKinley."

I frowned up at the crummy fluorescent fixture suspended overhead. "The light out in the stairwell is better."

"It's the same all over the precinct," grumbled Turner.

"Back in a second. I just want to make sure."

"Waste of time," said Turner.

I made no further comment. I was already gone.

With a glance behind to be sure Turner wasn't on my heels, I dashed into the stairwell. I was in luck, it was empty. No one was sneaking a smoke break, although from the smell, it seemed someone recently had.

Working quickly, I propped up the picture on the banister. Chuck's camera was tiny, virtually weightless, easy to use, and silent. In moments the entire operation was over and done.

I pushed the camera down into the bottom of my purse. Then I returned to Turner's cubicle, shaking my head in mock disappointment.

Turner was standing by his desk, heartily pumping Tommy's hand, solemnly pronouncing the official boilerplate good-citizen speech. "Thank you for coming by. It was the right thing to do. It's citizens like you who make a difference."

"Thank you," said Tommy, "and I apologize for the time before."

Turner turned to me. "Was I correct about the light?"

"You certainly were," I said. "It's bad everywhere. The city ought to do something about the atrocious work conditions around this place. It's a wonder you don't get headaches."

"Believe me, Ms. Midnight, I do. Constantly. Now, if you want to get a better look at the alleged mole on the woman's face, I have a magnifying glass in my desk drawer. We're better equipped than you might think."

"Thanks, but that won't be necessary. What I thought was a mole must have been a speck of dirt. It fell off. See? It's gone now."

"And that, Ms. Midnight, is what I wish you were."

Tommy and I took the hint.

We left the precinct and headed up Hudson Street.

Tommy let out a huge sigh of relief. "Well, I'm glad that's over." He unbuttoned his jacket. His arms were swinging, his step lively. He seemed much more relaxed.

"I told you it wouldn't be a big deal."

"Yeah, well, if there's one thing I learned from years behind the bar listening to people it's that one person's not so big deal is often another's really big deal. Tell me, what were you up to with the bit about the mole? I didn't see any speck of dirt on that poor dead woman's face."

"It was that obvious?"

"Afraid so."

Damn. If Tommy had seen through my act, so probably had Turner. No harm now in leveling with Tommy. "I needed an excuse to be alone with the picture. I photographed it to show to Ria Kleep. I've got a hunch she knew the victim. It's just too weird, the other woman's body turning up like that. It's not like we get a lot of dead bodies in the Village."

"No, we don't. I take it then you'll be seeing Ria again?"

"I hope so."

"Well, when you do," he said, "please give her my best, and tell her the regulars are still grieving her loss. She'll probably be flattered."

"I could think of better ways to get popular."

"I don't know," said Tommy. "She's a strange one, that Ria. I must have been crazy thinking I should lie to help her out. Lots of people hang around Angie's. I might let them run up a tab, but this is the first time I've done anything like this. Believe me, it's the last time. From now on, I'm sticking with the truth."

"Always the best policy," I said.

"I'm glad you convinced me to straighten things out with Detective Turner. It would be a damned shame, after all these years running a bar, and having no serious run-ins with the law, if something should happen, especially now, now that . . ." Tommy's voice faltered. He took my elbow, and guided me around the corner onto a quiet side street.

I had a good idea what he was going to say.

His eyes met mine. "Angie's is closing."

"I know. I'm sorry."

"How do you know?"

"The other day I was buying paint from One-Coat and he mentioned something about it, but I thought— hoped—it was a rumor. You know how stuff gets around in this neighborhood."

"It's no rumor. What did One-Coat tell you?"

"He was mostly griping that his paint job got canceled, after he'd done up an elaborate estimate with his new computer. He told me your ex-wife—"

"Nancy, my ex, she owns the building. We've got an okay divorce, she's not being mean or vengeful, but some big-time developer came along and made her an offer she couldn't refuse and all of a sudden she decides she wants to move to, of all places, L.A. It's amazing. Twenty years of marriage and you think you know somebody, then wham bang all of a sudden they turn into somebody else with a whole other set of desires.

HATFUL OF HOMICIDE

Says she wants a golden suntan and a silver sports car. According to the divorce settlement, I get first option on the building, but I can't come close to matching the money the developer is throwing around. He's going to tear it down and put up a luxury apartment house."

"It's happening all over the city, even in the East Village."

"Can't say as I blame Nancy. She'll be set up for the rest of her life. Given half a chance, I'd probably do the same—well, not L.A., but you know what I mean."

"How much longer do you have?"

"Let me put it to you this way," said Tommy, "I've been saving a hundred-dollar bottle of champagne to crack out the next time the Yanks win the World Series. No matter how good the boys do this year, Angie's won't make it through the summer. I'll pop the cork tonight if you want to come by for a toast."

"Thanks, but I can't tonight. I'll take a raincheck."

"Don't wait too long."

Jackhammer skidded to a stop in front of me and scrambled around my ankles. I picked him up and carried him into the room with me. "We'll go out as soon as I check my answering machine."

No calls.

I got Jackhammer's leash out of the closet, snapped it on, and off we went to Midnight Millinery. It was depressing to see the shop in such disarray—hats hidden away, and the paint mess—but I had to know if anyone had called me. I needn't have bothered. No calls there either.

I dialed Johnny on the slim chance he was home and answering his phone. Like I said, a slim chance. I slammed down the receiver without leaving a message.

Jackhammer streaked through Chuck's door, eager to explore unfamiliar territory.

"Hey, little doggie, nice to see you, buddy," said Chuck. "You too, Brenda. Did you get the shot?"

I handed him the camera. "I think so. I got several

shots, did exactly what you told me. It seemed almost too easy."

"Welcome to the digital age, Brenda Midnight."

Chuck poked a cable into the camera, stuck the other end in the back of one of his many computer setups. He sat down and tapped a few keys and slid his mouse around. "That's it. Like I told you—a piece of cake. The photographs are stored in the camera's memory. All we have to do now is wait for them to download."

One by one the images of the dead woman formed on Chuck's gigantic computer monitor. The process was much slower than I'd anticipated. "How come it's taking so long?"

"Technology marches on," said Chuck. "The camera is state-of-the-art, but the computer is last year's model. The processor is slow for the job."

"You always have the biggest and the fastest, the latest of the latest. Are you slipping?"

"No, I'm not. What I am is a damned nice guy. My brand-new real fast number cruncher is upstairs at Urban Dog Talk's place. They borrowed it to make a demo. Music takes mucho power."

Until Chuck mentioned Urban Dog Talk, I hadn't noticed the silence. All hours of the day and night the band shook the rafters of Chuck's building. They were a good band; I missed hearing them play. "They're working now? It's so quiet."

"They're either mixing or going direct."

I nodded, pretending to understand.

Eventually the images came up on the screen. I picked out the best of the batch. Chuck used a photo editing program to lighten it up a couple of notches, then printed out several copies on his color printer.

I put them in my purse. "Thanks a million, Chuck. I owe you a pizza."

"Make it two. Extra cheese, double pepperoni."

I found Jackhammer curled up asleep in one of the red beanbag chairs. I scooped him up and took him home.

20

It was late and I was tired. I craved a long, hot bubble bath and a good night's sleep. But I had the photograph of the picture of the dead woman and if I didn't take care of it tonight I'd have to do it tomorrow, and I planned to spend that entire day on the butt end of a paint roller.

I downed a cup of coffee.

Dweena picked up on the first ring. "S.O.B. headquarters," she said, using her best business voice. "Striving to preserve a slice of historic old New York."

"It's me, just checking to see if you and Ria are still around."

"Where else?" said Dweena. "Ria latched on to your idea of staying here, and you know me. Your pal Dweena is up all night, every night, toiling away for the good of Greenwich Village, a thankless job, which I should mention is precisely why, much as I'd like to, it's damned near impossible for me to get up at the crack of dawn to help you paint. Maybe I could pitch in, kinda latish, some afternoon."

"Tomorrow. I'll be painting all day. You're welcome to come by any time and sling a roller."

"Tomorrow? Oh. That's a mere few hours away. I'm not sure. Let me check my calendar before I commit. Hang on a minute."

"Forget it," I said. "If you show up, you do. If not, you don't. Right now, I need to see Ria. I'll be at Suite Sixteen in a few minutes."

"Fabulous. You can help us stuff envelopes for the cause."

"Make sure Ria sticks around."

"No prob. Ria is very happy here. Isn't that right, Ria?"

I heard Ria, but I couldn't make out what she said.

"She's really into S.O.B.," said Dweena. "Says it's the best thing since the defeat of Westway. Remember that?"

"No."

"You were probably still back in Belup's Creek or wherever the hell it is you're from. Let me tell you, it was a long series of very hairy confrontations and political machinations. Thought it would never end, then at the last possible minute, snail darters saved the day."

"What's a—"

"Never mind. It's too much to go into. Ria has caught up with me. I must get back to signing these letters."

"I can't believe you two are getting along so well."

"Ria's a great help and she's quite pleased with the deal on Dover's office. Considering we're talking prime midtown Manhattan real estate, and a short-term high-risk lease, I was quite generous."

"Should I take that to mean you're charging Ria rent on the office you commandeered?"

"Strictly speaking," said Dweena, "yes, I guess you could say that. But all for the good. The money is going straight into S.O.B.'s coffers. That makes it okay in my book."

I'd like to have thumbed through Dweena's book.

Tall gray buildings with darkened windows rose from barren sidewalks. Not a single deli was open. Not a single person was out. I felt like the last person on earth. Or rather, me and the cab driver. I tipped him extra.

"Stick around a minute to be sure I get into the building, okay?"

The way he palmed the money and sneered, I didn't trust him one bit. To make sure he hadn't misunderstood, I left the back door wide open when I exited the cab. By the time he got out, flipped me the bird, called me a crazy bitch, circled around to the back of the cab, and slammed the door shut, I'd whooshed through the revolving door of the building and was safely inside—that is, if you call traipsing through the lobby of an unlocked deserted midtown building after midnight safe.

Oh sure, the night guard was on duty, but he was far in the back of the lobby, and totally absorbed in a movie running on a personal DVD player. From the loud crashing sounds and screaming of the frightened masses, I figured it had to be an end-of-the-world disaster film.

I crossed the lobby, stopped at the desk, signed a fake name in the book. The whole time the guard's eyes stayed riveted on the tiny bright screen where a truck-size flaming object swooped down between the World Trade Center towers, then continued to carom its way uptown. After watching it flatten the Flatiron Building, I headed over to the bank of elevators.

Up at Suite Sixteen, a big burly guy dressed in camouflage fatigues sat behind the reception desk. His masculine presence must have been a nod to increased late-hour security, although I'm not sure how effective he'd be against the forces of evil. He was busy painting his perfectly sculpted fingernails. Unlike his female counterpart, he made no attempt to hide the fact. He spread open the fingers of his right hand and blew on his nails.

"That's a pretty shade of green," I said when he acknowledged me. "It goes well with your outfit."

"How nice of you to notice," he said.

I didn't know whether to ask for Gintoflakokia, P. G. Dover, Dweena, S.O.B., or Ria Kleep, so I lowered my voice to a conspiratorially low whisper, winked, and said, "No need to announce. They're expecting me."

It was hard to imagine, but for once Dweena hadn't lied. She and Ria really were stuffing envelopes. How quaint, how very 1960s.

"Yo, Brenda," said Dweena. "Pull up a chair and help collate."

I situated myself at a shaky little table directly across from Ria.

Dweena showed me what to do. "I sign and collate and pass to you. You staple and fold. Ria stuffs and seals. Got it?"

After a dozen or so I got a pretty good rhythm going. Tap, tap, chunka, two folds, and slide the finished piece across to Ria. The mindless work was very relaxing.

When I thought we were all sufficiently lulled, I extracted the photograph of the picture from my purse without breaking rhythm and slid that over to Ria. Tap, tap, chunka, slide.

Ria furrowed her brow at the picture.

I stopped mid-tap and focused on Ria's face.

"What's this?" she asked.

I thought I detected a hint of recognition, or perhaps dismay. "I got the picture from Detective Turner. This is the woman they thought was you."

Dweena picked up the picture. "This lady's dead? Yuck." She dropped it back down on the table.

Ria looked ill.

"Do either of you recognize this woman?" I asked.

Dweena shook her head. "Put it away. It gives me the creeps."

Ria didn't say anything. I nudged the picture toward her. "Do you know her, Ria?"

"No. Never seen her before."

"Oh well," I said. "It was a shot in the dark."

I got back to work. Tap, tap, chunka, two folds and . . .

Ria was no longer seated across from me.

She had stood up and moved away from the table. She now stretched and let go of an exaggerated yawn. "It's been a long stressful day and I'm dead on my feet, so if you don't mind, I'd like to turn in now."

"Go ahead," said Dweena. "We've got a great start. Brenda and I can finish up without you."

And that's what we did.

Then we left.

I bet Dweena five dollars that Ria would be out on the street within five minutes.

"You're wrong," said Dweena. "She's curled up on Dover's cot, sound asleep."

"She might be curled up, but she's faking the sleep. Did you catch the expression on her face when she saw that picture?"

"Yeah. Aghast. Like me, a perfectly normal reaction."

"Only she looked that way *before* I mentioned that the woman was dead. That's not obvious from the picture. Mark my word, Ria Kleep knows the dead woman. She's going to do something. I don't know what, but it won't be from Dover's office. That would be too risky. It could be bugged."

"Okay," said Dweena. "You're on. Five bucks." She glanced at her watch. "Five minutes and counting."

Exactly four minutes twenty-five seconds later Ria spun through the revolving door.

"I can't believe it," said Dweena. She handed me a five-dollar bill.

Dweena and I were waiting, hunkered down in piece of junk clunker that most certainly did not belong to a diplomat. I felt guilty that I'd actually encouraged Dweena to do her stuff and hotwire a car, especially since I was always harping on her to go straight, but extraordinary circumstances called for extraordinary measures. I promised myself that when we had finished, I'd have Dweena return the vehicle as close as possible to where it had been parked when she took it.

*   *   *

Ria walked one avenue east, stepped into the street, and stuck out her arm. Traffic was light. It was several minutes before a vacant on-duty cab cruised by and stopped for her.

Staying half a block behind, we followed the cab up to the East Eighties. Ria got out of the cab and scurried into the foyer of a small apartment building.

"Where do you think she's going?" asked Dweena.

"Don't know. I'm hoping this is where the dead woman lived."

"That's kind of a stretch."

"Not so much. I put myself in Ria's shoes. If someone showed me the picture of a dead person whom I knew, I'd want to see if the person was really dead."

"That's nuts. Even if you're right, why would she go chasing around town in the middle of the night? Why not just call?"

I shrugged. "Maybe she wants into the apartment."

And that did seem to be the case.

Dweena backed up the car so we had a good line of sight into the foyer. As we watched, Ria went through the tried-and-true method of getting into a locked apartment house. One by one she rang all the buzzers. The method works a lot better around dinnertime when half the population of New York City is expecting a Chinese takeout delivery. This time of night nobody buzzed her in.

Ria was damned lucky to get another cab, but she eventually did. We followed it back to the Suite Sixteen building.

"Want to go tuck her in and ask her what the hell she was doing?" asked Dweena.

"No. I want to go back to the Upper East Side."

Dweena was happy to take me. She loved to drive.

"Now what?" asked Dweena when we got back to the apartment building.

"Wait in the car. Keep the engine running."

I went into the foyer and wrote down all the names on the mailboxes. None of them was familiar to me. I didn't expect that they would be.

"That was quick," said Dweena.

"There wasn't much to do," I said.

"Are we finished now?"

"Almost, except for dropping the car back where we got it."

"How will we get back to the Village?"

"Cab. Bus. Subway."

"You're still no fun, Brenda."

I had information. I wanted Turner and McKinley to have that information. I didn't want them to know the information came from me.

I came up with a solution.

"I changed my mind," I said to Dweena. "We're not quite done yet. Pull over, I want to make a call."

I got back in the car. "I never knew that before," I said. "It doesn't cost anything to call nine-one-one."

"Cool," said Dweena.

We experienced a New York–style miracle. The exact parking space from where Dweena had boosted the car was vacant.

"Nobody will ever know," said Dweena.

"I hope not."

We got out, made sure the doors were properly locked, and hailed the first downtown-headed cab that rolled along.

I was totally tired.

At least my efforts had paid off. Thanks to me, Turner and McKinley would get information to solve the case. They'd soon know whatever Ria knew about the dead woman, including I hoped, who she was. I could stop worrying about who'd lied about what to whom. Tommy had told the truth, and with Ria alive, Dweena's lie was less significant, as were my nondisclosures.

I leaned back in the cab and breathed out a huge sigh of self-satisfaction. I dozed off, barely noticing when the cab quit its crosstown cruise to head downtown or when Dweena got out.

The next thing I knew, I was home, dragging the mattress out of the closet, getting ready for bed, and relating the events of the day to Jackhammer. I assured him it had all been worth it. When I got to the part about my anonymous call to 911 I stopped short.

What had I done? Anonymous 911 call? Yeah, right. Anonymous. Using my own voice. As if they didn't record every single call that came in.

If it hadn't been so late and if I hadn't been so tired or if I'd checked in with my brain before plunging in headfirst, I never would have made that call. I would have altered my voice or had someone else do it or written a letter or—

It was far too late. I finished making the bed, fell in, and was out.

21

My anxiety about the 911 call festered overnight. The next morning I awakened brimming over with dread.

I'd made that call in under one minute. I would suffer the consequences for much longer.

I remembered my exact words to the 911 operator. First, real casual like, "You know, that body found in the West Village? It's not who you think."

That was me playing dumb. At the time I thought that was a clever way to conceal my true identity. The cops, at least Turner, already knew the body wasn't who they'd originally thought, but I was one of the few outsiders who knew, and by pretending not to know, I figured they'd never figure out I was the snitch.

Then, I went on to leave the address of the building where "I'm pretty sure the dead lady lived."

All of this in my own voice. Which Turner and McKinley would recognize the instant they heard it.

And I thought I had trouble before. Once they knew it was me on the phone, they'd want to know how I knew, and I'd have to divulge everything. Just thinking of the potential trouble made me break out in a cold sweat.

Unless . . .

A small glimmer of hope surfaced. I didn't know the procedure. I supposed my 911 call, no more than a few inches of tape or a few blips in a computer, had been preserved along with hundreds of other calls at some central location. If that were so, maybe Turner and Mc-Kinley wouldn't actually hear my voice. Maybe they'd just receive the information, check it out, make some calls, go to that apartment building, get the facts, and then go on to solve the crime.

Or maybe they'd get a cassette, hear my voice, and . . .

To the beat of the ticking 911 tape time bomb, I headed over to Midnight Millinery with Jackhammer. I'd resolved the spend the entire day painting. Nothing was going to stop me.

In desperate need of distraction, I turned on the radio and got right to work. I didn't even waste time waiting for Dweena not to show up.

I poured a glob of paint into a roller pan. The cheap pan buckled when I moved it, slopped paint on the drop cloth, which I stepped in and tracked all over.

Not a good beginning. But once I loaded up the roller, pushed it up the wall, and sucked in the paint fumes, I got into it and became lost in thought.

Swoosh. I covered up a smudge of time, a blotch left over from that tense afternoon when I heaved a hat block at an intruder, a hit man actually, but that's a long story. The block connected with my intended target—the guy's head—then bounced off and grazed the wall.

Smudge gone, memory intact. If only I could so easily paint over my 911 call.

I found traces of previous tenants. I knocked a jagged chip of paint off the baseboard and studied the many layers. I thought about the individual who'd painted the gray-green layer over the red-brown. I tried to feel his sense of hope and renewal. Who had stared at the dark gold wall? Had they hung a painting on it? Was the soft peach from a long-forgotten candlelit cafe where a couple got engaged? Did they go through with the wedding? Had they stayed married? Did they ever walk by Midnight Millinery, look into the window, past all the hats displayed, and remember what the place had been way back whenever?

I grew up in Belup's Creek, a small town trying hard to pass itself off as a suburb of a mid-size Midwestern city where everything was too new, too contrived, too much fast food and fake wood paneling. In Belup's Creek I couldn't chip away at the layers, so I moved to New York, where old soulful buildings tell wonderful stories. And that, I reminded myself, was what Dweena's S.O.B. was all about.

Well, I thought, if buildings could tell stories, why not a fib or two? And why not Angie's?

Now that was an idea worth thinking about. I stopped rolling and flopped down cross-legged on the drop cloth. Just maybe, I'd come up with the answer to Tommy's problems. Like most truly great ideas, once I had it, it seemed so obvious, I wondered why I hadn't thought of it earlier.

All I had to do was get Dweena to declare that the Angie's building was a former brothel. When the developer got wind that S.O.B. was on the case, fearing protracted court battles, he'd probably do the sensible thing, withdraw his offer, and go in search of another building to knock down. Tommy's ex-wife Nancy would be plenty pissed, but Angie's little corner of the Village would be preserved.

I needed to check with Dweena before running over to Angie's to spread the good news. There might be some complication in this brothel declaration business, and I didn't want to get Tommy excited over nothing. I glanced at the clock—later than I thought, but still too early to disturb Dweena.

The chatter on the all-news radio station got on my nerves. I already knew it was a mild sunny day and traffic was snarled. A breaking story that police had identified the body would have relieved my anxiety about the 911 call. If Turner and McKinley had managed to ID the body without storming in to grill me, it might mean they truly didn't know I'd made the call, or they knew and didn't care, and I was off the hook. No news meant I was still very much on the hook.

"Yoo hoo, anybody here? Earth to Brenda Midnight, wake up."

I stepped down from the ladder and put the roller in the pan. "Elizabeth. Hi."

"What's wrong with you?" she asked. "I've been standing here for five minutes. You were somewhere way far away."

"I've been thinking," I said. "Past, present, layers of paint, all that kinda heavy stuff. Angie's. Life and death. Ria."

"Deep," said Elizabeth. "These days I stick to shallow waters. It's more fun to splash around with my feet touching bottom. Know what I mean?"

I shook my head no.

"Well, when you get to be my age, you'll understand."

"I suppose," I said, although I really didn't believe it.

"So," she said, "I see you changed your mind and went with blue paint."

"I was all set to buy pink, but One-Coat made a comment that turned me off."

"That man has a way with words. Did he ask you out?"

"Naturally. He also offered to help me paint."

"You should take him up on that."

"I ought to. Dweena punked out."

"Surprised?"

"No."

"What about Johnny? Ask him to help. You two seem to be getting along well."

"I want to keep it that way, so I didn't even ask. Besides, I think he went back to Boston to finish up that shoot. I haven't seen or heard from him since we went to Angie's."

"That shoot is taking an awfully long time, isn't it? I mean, it's only one hour of TV."

"It's probably more complicated than usual because of the two series involved, two sets of egos." I stood back and regarded my work. "What do you think about the blue?"

"Kind of streaky, now that you ask," said Elizabeth. "And you're leaving roller fuzz and bristles behind. No wonder. Look at the crummy tools you're using. Did you find it in the garbage or what?"

"I bought it all at One-Coat's when I got the paint."

"Shame on One-Coat. He shouldn't sell inferior supplies."

"It's not his fault. He warned me. I'll just have to work a little harder to make it nice. Right now, I have a lot more energy than money."

It would probably look better once it dried.

I painted until I was too weak to paint anymore without refueling. It was late for lunch, and early for dinner—in other words, a great time to talk to Tommy.

First, I called Dweena at Dover's office.

"Oh no," said Dweena. "You're calling to see if I can help you paint and I just this minute set up a meeting with a very important—"

"Forget about painting. I need S.O.B. to declare Angie's a former brothel. Can you do that?"

"Sure. I'll need some kind of proof, but that's easy enough to find. If not, I'll make it up. But why?"

"It's complicated. I'll explain later. Is Ria around?"

"Yep."

"How is she?"

"I really can't say."

"She's within earshot?"

"You got it."

"Is she nervous?"

"Oh yeah. I'm beginning to think you might be right about that."

"Keep a close watch on her, okay?"

"Wouldn't dream of doing otherwise."

I pulled up a stool and sat. Jackhammer climbed out of his bag and rested his chin on the bar.

Raphael came out of the back. "Jackhammer, good to see you. How's it going?"

Jackhammer wagged his tail stub.

"Good to see you, too, Brenda. You want the regular?"

"Make it a double grilled cheese, hold the wine, and one burger ball for Jackhammer."

"Hard at work making hats?"

"You better believe I'm hard at work, but not hats. I'm painting Midnight Millinery. The walls were in terrible condition."

"That's an awful job. You have my sympathy." Raphael gazed around at Angie's and sighed. "The walls here are probably worse than yours. They've got a thick layer of smoke and grease and dust and sticky beer. We were all set to have the whole place painted, but then . . ." Raphael trailed off. He must not have known that I knew about Angie's closing.

"Tommy around?" I asked.

"Upstairs."

"Is it all right if I go up? I need to talk to him."

"Sure. The door's open. I'll bring your food when it's ready."

Tommy's desk was covered with paperwork. He looked up and gave me a big smile. "Greetings, Brenda. Thanks again for convincing me to see your detective friend. It wasn't so bad and I feel a lot better."

"You're welcome."

"What brings you here today?"

"I had a brainstorm about Angie's. I think I know a way to save the building."

"You've got my attention," said Tommy.

Jackhammer squirmed in my arms. I let him down. He put his nose to the ground and raced off.

"Did it ever occur to you that maybe Angie's was a brothel?" I asked.

In a nanosecond, Tommy's smile was gone. His face contorted in anger. "What are you insinuating, Brenda? You know goddamned well I run a clean joint. That is, except for allowing your little dog on the premises."

"No, no," I said. "Calm down. I don't mean now. I mean a long time ago, before you were even born."

"What the hell has that got to do with now?"

"I was thinking if it had been a brothel, the building might fall under purview of Dweena's S.O.B."

"What's S.O.B.?"

I explained the S.O.B. mission and what I had in mind.

When I finished, Tommy's smile again flashed full force. "Brilliant, absolutely brilliant."

I asked him again if he thought maybe Angie's had been a brothel.

He pulled on his sideburns thoughtfully, and mused, "Well, you know, come to think of it, now that you mention it, maybe I did hear something along those lines. Yeah, I'm pretty sure I did. You're right, Brenda. Before it was a speakeasy, Angie's was a brothel, with a tough madam you wouldn't believe."

"I'm so glad," I said.

"Go for it, Brenda."

Raphael bustled in with food. I tried to pay, but Tommy wouldn't hear of it. My hand went for my purse, his hand clamped down on mine. "No."

Raphael excused himself. He couldn't leave the downstairs unattended for very long.

Tommy called after him, "Raphael, my man, Brenda has an idea that might save our asses."

Raphael gave a little hurrah, then was gone. His footsteps rat-a-tatted down the stairs.

Jackhammer trotted over, planted himself directly in front of me, and stared until I gave him his burger ball, which he swallowed in one gulp.

"Tell me," said Tommy, "how does one go about getting certified as a former brothel?"

"Dweena does the research. She'll find out when the building was built, the former owners, former businesses. She looks at old newspapers for stories of raids, then she does an on-site inspection, pokes into the nooks and crannies."

"What's she look for?"

"I'm really not sure. Don't worry, she's very good at exaggerating."

"I can imagine. She seems the creative sort. Let me know when she's coming. I'll make sure the cobwebs are swept up."

22

On the way home from Angie's, I stopped off at Midnight Millinery to see if the walls had improved any in my absence. I hoped they'd look better once they'd dried.

They did not.

The walls were still badly streaked.

I pried out several brush hairs from the fresh paint. There wasn't a whole lot I could do about the roller lint. Splatters of blue paint dotted all exposed surfaces, and most surfaces were exposed because the drop cloth shifted in the slightest breeze. I should have saved money and skipped the drop cloth altogether for the good it did.

It was sadly evident that one coat wouldn't to do the job. I couldn't blame One-Coat's paint, or even the bargain basement equipment I'd insisted on buying. I took full responsibility. I'm a lousy painter.

I hated to admit defeat, but Elizabeth was right. I needed help.

But who? Elizabeth had skillfully weaseled out of volunteering for the job. I absolutely could count on Dweena not to come through. Chuck was too hyper to be trusted with a roller in his hand. No way would I ever give in and ask One-Coat.

And Johnny—the most obvious choice—must have gone back to Boston. He hadn't returned any of my calls.

I really wanted to talk to him, now more than ever. He might know how 911 calls were handled. I wondered how much longer they'd be shooting. Like Elizabeth had said, it was only TV, an hour-long show.

Johnny's agent, Lemmy Crenshaw, would know. I decided to give him a call.

Lemmy might come off as a short, bald, feisty hothead, with an attitude toward women far worse than One-Coat's. Lemmy was so unenlightened it was almost inspired. I mean, the man collected brassieres—old, new, big, little, plain, fancy, flat, pointy, whatever. He mounted them all on his living room wall. Yet, deep down, Lemmy was really okay. A genuine good egg.

I picked up the phone and punched in Lemmy's number.

"Brenda," said Lemmy. "Long time. How's my favorite little milliner?"

"Not bad. Yourself?"

"Hanging in there."

"I was wondering, do you know when Johnny'll be back? I need to talk to him, but I don't want to bug him in Boston, so I thought if he'd be back reasonably soon—"

"Boston? Whaddya mean Boston?"

"The shoot, Johnny's guest appearance on the Boston-based cop show."

"Didn't Johnny tell you? He got pulled off of that."

"Pulled off? You mean like fired?"

"That's a harsh word, but it does fairly well describe the situation. Canned. They axed his ass."

"Why would anybody fire Johnny?"

"Believe me, it's not Johnny personally, but when word got out that *Tod Trueman* was canceled—"

"What!"

"Johnny didn't tell you that either?"

"No."

"I guess he didn't want to disappoint you. He likes how you're so proud of him. Anyway, without a *TTUD*

show, there's no viable tie-in to the Boston show, so
they gave Johnny the boot."

"Back up, Lemmy. How could *Tod Trueman* get canceled? The ratings are—"

"—down the freaking toilet, according to the latest
numbers. You can't say I didn't warn him. Johnny Verlane made a big mistake when he turned down that
movie offer I got for him."

"Come on, Lemmy. That was a stupid movie. Imagine, Tod Trueman, Urban Detective, suddenly trans-
formed into an Iowa sheriff and pig farmer. When
Johnny turned down that project they had to go with a
different high concept."

"That movie did swell," said Lemmy. "Of course, it
would have done even more swell if it had been a *Tod
Trueman* vehicle. But no, my stubborn former client had
to stick to his guns. Integrity, he said. He didn't want to
compromise the Tod character. What a joke."

"Did I hear you right? *Former* client?"

"Oops, Brenda, I've got another call coming in. Hang
on a sec."

Poor Johnny . . . before I could finish the thought
Lemmy clicked back on the line.

"Sorry, Brenda, I've gotta take this. It's Blanner—
Blanner Doosen, my cooperative client. He's the guy
who took the sheriff role."

"The Iowa pig farm gig."

"Right. You'll be hearing a lot more of Blanner in the
future."

I felt bad for Johnny. He'd worked so hard.

I was also hurt and angry. What the hell did he think
he was doing, keeping me in the dark about the demise
of *Tod Trueman, Urban Detective*? Granted, our romance had extreme ups and downs, and our current
status was confused, but except for a couple of times
when we weren't on speaking terms, we'd always been
good friends.

Johnny needed a friend now.

I hung on to that thought, swallowed my pride, and called him. I didn't expect him to pick up and he didn't. No more vague messages that he wouldn't respond to. I kept it short. "Call me. It's urgent."

I surveyed my streaked blue walls one last time, then locked up Midnight Millinery for the night.

Jackhammer and I walked west, all the way to the edge of Manhattan. He lifted his leg on all protuberances. I stared out across the Hudson River at the state of New Jersey and reflected on the unfathomable fact that I lived on a small island, and that my apartment was only a few blocks inland, and that *Tod Trueman* had been canceled.

I didn't know what to do with myself.

The TV was still out from the other night. And so, like millions of people I didn't want to be like, I sat down in front of the tube. I even turned it on. And got lost in prime time.

Yep, I was depressed all right.

During a break, the station ran a promo for the local evening news. It promised a late-breaking story about the body of the woman found in the Village. "Police, admitting earlier error, now have positive identification."

What a relief. My 911 call had worked and it looked like I got away unscathed.

I doused the situation comedy and turned on the radio. In a few minutes the news announcer devoted ten breathless seconds to the story. "No one knows why Minetta Carlton, a secretary living on the Upper East Side, was murdered. Detectives are working on a several leads. A police spokesperson attributed the earlier mistake in identification to a clerical error."

I thought that was very generous of Turner.

I checked the list of names I'd written down from the mailboxes in the building Ria had gone into. There it was: Minetta Carlton, third floor. I was right. Ria Kleep knew the victim.

Sometimes, some things do work out.

I'd done my duty, Turner and McKinley knew the victim's real identity, and I could sign off on the entire mess. If that seems coldhearted, it's not like I didn't feel terrible that this woman, Minetta Carlton, had been shot. Considering she was a total stranger, I thought I'd done enough already. If not for me, police wouldn't have a clue as to her true identity.

I was proud of myself. I'd fixed the havoc wreaked by Dweena and Tommy, P. G. Dover would be turned loose, I was in the clear, Turner and McKinley would find the killer, and I could get back to making hats.

Yes, at long last I was ready—actually itching to get back to millinery. Somehow in the middle of worrying about who had lied to whom, when everything I did to make things right only seemed to make them more wrong, my self-indulgent artistic crisis had showed definite signs of expiring.

Bubbling up from the back of my brain, making brief flit-throughs on my screen of consciousness, was an idea for a new line of hats. Escaping back into my own reality looked pretty damned good.

Except for that part about Johnny.

As Lemmy had said, I was proud of Johnny's success. I was even prouder that his success hadn't changed him. At the same time, I knew his success had changed me. I tried, but never got comfortable with the idea that 99 percent of adult females in the whole country had the hots for him. Maybe now that would be different. Maybe now we had a future.

My mind filled with visions of Johnny, of Johnny and me, me and Johnny, thoughts racing so far ahead of reality, I just barely caught the name Minetta Carlton again.

The news announcer was back with an update. In the Minetta Carlton case, police were now looking for Ria Kleep, coworker of the victim, previously thought to be the victim. They wanted to question her in connection with the murder.

23

"Gone," said Dweena.

"Damn." I banged the receiver on the table a few times, then put it to my mouth again. "Where the hell did she go?"

"For chrissakes, Brenda. Cool it. How would I know? I'm not Ria's keeper. She just up and split. That's all."

"You were supposed to keep an eye on her."

"I only went out for a couple of minutes to pick up some Chinese takeout, late dinner for both of us, or so I thought. When I got back, no more Ria. I figured there's no way I can eat all this broccoli in garlic sauce so I offered some to that receptionist, you know, the guy with the camouflage and the long green fingernails, and he told me that not long after I left, Ria ran out of here like a bat out of hell. And get this—she was wearing one of my wigs."

"I'll bet you two had the radio on in the office."

"As a matter of fact, we did. How'd you know that?"

"Good guesser."

"I can't stand that racket while I work, but Ria insisted. I decided to be nice since she'd been such a big help with S.O.B. When I got back with the food the radio was cranked up so loud I could hear it halfway down the hall. So, Brenda, are you gonna tell me what's going on?"

"It's quite simple, really. We're in big trouble."

*   *   *

"You hungry?" asked Dweena. "I've still got some of that broccoli if you want."

"No thanks. I'm too upset to eat."

"You're overreacting, Brenda. I don't get what the big deal is."

"As I suspected, Ria Kleep knew the victim, Minetta Carlton. According to the news story, they worked together."

"At the import-export firm?"

"Right, Minetta Carlton lived in that building we followed Ria to. And now the cops want to question Ria in connection with the murder. She must have heard it on the radio. That's why she took off."

"So what? The cops want to question Ria Kleep and she disappeared? Not my problem, although I do want my wig back."

"It *is* your problem. Mine too. Don't you get it? We've been harboring a criminal, a murderer maybe."

"Not me," said Dweena.

"Yes, you. If not harboring, then aiding and abetting or something. Whatever it is we did, we shouldn't have."

"I thought you were more creative than that, Brenda. Here's what I'll say if anyone asks: A concerned Village resident whom I barely knew showed up out of the blue, at offices that do not belong to me, and volunteered to do some typing for the S.O.B. organization, a worthy cause. Volunteer help is notoriously hard to come by and undependable. You say she was hiding out here? News to me."

"Do you really think the cops will believe that?"

"Sure. Why not? Anyway, who said Ria was a criminal? Or even a suspect? The cops question lots of people."

"I say so. Ria Kleep killed Minetta Carlton."

That was an overstatement. It was only one of many ideas that had been thrashing around in my head. Because of the connection to Dweena and me, it was the one that required immediate attention.

Dweena laughed. "Give me a break. Ria Kleep? A killer? How'd you come up with that?"

"When I showed Ria that picture of Minetta Carlton, she claimed she didn't know her. We now know for sure that wasn't the truth."

"So? Ria's a liar. If everybody who told a lie also killed somebody there'd be nobody around to tell lies to. Besides, if Ria killed this Carlton woman, why would she go to Carlton's building immediately after you showed her that picture? At the time you said she'd gone there to confirm that Carlton was dead. If Ria was the killer, she'd already know Carlton was dead."

I had to admit, Dweena had a good point, one I readily latched on to.

Dweena continued, "Not only did we not harbor a criminal, you provided the police with important information about the crime. Commendable, Brenda. I applaud you. It had to be your tip that led the cops to identify Minetta Carlton. Once again, you've come through for Turner and McKinley. They owe you. You ought to tell them it was you who made that nine-one-one call. Maybe you'll get a good citizen plaque. Or a free round of doughnuts."

"I'd just as soon not tell them. Don't you either. Okay?"

"Don't worry. I plan to stay far away from those two public servants."

"Good."

"Now that we've got that straightened out," said Dweena, "tell me what Tommy said."

"He's thrilled. So am I. If you save Angie's, you'll be a heroine in the West Village."

"Fabulous. I've always aspired to be a heroine. Decades from now a buncha drunks will be sitting around singing songs about me. I like that vision. How much time does Tommy have left?"

"Not much."

"Then I guess I better get on the stick."

"And I better get home. I'm exhausted from painting."

"How's that going?"

"Fine."

The phone rang, yanking me out of a good dream. I would have let the machine pick up, but I thought it was Johnny finally returning my call, so I answered live and in person and almost fully awake.

"On the other hand," said Dweena, "you could be right."

Not Johnny.

"Right about what?" I asked.

"I'm sitting here, stuffing envelopes, and I start to think. When Ria went to that building, perhaps it wasn't to see if Minetta Carlton was dead. Just because you thought so at the time doesn't make it so. We don't know why she went. Maybe when you showed her that picture of Minetta Carlton she realized that the body would be identified soon and went to the apartment to remove some kind of evidence."

"But she didn't get in."

"My point exactly. That means the evidence was still there when the cops arrived, which could be why Ria split as soon as she heard the cops wanted to talk to her."

I hated this. I'd grown very comfortable with the idea that Ria was innocent. Now Dweena was flipping it all around. "But why would Ria kill Minetta Carlton?"

"Easy. They worked together. You know how tempers flare in the workplace. Office politics are hell. There's plenty of people I'd love to have whacked when I was at that brokerage firm."

It was true. In Dweena's previous life, when she was Edward the Wall Street broker, one of her coworkers screwed her over royally, causing her career to crash and burn.

"The thing is," I told Dweena, "much as your co-worker deserved it, you didn't whack him or anybody else."

"Well, I should have."

"Nor did Ria kill Minetta, unless you're trying to convince me she had a better motive than you did."

Dweena snorted. "I sincerely doubt that."

"Probably no one in the history of murder ever had a better motive for murder than you."

"Thank you," said Dweena.

"Yet you didn't do it. Motives for murder are a dime a dozen. When push comes to shove, most people won't do the deed."

"Ria could be a shover," said Dweena.

I sincerely thought not. "I'm hanging up," I said.

"You know what really bothers me?" said Dweena. "Now that the body is properly identified, the police investigation will move away from Dover, and he'll get out of the clink."

It seemed like eons ago, but that had been my original intention. I was glad Dweena couldn't see my big grin through the phone.

"Which means," Dweena continued, "sooner or later, and probably sooner, that asshole fake diplomat is gonna show up here."

Back to sleep, but not for long.

The phone rang. Probably not Johnny, I thought. Most likely Dweena, who knew I was home and would keep calling until I picked up.

I fumbled for the phone. "What do you want?"

"Now, Brenda," said Brewster Winfield in his deep-as-the-ocean mellow voice, "you've got to stop your friend Dweena from calling me. Her behavior approaches harassment. Both you and she know perfectly well that I can't speak to her about the money she constantly refers to as hers, due to the fact that said money . . . well, to simplify the legalese, I'll just say that merely talking to her could be construed as a conflict of interest on my part."

I knew it would be a waste of breath to remind Winfield that Dweena had been his client before P. G. Dover.

Instead I inquired about Dover. "How soon will your client be turned loose?"

"Privileged information," said Winfield. "However, since you were so cooperative about a certain matter of a certain file, I suppose there's no harm in telling you that Mr. Dover might not get sprung so soon. Naturally, I'm trying every trick in the book, but the law, as you know, is very twisty. Once police found the corpus, my job became considerably more difficult."

"But," I said, "now that the cops know that the said corpus is not Ria Kleep, I just assumed they'd let him go."

"What do you mean 'not Ria Kleep'?"

"You don't know? It was all over the radio and TV."

"I don't have time for such media foolishness. After a hard and long day's work, Myrtle and I have been rehearsing her role. What happened? Why did the police change their minds?"

I could see no reason to divulge to a turncoat lawyer my role in the proper identification, or that Dweena and I had both seen Ria alive. "Apparently there was some kind of screw-up in the identification process. The body is not Ria Kleep. It's a woman named Minetta Carlton. Even if you didn't hear about it through the media, I'm surprised the cops didn't inform you."

"You kidding? They don't do that. You must live in a fantasy world."

"Oh. I thought they had to."

"They don't. So, thank you, Brenda, for telling me. This bit of good news may indeed shorten my client's incarceration ordeal."

"Only shorten? Won't he be set free immediately?"

"You will recall those trumped-up charges the authorities used to detain Mr. Dover. Tragically, some of those charges are sticking. My client is a rather shady character. Nothing as serious as murder, mind you, but getting him released has proved to be more of a challenge than I originally thought. It could take awhile."

And many more billable hours.

Poor Dweena. I'd never let her hear me say it, but in a way, I agreed with her. It sort of was her money.

I called Dweena.

"Brewster Winfield says you're harassing him."

"Winfield's full of shit. I called him and made a polite inquiry as to when he thought his client, Mr. P. G. Dover, might be back out on the street. He's the one who yelled at me. If anybody did any harassing, it was him. I ought to report him to the bar association."

"I doubt it would do much good."

"Did he tell you when Dover's getting out?"

"The good news for you is not so soon. They've run into some difficulties, prior misdeeds."

"In other words, Winfield's milking the case."

"Probably."

"That's not good news. Dover's using my money to pay Winfield. My fifty thousand is literally going straight down the tube. Specifically, that ugly orange and black tube known as Myrtle."

24

The early morning light did not improve my newly painted blue wall. If anything, it looked streakier today than yesterday. I don't know what I expected. Did I think the paint would somehow adjust itself overnight to stretch smoothly over the plane?

According to the newspapers and radio, the murder of Minetta Carlton hadn't somehow solved itself overnight either. No deranged killer, someone preferably not connected with Ria Kleep or P. G. Dover or Dweena or me, had marched into the precinct and confessed.

Too bad.

It's a cop-out to blame tools for bad craftsmanship. I've always been proud of my ability to make do with whatever is on hand, but after a thorough analysis of the situation, I reluctantly concluded that One-Coat and Elizabeth were right. I needed better equipment.

Perhaps a more highly skilled painter could work with cheap stuff, but I needed rollers that didn't disintegrate, paint pans that didn't buckle, and a drop cloth that didn't rearrange itself every time a cockroach sauntered by.

Admitting this to One-Coat would be a humbling experience. The sooner I got it over, the better. I snapped on Jackhammer's leash. We took the shortest route to the paint store.

* * *

The early morning rush of contractors had come, bought their last-minute supplies, and gone. One-Coat was alone in the store. Spread out on the counter in front of him was the newspaper. Off to the side, a round container with a half-eaten takeout breakfast of waffles and sausage.

"Well hello, Brenda. Did you see this?" He jabbed his finger at the paper. "Possibly some very good news about Ria Kleep. That body they found over in the meat market wasn't her after all. It was a lady she worked with."

"I heard."

"Cops sure messed that one up. I guess we still don't know what happened to Ria. But we can always hope she's okay, can't we?"

"No news is good news, I guess."

He folded up the newspaper and slipped it under the counter. "Now, what can I do for you on such a glorious day? How's that paint job going? Would your little doggie care for a bit of sausage?"

I answered his last question, the easy one, first. "No on the sausage. Jackhammer would love some, but it's too spicy. It'll make him puke, but thanks anyway." I paused a couple of beats before continuing. "As to the paint job, not so hot. You were right. And that's why I'm here. I need better tools."

Joe's lips turned into a knowing smirk. "Can't say I didn't warn you."

"No, I sure can't." I readied myself for the lecture I knew was certain to follow.

"You could have saved yourself a whole lot of trouble if you'd listened to me from the get-go," he said, shaking his head. "I notice with women especially, you all insist on learning the hard way. Do you know what's going to happen now? You're gonna need more paint than you bought originally. You know I can guarantee a perfect match only if I mix all the paint at the same time. I'm sure you realize the consequences."

I shrugged. "Guess I'll have to live with it." He made me feel like I was back in third grade.

"And don't think you can get away with watering down the paint you already have."

"No, never. I know better than to do that."

One-Coat stood up and came around the counter. Then, with Jackhammer trailing behind, he strode up and down the center aisle. While continuing the lecture, he gathered up high-priced premium brand supplies and put them in a red plastic shopping basket.

Since it was One-Coat who had first told me that Angie's was closing, I considered telling him that Dweena and S.O.B. were on the case. Afraid I'd somehow jinx it if I spoke before it was a done deal, I kept my mouth shut.

In a gesture of generosity that surprised the hell out of me, One-Coat gave me a 10 percent professional discount. "We're all in this together," he said, with a wink. "And Brenda, my offer to help you still stands. I'd be more than happy to come over and teach you a thing or two about paint."

"Thanks, Joe, that's very kind, but I'm not ready to admit defeat yet. Let me give it another try with these tools."

The new equipment was a pleasure to use. The right tool can make all the difference. The canvas drop cloth draped with authority, the paint pan had a nice solid feel, the roller fuzz stayed on the roller, and brushes held on to all their bristles.

I'd been working an hour or so when the phone rang. Taking a lesson from last night's experience, I let the machine answer the call while I listened in.

It was Dweena. "Get over to S.O.B. ASAP," she screeched. The line went dead.

What now? She'd sounded desperate. Then again, she's easily excitable and tends to overdramatize.

I called back to see what was wrong, but the phone

rang and rang. Neither of P. G. Dover's answering machines picked up.

Remembering what happened the last time Dweena called for help, I snapped into immediate action. I recapped the paint cans, threw the brushes and rollers into the sink, took Jackhammer back to the apartment, patted him on the head, and ran out the door.

A cab had just dropped off a neighbor outside the building. I jumped in, buckled up, and told the driver to step on it.

The Suite Sixteen day receptionist, Deb, was on duty. She was a wreck. She paced the reception area and gnawed at her recently manicured fingernails.

"Thank god you're here," she said.

From the office area in back came a crash. It sounded like a chair smashing against a wall. Next came loud angry voices. One voice I recognized as Dweena's, cursing like crazy. The other, also spewing invectives, I wasn't so sure about. However, given the location, and who he was fighting with, I had a pretty good idea the fake Gintoflakokian ambassador, good buddy P. G. Dover, PI, was out of the clink, somewhat earlier than lawyer Winfield had predicted.

"If they don't stop it with the yelling and throwing stuff," said Deb, "I swear I'm going to call in the cops. I don't care if it is against the rules."

"Against the rules?"

"Absolutely. Here at Suite Sixteen we do not to interfere with the business affairs of our tenants. Confidentiality, you know. Ms. Gates is the only one who's got the authority to call in the police. She's out of the office today with one of her migraines, so I guess that leaves me in charge, but nobody ever actually told me that was part of my job, and I could get in big trouble. It's a crummy job, but until my acting career takes off, I've got to pay the rent somehow. I don't know what to do."

An actress. I should have known. Another crash, harder and sharper than the last. "Do you know what's going on?"

"Only that your friend came in this morning. She had on this cool purple plaid outfit, a little short for business purposes if you want my opinion, but very chic. Not long after, Ambassador Dover came in. He didn't look so good though. Kinda rumpled, like he'd slept in his clothes. I didn't know what to do without Gates here, so I let him go back. Now I'm thinking maybe I shouldn't have."

"What else could you do? Stand between him and the door?"

"Good point," she said. "Remind me to mention that to Gates when she terminates my butt. Anyway, a minute or so after the ambassador went into the back, the shit hit the fan."

I rattled the doorknob. Dover's office was locked from the inside. From what I could hear, the shit was still hitting the fan, and pretty hard.

I banged on the door. "Dweena, I know you're inside. Open up. It's Brenda."

I heard the deadbolt slide, metal against metal, then a clink and the door swung open. Dweena grabbed my elbow, yanked me inside, and slammed the door shut again.

Standing on top of his desk, red-faced, arms flailing, kicking papers around, was P. G. Dover, PI. His ridiculous caterpillarlike mustache was still perched on his upper lip even after his stay in jail. I had to assume it was real.

"I don't believe you two have been formally introduced," Dweena said sarcastically. "Ambassador, this is my friend Brenda Midnight. You may remember her from the chaotic payoff. Brenda, this is the son of a bitch rat bastard who kidnapped me and ran off with my fifty thou."

Dover regarded me. "I remember you. You're the one who brought that cop." He had dropped all pretense of a foreign accent. The man was straight out of Brooklyn.

"He wasn't a cop," I said.

"Looked like one to me. I don't get it. First you screw up the payoff, then you get me that mouthpiece, Brewster Winfield, which may or may not turn out to be a good thing."

I had to chuckle. People often felt that way about Winfield. I hadn't actually gotten Winfield for Dover, but it was too hard to explain. It didn't matter. He and Dweena were railing at each other again. Neither paid any attention to me. I hoped Deb wouldn't make good on her threat to call in the cops.

The fight was over territory and money. Dover wanted his office back and Dweena didn't want to give it back. He claimed legal rights; his name was on the lease. She claimed moral rights; her money had paid his rent.

During a lull when they both wound down to catch their breath, I spoke up. "Why don't you call Brewster Winfield? Maybe he can help you two come to terms, or negotiate some kind of a settlement."

"I already called him," said Dover. "He said I should handle this on my own. He doesn't want to have anything to do with her." He jutted his chin in the general direction of Dweena.

"I called him too," said Dweena, "He reminded me again that he's not my lawyer. Then he said he's busy. He refuses to leave Myrtle alone at rehearsal."

"Who's Myrtle?" asked Dover.

"Winfield's snake," said Dweena. "A temperamental Broadway actress."

"Some lawyer," said Dover. He gave me a dirty look like it was all my fault.

That was the last straw. I'd had all I could take from Brewster Winfield. I reached him on his cellular.

"Where the hell are you?" I demanded.

"Why, Brenda Midnight, how nice to hear from you, and so soon. Didn't we just speak last night, mere hours ago?"

"Yes, we did. Tell me where you are."

"I'm with Myrtle at a rehearsal studio. Is that anger I detect in your voice?"

"Damn right. I'm calling about P. G. Dover and Dweena."

"Then you must know I got Mr. Dover freed much sooner than I'd anticipated. You should be pleased."

"Okay, I'm pleased about that. But I am not pleased about the fact that you're not where you should be. You're a professional. You have two clients in trouble, Mr. Dover and Dweena. They've each asked for your help, only to be brushed off."

"I did not brush anyone off. Mr. Dover is quite capable of handling this matter himself. As for Dweena, as I told you last night, I have but one client. To represent both parties in this matter would be a conflict of interest."

"Look, Brew, either you get your ass over here, or I'll come and get you."

"Idle threats don't scare me in the least."

"This is not an idle threat."

"Sure it is. You don't know where I am."

"You're at a rehearsal studio."

"Do you have any idea how many rehearsal studios there are in this town? You know what they say about a broken heart for every light on Broadway. Well, there's a rehearsal studio for every two lights."

"I'll find you. I'm one second away from asking Chuck Riley to track you down. Don't think he can't." I came up with what I thought was a plausible-sounding spiel. "You see, Brew, your cell phone constantly produces ultrasonic beeps in a pattern as unique as fingerprints. Through these ultrabeeps Chuck can home in on your exact position. And to get back at you for what you've done, I'll tell him to jam your phone. You'll be an incommunicado sitting duck."

"Pardon my French, Brenda, but you're full of shit. Even the extremely talented Chuck Riley couldn't do that, especially if I hang up right this instant."

"Chuck will be more than happy to prove what he can do."

Winfield was silent for a few seconds, weighing the risks. He'd seen Chuck in action. For all I knew, maybe Chuck really could track him down.

"All right, Brenda, you win," said Winfield. "But I can't leave Myrtle all alone."

I had a good idea what was coming next. "Don't ask. The answer is no."

"Please, Brenda, work with me on this. If Myrtle leaves the rehearsal, she'll get an undeserved reputation as a prima donna. You know what a sweetheart she is. Such action would irrevocably damage her career. You wouldn't want to be liable for that."

Liable? I didn't like it when lawyers talked about liability.

He gave me the address.

And that is why, instead of finishing up the Midnight Millinery paint job, I found myself at a dingy Upper West Side rehearsal studio, baby-sitting for an ingenue snake, hoping Winfield would wrap things up with Dweena and P. G. Dover before it was time for Myrtle to come out of her custom-made leather carrying case.

I'm not a theater fan. Especially musical theater. I don't want to hear them run through it one time perfectly with all the lights and costumes and stage magic. I sure as hell didn't want to hear them run through it time after time after time imperfectly.

Still, I had to admit, one of the tunes had a nice melody.

Lucky for me, Winfield came back before it was time for Myrtle to get out of her case and do whatever it was she did.

"How did it go with Dweena and Dover?" I asked.

"Peachy keen," said Winfield. He unlatched Myrtle's carrying case, opened the lid a crack, and made smoochy sounds. "How's my girl?"

"What happened?" I asked.

"I suggested that Dweena invest a portion of the money. My clients decided it is in their mutual best interest to cooperate."

"Clients? With an S?"

"Thanks to my superb negotiating ability, Dweena and Dover are getting along better now, so it's no longer a conflict of interest for me to represent both of them."

"Thanks, Brew."

"Think nothing of it, Babycakes."

25

"You're perfectly welcome to stick around and watch Myrtle do her stuff on the stage," said Winfield. "When my little lady shakes her booty, she positively oozes charisma."

I politely turned down Winfield's generous offer and left the rehearsal studio. On the way out I ran into a friend of Johnny's, a guy he'd known in acting class. "Is that you, Brenda Midnight, without a hat?"

"Good to see you again. How's it going?"

"Can't complain. I'm an extra."

"That's wonderful. Congratulations."

"It's a step in the right direction. Maybe some day I'll be as big as Johnny. What's he up to? *TTUD* must keep him real busy."

He must not have heard. "Oh you know . . ."

"Yeah, it must be tough to be a famous prime-time star. Well, I gotta go or I'll be late. You be sure and give Johnny my best."

For one second I considered stopping by Dover's office to check up on Dweena and P. G. Dover. As seconds do, that one passed very quickly, and when it was gone, so was that stupid idea. Vanished. I came to my senses, flagged down a cab, and headed back to the Village.

I had the cab drop me off at Balducci's so I could pick up a special treat for Jackhammer. On the way to the green bean display, I succumbed to the temptation of mounds of fresh baby lettuces and ended up buying a bagful of salad makings.

I rinsed the green beans, chopped off the ends, tossed those into the garbage, dropped the beans into the steamer, and turned on the flame.

Jackhammer's big round black eyes tracked every move. As a normal healthy small dog he has a normal healthy extremely short attention span. But whenever green beans are involved, he possesses the concentration of a Zen master. He stared unblinkingly at the pot for the entire seven minutes it steamed. After a quick cool-down I gave him a velvety green bean. Then two more, which was his limit.

I put together a huge salad and called Elizabeth.

"Had lunch yet?"

"Now that depends on what you call lunch. Does half a stale poppy-seed bagel qualify?"

"Come over and join me for a salad. I've got lots extra. And a terrific lawyer story."

Elizabeth swirled a piece of dark green arugula around the plate, loading it with dressing. "You know, Brenda, you're a not much of a cook, but you do whip up one mighty mean salad."

"Thank you," I said.

"You also tell a good story. That Brewster Winfield is too much. Interesting fellow, but you know, the next time I get in trouble, I sure wouldn't want him for a lawyer."

"What do you mean the next time you get in trouble? You haven't been arrested since the sixties."

"Yeah well, some things in this city have been pissing me off lately. I'm thinking of taking to the streets again."

"Be careful, the streets aren't what they used to be." Actually the streets were probably safer now than they ever had been. I was afraid to say what I really meant, that Elizabeth was a few decades older.

She acknowledged me with a frown and a "hmpf," then said, "I'm glad Winfield was able to work out a truce between Dweena and her fake diplomat."

"It's too soon to celebrate. P. G. Dover strikes me as a powder keg set to go off, and Dweena would never back down from a good fight. I plan to steer clear of that office for a while."

"I don't blame you. I wouldn't want to hang around there either. Poor Ria Kleep. Is she still staying there now that Dover's back?"

I wished I hadn't told Elizabeth about Ria. If she knew the total extent of my involvement, she might worry, and if she got worried enough, she might tell Johnny—that is, if she could find him—and he had enough problems with his career nose-dive without worrying about me.

However, since she brought it up, I had to say something. I went with the truth. "Ria took off the instant she found out the cops wanted to question her about Minetta Carlton."

"I'm glad you decided to mind your own business." It was hard to tell if she was being sarcastic.

"Me too."

"They were coworkers, you say?"

"Yes. At an import-export firm."

"Do you think Ria killed that woman? Office politics can be brutal."

I shrugged. "At first I thought so, then I didn't, and now I'm not so sure. All this wavering back and forth is driving me crazy."

"If she is the killer, the police are on the right track. Although personally, I don't think she did it, even if she is a boor." Elizabeth rolled the last remaining cherry tomato around her plate, stabbed it with her fork, and popped it into her mouth. "How's the paint job going? Does Midnight Millinery look good in blue?"

"The blue's okay, I guess, but the job is a disaster. I totally messed it up and had to invest in better equipment."

"What did I tell you?"

"You and One-Coat both. I thought I could get away with cheap junk. That mistake cost me time and money. One-Coat gave me a discount on the new stuff."

"That was certainly nice of him. I haven't been by One-Coat's in quite some time. What's he up to?"

"Same old, same old."

After Elizabeth left, Jackhammer and I went to Midnight Millinery.

Good news. The section I had repainted that morning looked as a wall should—smooth. My efforts were beginning to pay off. I got back to work with a more positive attitude.

Before I knew it, I'd rolled up an entire wall. I stood back to appraise my work and was hit by the realization that square inch for square inch, Midnight Millinery had officially become more blue than pink. That was an accomplishment. From now on it was all downhill. It wouldn't be long before I'd be making hats again.

The bells on the door jangled. Jackhammer gave a friendly woof. I turned around and saw Tommy standing in the doorway. "Okay if I come in?"

"Of course."

He lumbered in and leaned against the last remaining section of pink wall.

I put down the paint roller. "Is something wrong?"

"I see you're hard at work. I hate to barge in and disturb you like this. It's just that my ex-wife Nancy is getting mighty antsy. She wants to close on the building. My option expired. For what she calls old time's sake she's willing to delay the deal, but not for long. She gave me one lousy week to match the developer's offer. That's not gonna happen, so I was wondering how things are going with that brothel idea."

"You should check with Dweena about that. She's the expert. Tell her that your ex is putting on pressure. She'll come through for you."

"Oh. All right. What's Dweena's number at that private dick's office?"

"Hang on a sec and I'll get it for you."

Sidestepping around the mess, I made my way over to the work table. Somewhere underneath the mountains of junk I'd piled up, and the drop cloth that lay over it all, was the scrap of paper with the numbers for Dover's two telephones. Halfway across the room, I realized an easier way.

I told Tommy Dweena's home number which I knew by heart. "She's got call forwarding," I said. "Call her at home and it'll get bounced to Dover's . . ."

Hold the line—

My brain did a fast rewind. I went back over my recent conversations with Tommy trying to remember if I'd ever mentioned that Dweena had commandeered Dover's office. I concluded that I definitely had not.

Okay, it wasn't exactly a secret. Dweena, proud of her conquest of prime midtown real estate, had no doubt bragged about it to anybody who would listen. But she hadn't talked directly to Tommy, or if she had, she didn't tell me, which, I told myself, didn't necessarily mean she hadn't talked to him.

I supposed she might have called him in connection with S.O.B. No reason for me to always be the go-between. And if she had called him, it would be natural enough for her to tell him she was now working out of Dover's office. But if that were so, wouldn't she have given him the office numbers herself?

Maybe she forgot. Or maybe it hadn't even occurred to her to do so, and it hadn't occurred to Tommy to ask, which was why he was here now asking me.

Then again, maybe somebody else told him. Dweena could have told somebody who told somebody else who told somebody else. Angie's is a prime switching station in the lightning-fast West Village gossip communication network. So it was perfectly plausible to believe that Tommy might find out that Dweena had taken over Dover's office without either me or Dweena telling him.

There were probably a million other perfectly plausible scenarios by which Tommy could have known that Dweena had taken over Dover's office. But none of them could explain the intent way Tommy was now watching me, as if gauging my reaction, like he really had slipped up and said too much and was trying to figure out if I'd noticed.

Well, I had noticed.

I chose my next words very carefully. I said, as casually as possible, "Oh, so you know about that office." I left it wide open so he could interpret any way he wanted.

He replied with a tight voice, "Sure. You told me."

Wrong answer, Tommy.

I looked him straight in the eye, no longer casual. "No, I did not."

"Really? I could have sworn. But if you say so, I must have overheard somebody talking about it at Angie's. You know how it is. Sooner or later I hear just about everything that happens."

"I don't think so, Tommy."

My disbelief was based not so much on what he was saying, but more on the way he looked when he was saying it. "So," I said, "you want to level with me?"

He didn't want to, not at first, but the more he talked, the more he seemed to appreciate the opportunity to unburden.

Ria's plan, which he'd known about from the very beginning, had been much more than a simple disappeared-and-presumed-dead scheme. It was Tommy's impending loss of Angie's that gave Ria the idea to disappear in the first place. "She wanted to save Angie's."

A noble endeavor. "How?"

"Ria said she knew a way to get her hands on lots of

money, enough so that she could be someone else, somewhere else, and for me to buy the building from my ex.
You can imagine, being a bartender, the kind of bullshit
I hear, day after day. I didn't pay it much mind, that is,
until Ria actually disappeared."

"I assume by 'get her hands' on, you're not talking
about a withdrawal from her bank account."

Tommy shook his head. "No. You've got to understand, I thought it was all a crock, so it went in one ear
and out the other. I do remember her boasting that she
was positive she could get away with it. All she had to
do was disappear and if the cops thought she was dead,
so much the better. When that body turned up in the
meat packing district, I was afraid it might really be Ria.
But it wasn't, thank god, and . . . you know the rest."

"Only too well."

"Late last night, not long before closing, Ria came
around Angie's. At first I didn't recognize her. She had
on a long blond curly-haired wig and sunglasses. I don't
think any of the regulars recognized her either. Tell you
the truth, I thought she might be some kind of weirdo.
You get all kinds late at night. She sat by herself at one
of the front tables and stayed until the place emptied
out. I had to go over and ask her to leave. That's when
she started talking and of course I knew it was her. She
said she still wanted to give me money as planned, only
there was a slight problem."

"What kind of problem?"

"She didn't say. You've got to believe me, Brenda, if
I'd known Ria was serious about her plan I would have
put a stop to it from the start. I admit I was tempted,
but I told her no, dirty money brings on bad luck. Besides, I didn't need the money anymore because of
Dweena and S.O.B. I was surprised that she already
knew about that. That's when she told me shc'd been
hanging out with Dwcena at that P.I.'s office."

"What about the stalker? Did she make that up too?"

"I think so."

"Where's Ria now?"

"She wouldn't tell me. I'm sorry, Brenda."

To make him feel better, I said, "No harm done," then wondered if that was really true.

26

Tommy got one foot through the door, turned back, and apologized again.

"It's all right." All I wanted was for him to be gone. I needed to be alone to think about this latest bit of information.

"No, it's not all right," he said.

He stepped back inside the shop.

He had lots of excuses and seemed to feel the need to make them. He was embarrassed, he claimed, and it was hard for him to admit he needed money to save Angie's, and anyway he'd done right and turned the money down, but he still felt bad that he hadn't stopped Ria, and now she might be in some kind of trouble. "I should have leveled with you earlier, laid all my cards out on the table."

He was right about that. I hated getting the truth in tiny increments. The longer he went on with his lame excuses the sicker I got of trying to make him feel better and the more I realized what he'd done really wasn't all right at all.

Tommy had spent many years listening to other people's tales of woe. He must have felt he deserved equal time.

He showed no immediate signs of winding down, so I loaded up a roller and resumed painting. Every so often

I grunted a noncommittal response to make him think I was listening.

Tommy eventually caught on that I was pretty much ignoring him, and told me one last time how terribly sorry he was. "I'll call Dweena right away," he said on his way out. "And Brenda, I really am sorry."

One big section of wall to go.

Or maybe I should pack it in and quit for the day. I was beat, and despite the advanced state of entropic deterioration, it was highly probable that the wall would still be standing tomorrow.

Then again, I thought, it would feel great to finish the goddamned job. And what else did I have to do except worry?

So I painted, rolled blue over pink, and thought about what I'd learned about Ria Kleep. An interesting twist, that money.

I wasn't surprised to hear that Ria was a thief. I never did trust that woman. What surprised me was that she was such a *big* thief. It wasn't like Jackhammer swiping a green bean from the farmers' market, or Dweena shoplifting a tube of hot-pink lipstick. This was serious money. Ultra extreme grand larceny.

The building Angie's was in was worth a million, maybe two. Say Tommy needs 20 percent down to get a mortgage. Figuring for the worst case that would be four hundred thousand. Then, Ria needed enough money for herself to disappear and live on forevermore, maybe five hundred thousand. That would make the take around a million.

Ria Kleep was no criminal mastermind; she was a secretary who hung out most nights with a bunch of regulars in a neighborhood bar. Where could she get her hands on that kind of money?

I had to stop, yet again, to refill the paint pan, a task that was occurring way too often. I gauged the rapidly deplenishing supply of blue paint against how far it had to go and how fast the wall was sucking it up. I concluded that the paint would run out about thirty square feet shy of completion.

That was bad news. It was after five. One-Coat's would be closed for the day. No matter how long or how hard I worked, I couldn't finish until tomorrow.

So much for my incentive.

I stretched out flat on my back on a clean section of drop cloth. Jackhammer trotted over and stretched out across my belly. I stared up at the expanse of pressed tin ceiling, thankful that I didn't have to paint that.

Back to Ria.

Okay, so how does a mere secretary who worked at some import-export firm get her hands on a million dollars? That was the question. Once I phrased it that way, the answer came easy. The money was at the import-export firm. Ria planned an inside job.

I've witnessed plenty of dubious cash transactions in the garment center. I saw one buyer whip twenty thousand dollars out of her jeans pocket, and another pull a huge wad of cash out of the pointy toe of his red alligator cowboy boot.

I could easily imagine similar cash deals, only on a much larger scale, at an import-export firm. Lots of cash deals meant lots of cash on hand. I remembered Ria said that her boss was often out of the country.

I considered Minetta Carlton, who worked at the same firm and ended up dead. How did she fit in?

I didn't like where my train of thought seemed to be headed.

I took a break to keep from having the thought. I got up off the floor, walked over to the window, and took a look outside.

Not much was happening out on charming, cobblestoned West Fourth Street, nothing diverted my attention away from what came next. I fought the obvious conclusion, but I couldn't keep a good idea down for long. It roiled to the surface.

Ria Kleep killed Minetta Carlton.

It's not like it was the first time I'd thought that, but for the first time I had good solid motive—one that went way beyond office politics—to back up my hunch.

Hardly trying, I came up with several scenarios, all of which pointed to Ria as the killer. Minetta Carlton might have been in on the theft or pilferage or whatever it was from the very start, and the deal went bad. Or Minetta Carlton could have caught Ria with her hand in the till and demanded a piece of the action, and Ria wasn't into sharing. Or Carlton could have threatened to turn Ria over to the authorities. Or . . .

Whatever, Minetta Carlton ended up dead. And Ria was alive. According to Tommy, Ria said she was having a problem with the money. Was she looking for all or part of the money when she tried to get into Minetta Carlton's apartment building?

True, I didn't like Ria. She was a little crude, a little rude, and then there was that thing with Johnny. My dislike of Ria had fueled my earlier suspicions. How I felt no longer mattered. The evidence against her was strong.

During a violent confrontation over the money, Ria killed Minetta Carlton, probably in her own kitchen. Ria still had to disappear as she'd originally planned, only first she had to get rid of Carlton's body. She quickly adapted her original plan to accommodate one real dead body and one missing and presumed dead person. She'd cleaned up the mess and left behind a pool of her own blood, dumped Carlton's body in an abandoned building on Little West Twelfth, called the cops, took the PATH train to Hoboken, and disappeared.

Poor P. G. Dover. Now I knew how he fit in. Ria made up the stalker bit, hired Dover—set him up actually—so that once she had disappeared, he'd tell the cops about the stalker, and they'd be more likely to believe she'd met with foul play.

So far, so good. But soon my recap of possible events faltered. Why, if she killed Minetta Carlton, had Ria surfaced and turned up at Dover's office when she heard Carlton's body had been found and identified as her own?

Ria told Dweena and me she'd come back to find out if Dover knew what happened. Given what I now knew, that took on a new and ominous meaning. Ria was curious all right, but not about *what* happened; she knew damned well what happened. She wanted to know if Dover knew, because if he did, he could spoil her revised plan.

She was afraid Dover was on to her, and came back to kill him to shut him up, but he was in jail and Dweena was using his office. Ria stuck around. She didn't give a hoot about S.O.B. Ria agreed to stay because she knew that sooner or later Dover would show up and she could take care of business. Then when she heard the police had identified Carlton's body and wanted to question her, she freaked and left, changing her plan yet again.

She'd be back.

If I was right, P. G. Dover was in danger. And if he was in danger, so was Dweena.

I called Dweena. She answered.

"Brenda, you caught me on my way out. So sorry, but I really must run."

"No! Listen, Dweena, you're in danger."

"Look, Brenda, even if I didn't have this important meeting, I couldn't help you paint anyway. I hurt my—"

"This is not about painting. No bullshit, Dweena. You are in danger. Stay away from P. G. Dover's office."

"Not to worry, Brenda. That little pipsqueak won't harm a hair on my gloriously platinum-blond bewigged head. Ever since I beat the shit out of him earlier today, P. G. the PI and I are beginning to see eye to eye."

"Ria killed Minetta and now she's after Dover and if you're there she'll have to kill you too."

"You changed your mind about Ria again? What's

wrong with you lately, Brenda? You're usually so much more decisive."

"I got more information."

I told Dweena.

"Cool," she said. "Do you really think Ria's gonna whack Dover?"

"Goddammit, Dweena. This is no time to joke. I mean it, stay away from Dover's office."

"You're really serious, aren't you?"

"Yes, I am. So promise you won't go to Dover's office."

"You know Dweena never ever makes promises. But I assure you, Dweena also never ever comes between a weapon and its target, especially such a deserving target as P. G. Dover. Now, I really do have a meeting tonight."

Next, Dover had to be warned. After that surprise birthday party debacle, I probably didn't have too much credibility with him. Brewster Winfield wasn't exactly the man for the job, but in a pinch he'd do.

I tried Winfield at his loft. No answer. I called his cell phone. He didn't answer that either, which was unusual. I couldn't imagine him not answering, unless . . .

As P. G. Dover's attorney, Winfield also might have known too much for Ria's comfort. Had she already got to him? I envisioned Winfield mortally wounded, shot through the heart, facedown in a pool of blood, dreadlocks matted and sticky, his cell phone ringing, Myrtle slithering around his dying body, then stretching her jaws and swallowing the phone.

I shook my head to get rid of that vision. Get a grip.

To tell the truth, I didn't know much about Myrtle. To me, a snake is a snake and that pretty much says it all. I'd rather not think about what Myrtle ate or how she ate it. Was she the kind of snake that swallowed her meal whole? Kicking and screaming? Ringing and ringing? I imagined a cell phone shape moving sinuously along the length of her body . . .

"Winfield here."

I'd never been so happy to hear his voice.

"Oh, good, you're there," I said, having no idea where there actually might be. "When you didn't pick up I thought—"

"Tunnel," he said.

"Oh, so that was it." I didn't waste time asking where he'd been or where he was going. I got right to the point, but kept it vague because I didn't think cellular calls were secure. "Your client's client might be looking to ice him."

"Huh?" said Winfield. "Who likes icing?"

"Your client's client is about to be—"

"Brenda, you're voice is breaking up. I'll call you when I get back."

A crackle on the line, and he was gone.

Get back from where? I had no way of knowing. I waited half an hour for Winfield to call. When he didn't, I took matters into my own hands.

The machine hooked up to Dover's red phone picked up. A couple of seconds into the taped S.O.B. greeting, Dover came on the line. "What's this S.O.B. shit on my answering machine?"

I identified myself.

"You should be aware that I'm filing assault charges against that Dweena person."

"Mr. Dover, listen to me. You are in grave danger. I can't go into detail right now, but I have reason to believe Ria Kleep wants you dead."

"Yet another dissatisfied client. The PI's lot is difficult."

"I'm serious, Mr. Dover. Watch your back."

"I'm a PI. Danger comes with the job. Killer dames are a dime a dozen. Don't worry about me."

27

It wasn't until early the next morning that the esteemed Brewster Winfield finally got around to returning my call. The snake-doting attorney didn't apologize. No big surprise, but it sure pissed me off. Winfield was only reliable on matters that were billable or concerned Myrtle.

"Why the hell didn't you call me back last night?"

"And a cheery good morning to you too, Brenda. Now, what seems to be the problem?"

"I believe that your client, P. G. Dover, is in extreme danger from his client, Ria Kleep."

"What kind of danger?"

"I'm pretty sure she wants to ice him. And Dweena too, if she gets in the way. She could even be after you."

"You've certainly piqued my interest."

I recounted what I knew, how I knew it, and how that had led me to my conclusion. "I realize it might sound kind of farfetched that a woman like Ria Kleep could be involved in a major theft, but she told Tommy she could get her hands on lots of money, and she planned her own disappearance, and then her coworker was killed, and one thing led to another, and whether I'm right about Ria, clearly somebody is playing for keeps and P. G. Dover is right smack in the middle of it."

Winfield seemed to appreciate the gravity of the situation. "You know, Brenda," he said, "you just might be on to something."

"I'm glad *you* get it. Do me a favor and call Dover. Last night I called to warn him, but it seemed like he thought I was kidding."

"I wouldn't be so sure about that. My client is one flaky dude, his Gintoflakokia scam is a joke, but the man is no fool. Most likely he was putting up a front for you so as not to appear weak. It's a guy thing, Brenda, you wouldn't understand. However, to be on the safe side, and to reduce my own liability, I will call him."

"Thanks, Brew. Remember, watch your own back too."

"But of course."

Last night Dweena had sort of halfway promised to stay away from Dover's office. That didn't necessarily mean she would. It was all too possible that she'd wake up this morning, decide my fears were ungrounded, and head straight into danger.

I thought it would be a good idea to drop by her place to make sure she was heeding my warning.

Jackhammer had to go out anyway.

As we neared the meat packing district, he sniffed the ground madly. The neighborhood was changing rapidly, but there were still enough meatpackers around to send out thrilling odors of putrefied flesh. Thrilling to Jackhammer, that is. I breathed through my mouth and picked him up to keep entrails residue off his feet.

I went into Dweena's building, climbed up the concrete steps to the second floor, and banged on her door.

She answered almost immediately, which surprised me, still in her plaid flannel jammies, which did not.

"Yo, Brenda, Jackhammer. What's shaking? You knocked loud enough to raise the dead."

"You're already up," I commented.

"Damned tootin' I'm up. Got a big day ahead of me.

S.O.B. is about to happen big time." She started to detail her meeting and inspection agenda.

I cut her off. "I wanted to be sure you meant it when you promised to stay away from Dover's."

"I did not promise. Remember? Dweena never promises. But you can be damned sure you won't catch me anywhere near that office. I woke up this morning, thought over what you said, and concluded it makes sense. Amusing as it might be, I do prefer to miss the bloodbath. I just hope Ria strikes soon. If she whacks Dover before the end of the month, I can still get some use out of his office before the rent is due."

Dweena's callous act was a good sign that she was actually afraid and trying to cover up her fear. I was glad my warnings had impact.

"So Brenda, Tommy called all upset that Angie's is running out of time. I shuffled my schedule to squeeze in an inspection of the premises this afternoon. Want to come along?"

"Sure," I said. "What time?"

"Two o'clock. I'll treat you to lunch."

"A pint will do it."

"Whatever."

From Dweena's I'd walked straight to One-Coat's store. I got lucky; One-Coat wasn't around. The kid in charge didn't know I'd screwed up the paint job, so I escaped another lecture about how I should have invested in proper tools from the get-go. The kid squeezed in some pigment, jiggled the paint for a bit, took my money, and before Jackhammer and I were out the door, he had his nose stuck back in his wrestling magazine.

The pint did do it.

The job was finished.

Midnight Millinery was blue.

The last section hadn't yet dried. It was too soon to tell if the paint the kid mixed would match.

*   *   *

A bicycle bell sounded.

Elizabeth bumped the wheels of her hot-pink shopping cart over the doorjamb. The fuzzy dice hanging on the front collided and bounced off each other.

"Hey, Elizabeth. You're just in time to help me clean up this paint mess."

"I can't believe you finally finished the job."

"Well, I did. Only moments ago."

"Congratulations. This calls for a celebration."

Elizabeth walked around the periphery of the shop, casting a critical eye on my work.

"Careful," I said, "that section over there is still wet."

"I can see that."

"So, what do you think?"

"Not bad, Brenda, not bad at all. After a lousy start, you pulled off an admirable job."

"Thank you. Coming from you, that's a great compliment."

"You're welcome," she said. "Tell me, how do you feel about that blue now that it's all done?"

"I don't know. Okay, I guess. I mean, it's blue."

"It certainly is. Blue. That's definitely what you wanted, right?"

"Absolutely. I like blue. I mean, it's sky, faded jeans, and the blues. You know how I love the sound of a good blues guitar. Why, don't you like blue?"

"I was just wondering how you felt."

"I'm glad the job is done. I want to make some hats."

"That's good to hear."

"Where are you headed with your shopping cart?" I asked.

"For disaster probably."

"What do you mean?"

"I'm en route to Chuck's. It's demolition time. He's taking down that old computer magazine wall."

"What for? It's a good wall. So practical, so cheap."

"You know that band who lives above him?"

"Sure. Urban Dog Talk."

"One of the guys, I think Chuck said the bass player, flooded the joint."

"How'd that happen?"

"He was trying to steam creases out of his jeans. He hung them upside down on the shower rod, turned on the hot water full blast, shut the door, and went into the kitchen to rustle up some breakfast. While he was mixing up a batch of banana nut pancakes, a bunch of guitar picks fell out of the jean pockets, jammed up the drain, and the tub overflowed."

"What about the overflow drain? Don't all tubs have one of those, close to the top? That should have stopped the tub from running over."

"It would have except one of the other members of the band had duct-taped the overflow drain so he could fill the tub all the way to the top to practice snorkeling. While all this was going on, Chuck was out picking up a breakfast pizza. By the time he got back the wall was soaked."

"Now that I think of it, Chuck's wall isn't in line with the bathrooms. Wouldn't the water have gone straight into his bathtub and down his drain?"

"Old buildings leak in weird ways, water seeks its own level. Chuck's sagging ceiling got the brunt of it, and it broke through. He says the magazines are starting to smell moldy."

"He must be mad."

"Actually he's displaying a remarkably positive attitude. He thinks it's word from above telling him to open up his space, rethink his goals."

"Word from above?"

"That's what he said. I'm concerned though. Given the state of his building, I'd say that wall is about all that keeps his ceiling above his head. Over the years, it has become an important structural element. Hell, the whole building could collapse. Chuck knows electronics, he doesn't know a hill of beans about structural engineering. I thought I should go over and supervise. If it looks bad I won't let him take it down."

"Why the shopping cart?"

"Chuck says those old magazines are collectible, moldy or not. He's got a potential buyer, some Cooper Union geek he ran into at McSorley's. If the wall goes, I get to be broker and delivery person."

The problem with buying quality paint supplies was that I couldn't throw them away when the job was done. I cleaned the pans and rollers and brushes, dried them, shook out the drop cloth, and folded it up.

Then came the hard part. I had to make room to store it all.

I went into the storage closet, flicked on the light. My shelves, which sagged worse than Chuck's ceiling, were already jam-packed with millinery equipment and supplies.

Something had to go. Not my antique hatblocks. Not my spare steamer. Not my banding ribbon, or buckram, or felt bodies.

I had boxes and boxes of fabric, much of it unseen for years. Maybe I could part with a few yards. I pulled the boxes off the shelves, moved them out into the studio, and started to sort through. Editing the collection.

In the first box, underneath a couple of yards of black denim, I came upon a panel of 1950s barkcloth, a flea market find. Boomerang abstract shapes danced across in chartreuse and red and black with occasional splashes of silver. I'd be crazy to get rid of that.

The next box was filled with several different kinds of antique veiling. Veiling is too fussy and costumey for the kind of hats I make, but I could hardly throw away millinery history to make room for paint rollers.

I moved on to the next box. Bingo. In it were yards and yards of blue polished cotton. I wondered whatever had possessed me to pay good money for that stuff. Then I remembered I hadn't. The fabric had been a gift from a client who wanted to make amends for writing a bad check. I think she found it in the basement of her building. I didn't feel the least bit guilty about giving it the heave-ho.

I left it on my blocking table, put the paint supplies in the box, and put the box back in the closet.

28

Most of the lunch crowd had emptied out of Angie's. Sinatra was on the juke-box, the television was turned off. Dweena, as usual, was late. I pulled up a stool at the bar.

Tommy, deep in conversation with one of the regulars at the other end of the bar, raised his eyebrows to ask if I wanted anything.

I shook my head no.

About ten minutes later Dweena bustled in, clip-board in hand. She had on a skintight charcoal-gray pinstriped spandex pantsuit with sky-high bloodred plat-form pumps—her conservative get-up. She slid onto the next stool. "This building inspection gig is the best. How I love to be an authority figure. The power, the prestige, the potential for payoffs is positively intoxicating."

"I'll bet."

"Did you order lunch yet?"

"No."

"Good. If you don't mind, I'd like to get the inspec-tion out of the way first. Then we can eat and discuss our findings."

"Okay by me."

Dweena flapped her hand in the air to get Tommy's attention. "Yo, Tommy."

Tommy moved down to our end of the bar. "After-noon, Dweena," he said. "All ready for the inspection?"

"Ready, willing, and able. S.O.B. is on the job."

"Will you be needing me?"

"I don't think so. Brenda's gonna help."

"Well, if you do, you know where to find me. I sure hope you two gals are successful. The fate of Angie's rests in your hands." He took a ring of keys out of the cash register and presented it to Dweena. "These will get you anywhere in the building. The place is all yours. Any problems, give a holler."

On our way into the back room Dweena and I passed by the kitchen. Raphael was chopping onions. "Best of luck," he said.

The key ring Tommy gave Dweena held more than a dozen keys. The very first one she tried unlocked the door to the stairway.

"How do you do that?"

"Born talent, further developed by practice."

The building was only three stories high. We stopped on the second floor first.

"Four doors, four rooms," said Dweena, scribbling down the information on her clipboard. "What goes on up here?"

"Well," I said, "Over there is Tommy's office. These other rooms are probably for storage. Raphael lives in a couple of the rooms upstairs."

"Nice perk," said Dweena.

"It's also a smart move on Tommy's part. It's good to have someone around to keep an eye on the place when he can't be here."

Sound from the jukebox filtered up.

"How appropriate," said Dweena. "Brothel music. Sets the mood."

"What the hell is brothel music?"

"Bluesy sax, swishy drums," she said. "I thought everybody knew that."

She got down to business, unlocked each of the doors, and briefly stuck her head into each room.

It didn't seem like much of an inspection to me.

*   *   *

We climbed up to the third floor.

"Same room configuration as downstairs," noted Dweena. "Which is almost always the case." As she had downstairs, she unlocked each door and peeked inside, but only for a moment. "So tell me, Brenda, have you seen any outstanding brothel indicators yet?"

"What exactly are we looking for?" I was genuinely curious, especially since Dweena didn't seem to be looking very thoroughly.

"Can you keep a secret?" she asked.

"Sure, I guess so."

"We're not looking for anything. After I got a few of these inspections under my belt, I decided it was much easier to make it *all* up as I go along. Most of the buildings on my endangered list have no corresponding evidence whatsoever that they were ever brothels. The West Village was never a hotbed of brothel activity. In my research phase, I whirred through miles of microfilm at the library and managed to dig up a few instances of brothel raids around the neighborhood, but most of those buildings were torn down decades ago. So I fudge it."

"How can you fudge history?"

"Simple. Like for instance, I found a story about a legitimate brothel raid in a building that was torn down twenty years ago. I transposed the address, thus moving the raid across the street to where a building still stands. Nobody's ever gonna check. If they do, I can always say I made an honest mistake."

"Dyslexia."

"You got it. And you know those rundown buildings on Jane Street? I found mention of a raid in one of them, not a brothel, but an alleged lesbian bar. In my write-up, I simply disputed what the ladies had been doing. They'd be mighty angry if they knew, but fortunately all the concerned parties are long dead."

"This inspection of Angie's, then . . ."

"Is all for show, Brenda. Basically, you could say, I'm full of shit. S.O.B. is a sham, a scam, a flim-flam, my own personal Gintoflakokia. But the hoax is working. I've even got people at Landmarks calling me for advice—a true sign of success. What more could a girl ask?"

"What about Angie's? Did your research turn up any evidence at all?"

"Quite the opposite. In my expert opinion, Angie's was never a brothel. For that matter, despite what all the history books and tourist literature say, I don't think Angie's was a speakeasy either. It never got raided, or if it did, the raids didn't make the papers. Doesn't make a bit of difference though. People believe pretty much what they want, and everybody in the entire city wants to believe Angie's was once a speakeasy. It shouldn't be too hard to convince a couple of bureaucrats it was also once a brothel."

A telephone rang, startling both of us. It sounded like it was in the hallway right beside us, but it was down below in Tommy's office. After four rings, his machine picked up, the recording came on—Tommy—saying he was probably working in the bar and unless it was an emergency to please leave a message.

"Think he's got that thing turned up loud enough?" said Dweena.

"Shhh," I said. "I want to hear this."

"Aren't you the nosey one."

I felt guilty eavesdropping, and then when the call was over, foolish. The caller turned out to be a New Jersey tomato vendor who wanted to confirm an order.

I must have looked disappointed because Dweena asked what I'd been expecting.

"I don't know. Ria Kleep maybe."

"Yeah, right. Like she's gonna call up and confess on tape to the murder of Minetta Carlton, mention that she's also planning to off Dover, and reveal where she's hiding. Then you can take the answering machine tape to Turner and McKinley and be a crime-busting heroine."

"I just thought . . . well, I don't know what really. At

any rate, I'm pleased to find out that Tommy uses high-quality New Jersey tomatoes."

"Speaking of food," said Dweena, "that noise you hear is my stomach growling. I hereby declare the S.O.B. inspection of Angie's officially over."

"We didn't do the cellar yet."

"Very observant of you, Brenda. The omission is quite intentional. Cellars, especially in food establishments, tend to be dark and damp and groady and overrun with mice and rats and cockroaches. Dweena doesn't do cellars. Besides, my fabulous red pumps are killing me. It's time to take a load off."

Raphael cleared dishes away from my favorite booth. "The regular?"

"Actually, no."

He put the dishes back down on the table and pounded the side of his head with the heel of his hand. "Excuse me. Did I hear you right? You don't want the regular? What gives?"

"All of a sudden I crave tomato. So, I'd like the regular grilled cheese but with a slight variation, namely a big fat juicy slice of tomato slammed down in the middle between the two hunks of hot cheese. Can you do that?"

"No problem."

"That sounds good," said Dweena. "I'd like a cheeseburger with a slice of tomato on the side."

"Coming right up," said Raphael.

The tomatoes were delicious.

While Dweena and I ate, we tossed around some ideas. She filled out several pages of official-looking forms.

"Chuck designed those?"

"Yep."

"Nice job."

Dweena smiled. "My paperwork impressed the hell out of the red-tape people, that's for sure. The Landmark bigwigs are totally bamboozled. I've got them convinced that S.O.B. is an officially sanctioned city agency."

"You're amazing."

"Thank you, I like to think so. Now, help me decide what to say about this place." Thoughtful, she tapped her ballpoint pen against the clipboard.

"Why don't you make up something about the cellar? You didn't want to go down there. If cellars are as bad as you say, I doubt any city officials will check it out either. They'll go along with whatever you tell them."

"Good thinking, Brenda. An idea like that is worth the price of lunch." She scribbled some more notes. "Yes, I believe this will work out."

Raphael breezed by. "You two ladies okay?"

"Better than okay," I said. "This tomato really adds a nice punch to the grilled cheese."

"Be careful, Raphael," said Dweena. "Before you know, Brenda will be wanting a slice of onion."

"I can do that too," said Raphael.

Dweena and I were finishing up lunch when Tommy came by with a freshly uncorked bottle of red wine and three glasses. "Mind if I join you?"

"Of course not."

I scooted over and he slid into the booth next to me. He poured the wine. "To Angie's," he said.

"May it be here always," said Dweena.

"I take it, then, you found something," said Tommy.

"I did," said Dweena, lifting her glass again. "The news is good. If this place isn't a former brothel, Brenda will eat her hats."

29

"If you'll excuse me," said Tommy, "I should get back behind the bar."

The three of us made one last toast to Angie's.

I asked Dweena to come back to Midnight Millinery with me. "I've got something to show you."

"Yeah, I bet you do," she said. "This is a setup, right? It's a scheme to get me to help you paint."

"Nope," I said. "I don't need your help anymore. The paint job is done. All I want from you is an honest opinion."

"You finished? By yourself?"

I nodded.

"All right, I'll take a look, but only for a second. I have one more brothel inspection scheduled for today. After that I need to do a little paperwork."

"Not at Dover's office, I hope."

"No way. Although I'm still not totally convinced Ria Kleep is much of a threat."

"She is. The pieces fit."

"Face it Brenda, the pieces fit lousy. It's like you took a sledgehammer and pounded a square peg in a round hole. Now, if you want to see a good fit, I'll show you my new pink-and-black polka-dot capri pants. How I do love that Lycra."

"Ria Kleep is bad news," I said. "Sooner or later she's gonna show up at Dover's office, and you don't want to be around when she does."

"If you're so sure then why don't you go to the cops?"

"Because my proof isn't provable. They'll laugh at me." Or worse.

"Admit it, your proof is no more than a hunch."

I didn't respond.

"Well . . . I'm waiting."

"All right. It's just a hunch. But a strong enough hunch, that I want you to stay away from that office."

"I won't go back until you give me the all-clear signal."

Jackhammer bounded to the door to greet us. Dweena scooped him up in her arms. "Did mean old Brenda leave you all alone in her little hat shop while she was out gallivanting?"

Jackhammer, who hated baby talk, vibrated his tail stub, squirmed to get down, gave my ankles a drive-by sniff, and trotted off.

I gestured toward the freshly painted walls. "What do you think?"

Dweena wrinkled her forehead, as if she were actually giving my question a deep ponder. "Well," she said finally, "it certainly is blue, isn't it?"

Her reaction was the same as Elizabeth's.

Too blue? I didn't think so, although I had to admit, the new color would take some time to get used to.

"What's this?" asked Dweena. She pointed at the yards of polished cotton I hadn't yet put in the garbage. "Curtain material?"

"You've got to be kidding. I'm tossing this crap."

"What's wrong with it?"

"It's ugly. I hate it."

"It's not so bad. What specifically do you hate?"

"The color, I guess."

"Well, think again, Brenda. It's a perfect match for

your walls. You really ought to make cute ruffled café curtains for your window."

I gave her a look like she was nuts.

"I'll leave you with that thought," she said. Then, with a toodle-ooo, she was gone.

I extended my arm and held the fabric up to the wall.

The hue might be similar, but a woven surface reflects light quite differently than a flat wall. Dweena loves flash; she was unable to appreciate sophisticated nuances of color.

I looked away from the fabric and back again. Then again to make sure. The truth was that I didn't appreciate the nuances either. The fabric was the same color as the walls. My walls were blue, way too blue.

I missed the pink.

Okay, so Dweena was right about the walls, but goddammit, I was right about Ria Kleep. I hadn't pounded a square peg into a round hole, or forced the pieces to fit. Ria was a thief and a killer. I hadn't let my feelings about her cloud my perception of those two fundamental facts.

I looked at the wall again. And at the fabric against the wall. Damn.

Okay, maybe I'd overstated a bit. Those two things about Ria were not real facts; they were still in the realm of good strong hunches.

The only real fact was the sad and brutal fact that Minetta Carlton was dead. I tried not to get too hung up by the fact that even that fact hadn't always been a fact. Thanks to Tommy's false identification, it had once appeared as a fact that Ria Kleep was dead, not Minetta Carlton.

Leaving facts, I moved on to the far more fertile territory of assumptions and hunches, and tried to analyze a few of mine.

I was once at a party in a fancy Upper East Side

apartment. I glanced out the host's big picture window just as a bomb squad vehicle screeched to a stop in front of the dry cleaner across the avenue. A cop got out and hurried inside. Seconds later a patrol car zoomed onto the scene, siren blaring, and two ambulances raced up the street.

Naturally I thought terrorists had planted a bomb and the dry cleaner was about to blow sky high and shatter windows up and down the avenue. Before I could tell the host and alert the guests I looked out the window once again. The first cop exited the dry cleaner, a black suit shrouded in plastic draped over his arm. The second cop was writing out a ticket for the driver he'd just pulled over. The two ambulances had already turned onto another street.

In other words, there's a lot of coincidence in this world and actions sometimes aren't what they seem.

Back to my supposed facts. Ria told Tommy she could get her hands on a lot of money. That didn't necessarily mean she planned to steal the money, and even if she did, she hadn't necessarily stolen it from work, and even if she had, it didn't mean Minetta Carlton had found out.

For that matter, any number of people could have found out about the money. Ria herself had told Tommy. That, I knew for a fact, and . . .

Tommy?

What was I thinking?

Obviously, the paint fumes had gone to my head.

I stepped out on to West Fourth and sucked in some fresh spring air and was greatly relieved to remember, now that I could think straight, that Ria had offered Tommy enough money to save Angie's. Though tempted, he'd turned it down. He wouldn't have killed her for the money she was so willing to give. Tommy's honesty and talk of dirty money being bad luck must have shocked Ria. I could imagine the surprised expression on her face.

Glad I got that figured out.

Feeling much better, I went back inside and put the shop back in order so I could get back to my real work early tomorrow morning. Blue walls or not, for the first time in a long time, I looked forward to making hats.

My stomach growled. I hadn't eaten since the grilled cheese at Angie's. That tomato slice added the perfect counterpoint to the high fat sandwich. I'd have to tell Raphael to make that my new "regular."

I never would have thought to ask for tomato if I hadn't eavesdropped on Tommy's message from the tomato vendor. I didn't feel guilty about listening in. The way sound traveled in that old building I couldn't help but overhear. I happened to be at the right place at the right time.

Oh no. My next thought made me sick.

That's right. I happened to be at Angie's, on the third floor, at the right place at the right time, like anybody else who could have been there at the right place and at the right time, listening in when Ria told Tommy about the money.

I knew it couldn't really be just anybody. It had to be somebody who had access to the floor above Tommy's office. Somebody like Raphael, a man who stood to lose not only his job but also his home if Angie's was forced to close.

I knew of only one way to find out.

Angie's was a public place. I would be perfectly safe. I took Jackhammer with me. This time, I didn't want anybody to get the idea that my visit was anything special.

Raphael was manning the bar. "Back again so soon?"

"I only dropped by for a second," I said real casual-like. "You know how scatterbrained Dweena is. She left out a small detail on her brothel inspection report. Is Tommy around? He could clear this up in a second."

"He's in his office. You want to go up?"

"Sure."

Raphael buzzed Tommy and told him I was on my way. Then he ducked under the bar, escorted me into the back room, and unlocked the door to the staircase.

"Thanks," I said.

"Think nothing of it."

Tommy's office door was ajar. I stepped inside.

"Hi, Brenda, Jackhammer. What's up?"

I wanted to get Tommy out of the building so I could talk freely. Very loudly, in case Raphael was within earshot, I announced, "Dweena forgot to ask you about a structural detail of the building. If it's not too much trouble, I need you to come outside for minute. We can get a better view from across the street."

"Of course. Anything to help Dweena and S.O.B." said Tommy. "She's our last hope."

Tommy and I clomped down the stairs. He stopped at the bar briefly to tell Raphael he'd be back soon. Then we continued outside and across the street.

I pointed up to the roof. "See that?"

"You mean the crumbling facade?" said Tommy. "It's been that way for years."

No, not the crumbling facade.

I could either level with Tommy or not. In a split-second decision, in the spirit of returning a favor, I decided to go with the truth. Tommy had, after all, leveled with me about his lie to Turner and McKinley and then about Ria Kleep's offer of money.

"Keep looking at that facade," I said. "Pretend like you're worried about it. I wanted to get you outside so we could speak in private."

"My office is private."

"I wouldn't be so sure about that. When Dweena and I were inspecting this afternoon we discovered, quite by accident, that from the floor above, you can hear a conversation in your office."

Tommy shrugged. "So what?"

"When Ria told you about the money and her plan to disappear, where were you? In the bar?"

Tommy thought for a moment. "No, not the bar. We were in my office. I still don't see—"

I explained as best I could, given the fact I was still pretty shaky on the details.

All the time I spoke Tommy kept frowning up at the facade.

"So, what do you think?" I asked when I finished.

"I get your drift, and appreciate your interest, but there's nothing to be concerned about. You see, Brenda, nobody ever goes up to the third floor except me and Raphael."

I took a deep breath, considered how best to phrase what had to be said, decided there was no best way, and blurted out, "How well do you know Raphael?"

Tommy turned away from the facade and directed his attention to me. "What the hell are you trying to say, Brenda?"

"Nothing. It was just an idea."

"You be sure to let me know if have any more ideas."

With that, Tommy stomped across the street and went into Angie's, slamming the door hard behind him.

30

I stung as if Tommy had slapped me in the face.

I hate it when people get mad at me. I'll do almost anything to avoid it—turn the other cheek, let insults slide off me, walk on eggs. I should have done a little egg-walking with Tommy. I should have thought before I opened my mouth and insinuated that his friend and long-time employee was a murderer.

Tommy was much more than temporarily ticked off.

I didn't know what to do.

I let Jackhammer lead me through the Village streets. He sniffed whatever he wanted to sniff, lifted his leg on every fire hydrant and stump along the way. He had a great time.

I did not. What I had couldn't even be described as a time, because I totally lost track of that half a block away from Angie's.

We walked awhile.

Jackhammer yanked hard against his leash.

Half a block up ahead I saw a man in a long trench coat and plush gray fedora. Dover? No, too tall.

I pulled back on the leash.

The man made a quick turn and disappeared around the corner.

A shadowy figure, I thought.

Come to think of it, we were at the far edge of the Village, where there were more shadows than people, and it was probably much later than I thought. "Let's head home," I said to Jackhammer.

The most direct way home took me around the corner where the man had turned. Cautiously, I checked it out before proceeding. The man had vanished. The block had two restaurants, both open. The man had probably gone into one of them. I felt safe, and we went ahead.

Again, Jackhammer yanked at his leash, so hard that I dropped it. He took off at full speed, scrambled up the steps of an old apartment building, and across the stoop.

I dashed up the steps, made a grab for his leash. He scrambled back and forth, sniffing at the crack under the wooden front door.

"What's the big attraction?" I peeked through the glass window set into the door.

The shadowy figure in the fedora crouched in an awkward position in the vestibule of the building. At first I was scared, and jumped back, but then it didn't seem like the man was hiding in order to ambush me. It was more like he was hiding from me. I was just thinking how weird that was when the figure shifted in position. His fingers pressed against the tile floor for balance.

Have I ever mentioned Johnny's hands? Forget those devastating cheekbones, or the dark smoky eyes, or that thick black hair. For me, it's his hands. Slender, strong hands, expressive with just enough vein showing. Hands I'd recognize anywhere.

"What the hell are you doing crouched down like that?"

The shadowy figure looked up at me. "Oh, hi Brenda."

Johnny spun around so that he was sitting on the tile floor. Jackhammer climbed into his lap and licked his face.

"I see you're back from Boston," I said, fighting to

keep the sarcasm—and the hurt—out of my voice.

"Uh . . . yeah, Boston. Well . . ."

"Johnny, it's all right. Lemmy told me."

"Skulking? I wouldn't exactly say I was skulking around the Village. All I did was go out for some chocolate milk."

"Come on, Johnny, 'fess up. You've been avoiding me. Not just tonight either."

We were sitting on the stoop of the building in which he'd hidden.

"Have some chocolate milk," he said, passing the carton.

"No thanks."

He took a swig, wiped his mouth with the back of his hand. "I admit, I've been avoiding you, but definitely not by skulking. I'm washed up as an actor and out of a job. I have no skills or foreseeable future income. But I do not skulk."

"All right, Johnny, you're not skulking. Sorry I brought it up."

"Good. I'm glad we got that straightened out."

"Me too," I said.

For a while we sat in silence.

Finally I ventured to say, "I'm sorry about *Tod Trueman*."

"The show sucked."

"You were good in it. You transcended."

"Fat lot of good it did."

I touched the brim of the fedora. "Nice hat. A disguise?"

"Supposed to be. It helps, especially after dark, which is about the only time I go out anymore. You see, Brenda, it's not just you I'm avoiding. I'm avoiding everybody I know. That's why I came all the way over here to pick up a container of chocolate milk. Nobody expects to see me in this part of the Village. It used to be, before *TTUD*, nobody knew me, and that was swell. Then the *Tod* show hit big, and all of a sudden everybody knows me. And now I'm a colossal failure and everybody knows that too."

"You're not a failure, Johnny. You're an out-of-work actor, like ninety-nine percent of the actors in this city."

"There's a big difference between an out-of-work actor and an out-of-work-actor-whose-former-hit-show-got-canceled. It's not shameful to be an out-of-work actor."

"Don't tell me you're ashamed."

"Of course I'm ashamed."

"Shame on you for being ashamed when you've got so much to be proud of."

We talked for a long time. When we decided to move on, the streets were deserted. Johnny insisted on seeing me all the way home.

"Want to come upstairs?" I asked.

He shook his head no, turned, and walked away.

The single good thing about Johnny feeling so bad was that he was totally self-centered and hadn't asked me what I'd been up to. And so I didn't have to lie.

Aside from that, I felt utterly awful.

Hard to believe the night had started out so full of promise. I'd finished the Midnight Millinery paint job and looked forward to making new hats. Now, only a few hours later, my whole world had turned upside down. I hated the newly blue walls. I'd virtually accused one friend of murder, in doing so got another friend mad at me, and then I proved to be no help whatsoever to Johnny, who was probably the best friend I'd ever had.

Ugly blue walls, Tommy mad, Johnny sad. And Raphael . . . him I didn't even want to think about.

But of course I did.

I'd known Raphael for years, but what did I really know about him? Not much, except that he was a pretty good cook, seemed to be a loyal employee, always remembered everybody's regular order, and delighted Jackhammer with his special little burger balls.

Now that I'd cast Raphael in a whole different light, I recalled snippets of old conversations, an occasional sideways glance, and reinterpreted. Was he watching too carefully? Listening in on private conversations? Saying something between the lines?

Besides Tommy, Raphael was Angie's only full-time employee. He would lose his job and his home if Tommy lost the building. Tommy admitted being tempted by Ria's offer of money, but he'd turned it down. Maybe Raphael, who had more to lose, was more desperate. Maybe he'd gone after Ria once she had the money.

But if that were the case, how come Ria was alive, and Minetta Carlton was dead?

I backtracked. Yesterday I thought Ria Kloop killed Minetta Carlton to shut her up because she knew Ria stole the money, or to keep Minetta from getting the money herself. When Ria showed up at Angie's in disguise she told Tommy there was a problem with the money—in other words she didn't have it. Maybe Minetta Carlton stole it from Ria and that's what Ria was looking for when she tried to get into Minetta's apartment.

Ria told Dweena and me that after she trashed her kitchen she walked around to decide if she really wanted to go through with her disappearance. Would she have taken the money with her? Not likely. It's pretty stupid to walk around lost in thought with that kind of money. She probably left it in her apartment.

While Ria was walking around thinking, Minetta broke into the apartment to steal the money. Raphael, who also knew about the money, had the same idea. He battled it out with Minetta Carlton, killed her, and disposed of the body.

That worked.

I didn't like it. I fought the idea that Raphael was the killer. I'd much rather it be a total stranger, or if it had to be someone I knew, then Ria would do nicely. Unfortunately, what I wanted was not relevant. Each time I reevaluated, Raphael came up as the killer.

He had motive and opportunity and means to gain inside knowledge. And, as someone frequently left in charge of a drinking establishment, he most likely had a gun.

Oh sure, other people stood to lose something—though not nearly as much as Raphael—if Angie's closed. The regulars would lose their hangout. Also the tomato vendor would lose a client. And the liquor distributor and all the other suppliers, the guy who washed the windows, even One-Coat Joe had lost the job painting the place. He'd griped about the job being canceled after he'd taken the time and trouble to do an accurate computer estimate.

Now, that was something.

I remembered how One-Coat described how he'd painstakingly measured every inch of wall and input all the numbers into his brand new expensive computer program. To do so, he too, must have had access to the upper floors of Angie's. If he was at the right place at the right time, he might have overheard Ria talking to Tommy about the money and then . . .

Okay, it was really a big stretch, but I was grasping at straws. I wanted to prove it wasn't Raphael, and One-Coat sort of fit.

Motive was easy.

One-Coat needed money. His little mom-and-pop paint store suffered great losses from the competition of big hardware chains. He'd told me so himself. That's why he got the computer. I wouldn't be a bit surprised if he kept a gun stashed under the counter. He was certainly into protecting the store, and he hadn't always had the sophisticated security system.

I needed to find out if One-Coat had been at Angie's when Ria told Tommy about the money. I could hardly ask Tommy. I'd be lucky if he ever talked to me again.

Nor could I ask One-Coat, at least not outright.

Maybe though, if I put my mind to it, I could come up with another way.

I stayed up all night, thinking and scheming, and by the time the eastern sky lightened up and streaked with color, I had a plan. A devious plan, a plan so subtle that if One-Coat wasn't guilty, he wouldn't even notice I suspected him, but if he had done it, he'd be trapped.

31

I pulled the mattress out of the closet, dragged it across the floor, and flopped down on it, but I was too worked up to sleep. For two hours I tossed and turned, then gave up, got up, made a fresh pot of coffee, and went over my plan to trap One-Coat.

I steer clear of dangerous situations. I circumvent what I perceive as danger, and I see danger in places most people wouldn't even think to look.

I don't take large amounts of cash to the garment center, or eat too much cheese, or spend time alone with murderers who might at any moment perceive that I know much more than they want me to know.

That's why I ran through my plan forward and backward. And then I went over it again. And one more time for good luck. I took into account all kinds of possible screw-ups and devised countermaneuvers. I briefly considered dragging Chuck or Johnny or Elizabeth or Dweena into the scheme, but decided not to. Keep it simple, I told myself.

In the end, I concluded that I would be perfectly safe. The plan was a go.

Stage one of the plan was a snap. More than once One-Coat had volunteered to help me paint the shop. I would simply take him up on his kind offer.

He'd love to hear how my not heeding his advice at the beginning had made it impossible for me to salvage the job even with the proper tools. I'd tell him I'd come to grips with the harsh reality that I'd bitten off more than I could chew, admit failure, grovel a little, swallow some pride, and tell him that without his help I'd never get Midnight Millinery painted. I could say anything. If he was guilty, he'd never see that I'd finished the job. If he wasn't guilty . . . well, I didn't have to worry about that.

One-Coat's offers of help had probably been a bunch of hot air, more flirtatious than genuine. It was safe for him to offer what I would most surely turn down.

That's why I had to see him in person. It would be too easy for him to tell me no on the phone.

Jackhammer and I walked along the quiet streets. It was still too early for the nine-to-fivers to leave for work, but not too early for One-Coat's. It was his busiest time of day, servicing the contractors who dropped by to pick up last-minute supplies.

When I arrived, several such men were hanging around—just as I'd hoped. One-Coat wouldn't dare turn down a damsel in distress in front of an audience of macho male customers.

"Hiya, Joe," I said, loud enough that everyone could hear.

"Brenda Midnight," he said. "Always a pleasure. How's that paint job of yours coming along?"

I sighed dramatically. "You were right, Joe. I should have listened to you and bought your high-quality tools from the very start."

One-Coat smirked. "Live and learn. How are you doing now that you have my top-of-the-line tools?"

"The new tools work like a dream. Problem is I screwed up my walls so badly with the cheap stuff, I can't fix the damage. So, I was wondering, does your offer still stand? I could really use your expert help. Without you . . ."

With a knowing wink to the customers, One-Coat said, "What say I come by after I close up here, a little after five?"

"That'd be wonderful. You're a lifesaver, Joe, a real hero. I don't know how I'll ever thank you."

"Don't you worry your pretty little head about that. I'll think of something."

And so the first stage of my plan was done. It had, I'm pleased to say, gone off without a hitch.

My friends would be surprised to learn that I have, stuffed way in the back of my sock drawer, a bright yellow cell phone. I got it several months ago as an experiment to find out if I could make a hat that did double duty as a cell phone carrying case. The experiment was a success, but I decided to let some other milliner be the first on her block.

Meanwhile, I still had the thing.

I plugged it in and charged it up.

The rest of the day went by. I kept a low profile and avoided contact with friends. They could tell when I was up to something, and I didn't want anybody trying to talk me out of this. I couldn't hang out at Angie's, and I didn't want to go to Midnight Millinery and be surrounded by those awful blue walls, so I stayed home, worried, and played catch-the-chewy-toy with Jackhammer.

Around four-thirty, I began to execute the final stage of my plan. Armed with the cellular phone in my purse and this morning's *New York Times* tucked under my arm, I walked over to One-Coat's street.

I sat down on a wooden bench in front of the Laundromat half a block down from One-Coat's store. Once situated, I opened the *Times* and held it up so it hid my face. Every thirty seconds or so, I peeked over the top to check out the paint store.

At precisely five o'clock, closing time, One-Coat's assistant zoomed out like the place was on fire. At five minutes after, One-Coat himself left the store, clattered down the gates, padlocked them, and started to walk in the direction of Midnight Millinery.

I dropped the *Times* into the trash, and ran after One-Coat. "Joe, Joe," I said, "I'm so glad I caught you."

"Brenda, what are you doing here? I was on my way to Midnight Millinery. What's the matter, you don't need my help anymore?"

"You better believe I still need your help, more than ever. I've had one hell of a day since I saw you this morning."

"Sorry to hear that. What happened?"

I took a deep breath then launched into full bullshit mode. "I was stuck at the precinct all afternoon. Goddamned cops finally turned me loose a few minutes ago. I was afraid you'd beat me to Midnight Millinery, see the shop empty, think I'd totally given up, and leave."

"What'd the cops want with such a sweet thing like you?" He gave me that leer again.

"Red tape. It was stupid. You must have heard about what happened. I thought my friends were giving me a surprise birthday party, but it was actually Dweena and this fake diplomat guy, P. G. Dover, the one they thought killed Ria Kleep—"

The leer was gone now, replaced by an expression I didn't recognize.

"I'll never live that down. I was so embarrassed. Anyway, early this morning the cops caught P. G. Dover, who is some kind of private investigator, breaking into Ria Kleep's apartment. They arrested him again. The cops don't tell me much, but I was able to glean a bit of the story. Dover claims he broke into Ria's to retrieve his own equipment, a bunch of spy stuff, high-tech snooping equipment he'd installed after Ria hired him to catch some guy who'd been stalking her. They've got a team of cops going over the videotapes now. I don't know what they hope to find, but you know how cops are. Meanwhile they wanted to know if I'd seen any kind of electronic equipment in Dover's car, which is crazy because I only saw that car for a couple of minutes. The cops wanted to ask Dweena about the snooping equipment. They couldn't find her, so they came after me."

One-Coat looked sick, his face gray and worried. My long-winded bull spiel had the desired effect. One-Coat had shot Minetta Carlton in Ria Kleep's kitchen. He now feared his act had been captured on videotape.

One-Coat slowed his pace. He got very quiet, as if his mind were elsewhere. If my hunch was right, he was plotting his escape.

We walked another a block, then One-Coat slowed to a stop. "Dammit," he said. "I've got to go back and get some papers I left at the store. You go on ahead, Brenda. I'll catch up with you at Midnight Millinery."

Things were going according to my plan—so far. I mustered up the courage to take it to the next level. "Oh no, you don't, mister," I said playfully. "I'm on to you. You're as bad as Dweena. Once you go back to your store you're gonna come up with some excuse to get out of helping me paint. I'm gonna stick with you like glue until I see a roller in your hand."

He did not look happy. "Suit yourself."

We backtracked to his store. One-Coat unlocked the metal gates and shoved them halfway open. We ducked under and entered. After turning on the overhead fluorescents, he excused himself. "This might take awhile."

"I'm in no hurry."

One-Coat disappeared through the door to the back room.

I doubted he planned to come back.

He'd get the money out of his safe—money Minetta Carlton had taken from Ria Kleep's apartment, money he'd taken from Minetta Carlton during the confrontation that left her dead. Once he had the money, he'd take the back way out. One-Coat needed to get out of town fast.

I had to stop him, but not alone.

I walked behind the counter, reached beneath the cash register, and hit the panic button on his super-duper new sophisticated burglar alarm. Instantly, sirens honked and wailed and lights flashed. Most importantly, the cops and private security were also getting the alarm.

One-Coat ran out of the back screaming, "Goddammit, Brenda, what did you do?"

"I'm so sorry," I yelled over the racket. "I wanted to take a look at your paint jiggler, I tripped on something and grabbed on to the cash register to catch myself, and . . ."

"Now we've got to wait for the security team and the cops—" He cut himself short, perhaps calculating his chances of making a run for it.

He stayed put. His chances of escape didn't look so good.

"I'm really terribly sorry," I said.

The cops arrived one minute before the expensive private security force, probably because the siren on their vehicle moved them through traffic faster.

Humbly, I took full responsibility for the mishap and apologized profusely to the officers for my clumsiness. A minute later, I ran through the same bit for the private guys. "So, anyway," I said, "thanks to all of you for dropping by, but as you can see, it wasn't necessary."

To my great relief, the highly trained professionals didn't go for that. They diligently performed their duty. They made One-Coat prove he owned the store. I could tell One-Coat was pissed by the way he slammed several forms of identification down on his counter.

While One-Coat was busy proving who he was, I meandered down the big aisle of top-of-the-line brushes and rollers, pulled out my cellular phone, and pushed auto dial.

*   *   *

"Turner here."

"Good evening, Detective."

Turner came back with a thoroughly world-weary "What is it now, Ms. Midnight?"

"There's been some trouble at One-Coat Joe's paint store. I thought you'd like to know."

"Yeah? What sort of trouble?"

"It's kind of a lot to explain."

"Go ahead, I have all evening."

Unfortunately, I didn't.

"Okay," I said. "I'll hit the high points: Ria Kleep stole a bunch of money from her employer. Her co-worker Minetta Carlton found out about it and got some or all of the money. One-Coat also found out about the money and he killed Minetta Carlton. Because of some kind of complicated stuff that happened a few minutes ago, One-Coat is convinced that any minute the police will figure out that he did it, so he's ready to bolt. Right now some uniformed cops are detaining him on a non-related matter, and a couple private security guys too, but they'd never in a million years believe me, so if you and McKinley don't get here real quick, One-Coat's gonna get away."

32

"Is One-Coat Joe gonna do time?"

Turner looked down at me from aloft.

"Too soon to tell. The wheels of justice grind in slow-mo. He hired some hotshot mouthpiece who's trying to make a case that decades of sniffing paint fumes made One-Coat nuts. Claims he wasn't responsible for his actions."

McKinley said, "I, for one, believe it. Another hour of these paint fumes and I'm liable to kill somebody, perhaps a certain milliner."

"Now, now, Detective McKinley," I said, "that's no way to talk. Remember, you volunteered for the job. Besides, it's a water-based paint, not too smelly."

Seated at my antique vanity with Jackhammer on my lap, I supervised the two detectives as they restored the walls of Midnight Millinery to the original pale pink.

That blue, I don't know. Like everyone who saw it said, it certainly was blue. I decided it had to go.

McKinley was cranky because it was actually Turner who'd volunteered to paint. McKinley wanted to treat me to dinner at the restaurant of my choice. I insisted they do both. I didn't think it was too much to ask, not after I let the detectives get all the glory for nabbing the killer.

* * *

Poor Ria Kleep. She would do some time for that money she'd stolen from the import-export firm where she worked. When the police tried to round her up, she'd vanished. I had a hunch she'd gone back to Hoboken and was debating whether to rat on her, when she saved me the trouble.

Ria ratted on herself.

She had no choice. It was a desperate act of self-preservation. When her boss and Minetta Carlton's boss, partners in the import-export firm, returned to New York from a lengthy buying trip, they discovered one of their secretaries had been murdered, the other had disappeared, and the cash for their next not-quite-aboveboard deal had vanished.

When Minetta discovered that Ria planned to steal money from the firm, she told her boss, with whom she was having a torrid, yet secret, office romance. Minetta's boss then hatched a plan that Minetta steal the money from Ria. Ria would get the blame. Minetta and her boss would get the cash.

Things hadn't exactly worked out. By some convoluted logic, Minetta's boss blamed Ria for planting the seeds of crime. He couldn't bring Minetta back, but he sure as hell had resources to hire a good private investigator to track down Ria in her Hoboken hideaway. One way or the other she would pay for what she had done.

Ria, increasingly paranoid, felt she was being stalked. This time, she wasn't making it up. She put two and two together, and rehired P. G. Dover to look into it. When Dover reported back that she was indeed being stalked by an investigator hired by Minetta's boss, Ria decided the safest thing to do would be to turn herself in.

A funny thing about that money.

The police got it from One-Coat who'd stolen it from Minetta Carlton who'd stolen it from Ria Kleep who'd stolen it from the import-export firm. Counterfeit. All of it. That came as a big surprise to Minetta Carlton's boss, who shot Ria's boss in the leg. Ria's boss was arrested from his bed in the hospital. Minetta Carlton's boss was arrested in the airport.

P. G. Dover didn't get away clean either. His diplomat plates were confiscated and when word got out that he was an impostor, he was shunned by the diplomatic community. No more Mr. Ambassador. No more Gintoflakokia. No more parking in no parking spaces. Dover was reduced to being a full-time sleazy unlicensed private eye, who lived in his office—a much larger office now, due to Dweena's successful investment of the disputed fifty thousand dollars.

Back to Turner and McKinley. Working evenings after their shift, the detectives painted Midnight Millinery in four days. The very next night they took me out for a fancy dinner at La Reverie, a romantic restaurant totally unsuited to the occasion. However, that's where I wanted to go, so that's where I got to go. Heads turned when I descended the plushly carpeted curved stairway into the seductively soft-lit dining room with two extremely well-dressed, not bad-looking men—one on each side.

During before-dinner cocktails the detectives thanked me profusely. During the appetizers we talked about the weather. During the entrees they mentioned the party I'd invited them to. Party? Oh right, that party, the one I made up so I could grab the key from under McKinley's calendar. I regretfully informed them the party was off. During dessert they reminded me that I should to stick to millinery and leave the police work to them.

"I wouldn't have it any other way," I said.

None of us ever mentioned the 911 call.

The time had finally come to prove to myself that my artistic crisis was over. I got out my design head block and within hours came up with a design, different from anything I'd ever made. It was impossible to judge a new hat hot off the block while still caught up in a creative frenzy, but I had a real good feeling about this new direction.

Sadly, I stayed away from Angie's, afraid to face Tommy and Raphael. They were both quite aware that for a brief time I had thought that one or the other of them was the killer. It was kind of hard to be friends after that.

Dweena called me the morning of the day she was to meet with city officials to get the final S.O.B. rulings. "Meet me at Angie's this evening," she said. "It wouldn't be right to announce the good news without you there."

Reluctantly, I agreed to go. I really missed the joint.

I put on my new hat for the occasion. For the first time in way too long, Jackhammer climbed into his going-to-Angie's canvas bag. He quivered with excitement at the prospect of special little burger balls.

I was pretty excited too, but when I walked into the bar I sensed something had gone terribly wrong.

The jukebox was silent, the TV was off, the regulars moped, and Tommy looked more glum than ever. Obviously, Dweena's news had not been good. Maybe her whole S.O.B. scam had been found out.

I couldn't turn back. Tommy had already seen me.

"Dweena's in the back," he said, not the least bit friendly. He didn't even acknowledge Jackhammer squirming in the bag. As I passed by, he turned his head away. I heard his breath catch, his whole body shook. The man was sobbing.

When I walked by Raphael in the kitchen, he too turned away so I couldn't see him cry.

The back room seemed dimmer than usual. When my eyes adjusted I saw that except for Dweena, the place was empty.

"What went wrong?" I sat down in the booth opposite her and let Jackhammer out of his bag.

"Nothing went wrong," said Dweena. "S.O.B. was a resounding success. I've got those city officials wrapped around my baby finger. Angie's and all the other buildings are formally recognized former brothels, and as such immune to the wrecker's ball."

"That's fantastic!"

Dweena smiled.

"Wait a minute. Tommy and Raphael are sobbing. What's the deal?"

"They're not sobbing, Brenda. They're laughing their asses off."

Suddenly, the dim light darkened to pitch black. A few seconds later many lights blazed on.

"Surprise!"

This time it really was.

"Now this," said Elizabeth, "is what I call a proper venue for a surprise belated birthday party."

"Food's good," said Chuck. He was on his second jumbo order of french fries.

"Good company," said Johnny.

It was wonderful to see Johnny out in public among friends. Actually, it was plain old wonderful to see him. He seemed to be dealing better with his professional setback. Lemmy Crenshaw, once again his agent, was "talking with some people."

Everybody was there, even Brewster Winfield and Myrtle, who, at Dweena's request stayed under the table in her carrying case. Winfield didn't mind. "She needs her beauty sleep." He invited us all to the opening of her play.

When the party was well under way Tommy and Raphael came into the back room. Raphael gave Jackhammer a special little burger ball. Then they dramatically presented my birthday cake, shaped like a hat, thick with frosting, candles burning bright.

I made a wish, blew out the candles. Then, while

Dweena cut the cake, I pulled Tommy and Raphael off to the side. "I've got something to say to you guys."

Tommy held up his hand to shush me. "It's real good to have you back, Brenda."

And we left it at that.